A Cattleman's Daughter

Book Three of the Fairfax Family Series

Chris Taylor

LCT Productions Pty Limited

This book is dedicated to my husband, Linden. My life, my love, my true blue outback hero.
I love you.

Other books by Chris Taylor

The Munro Family Series
(in order)

The Profiler
The Investigator
The Predator
The Betrayal
The Deception
The Negotiator
The Christmas Vigil (A novella)
The Ransom
The Defendant
The Shooting

A CATTLEMAN'S DAUGHTER

The Maker

The Sydney Harbour Hospital Series (in order)

The Perfect Husband
The Body Thief
The Baby Snatchers
The Final Bullet
The Debt Collector
The Lab Test
The Stolen Identity
The Cliff-top Killer
The Likeable Fraudster

The Sydney Legal Series
(in order)

An Accidental Murderer
At the Hand of her Father
A Woman Scorned
Lies and Deception
Ordinary Evil
The Ties that Bind
The Perfect Crime
A Toxic Inheritance
Malicious Love

CHRIS TAYLOR

The Craigdon Family Series
(in order)

Callum
Joel
Isabella
Nicholas
Sophia
Flynn
Noah
Logan
Elizabeth

The Barrington Family Series
(in order)

Broken Lives
Broken Promises
Broken Bonds
Broken Spirits
Broken Minds
Broken Vows
Broken Hearts
Broken Dreams
Broken Homes

The Fairfax Family Series (in order)

A CATTLEMAN'S DAUGHTER

A Cattleman in Disguise
A Cattleman's Quest
A Cattleman's Daughter
A Cattleman's Secret Baby
To Catch a Cattleman
The Doctor and the Cattleman
To Rescue a Cattleman
A Cattleman's Heart
For the Love of a Cattleman

Bachelors and Brides Series (in order)

Matilda
Austin
Farrah
Benjamin
Verity
Denver
Ebony
Tyrone
Willow

Books by Chris Taylor
Writing as
Bella
Christian

Chapter One

♥

The cloud of red dust visible in the distance was the first tangible evidence of the imminent arrival of Maggie Fairfax's unwelcome visitor.

"That'll be him then," Bluey muttered and turned his head to spit up a globule of phlegm on the dry, hard ground.

Maggie stared at the approaching vehicle with a mixture of hopelessness and dread. The four-wheel-drive vehicle was nothing more than a speck in the distance, but she was in no doubt that when her new boss arrived, her life as she knew it would change forever. She cursed under her breath.

Stop being so melodramatic. There's always the chance he'll fall in love with the place. After all, it's now his.

According to the estate lawyer, Rafael Hetherington was a city slicker. Until now, he'd never set foot on his late uncle's farm. No doubt he'd be there only for as long as it took him to assess the value of the place so that he could put Hetherington Station on the market. The lawyer had already intimated as much. She was certain the nephew of her late boss wouldn't have any interest in an outback cattle station. Even less interest in the people who lived there and relied on the Central Queensland station for their livelihood. People like her and Bluey.

She glanced at the old stockman beside her. The shade of an ancient gum tree cast shadows over his face. His weathered skin and thick snowy hair showed a man well past his prime, but there wasn't a more capable horseman in the district. He'd been born on Hetherington Station, as had his father. In fact, Bluey and his wife, Daphne, lived in the same cottage where he'd grown up. That kind of thing often happened in the outback. The place had a way of taking hold of a person and never letting them go. She was a lot like Bluey in that regard.

As if sensing her scrutiny, he turned to her. Fear and uncertainty flashed in his eyes. "What's gonna happen to me and Daphne? Where are we gonna go?"

Despite her own concerns, Maggie squeezed his arm and gave him what she hoped was a reassuring smile.

"Don't worry about that, Bluey. Who knows? The nephew might want to keep the place and the employees along with it."

Bluey regarded her skeptically. "I thought you said the lawyer already told you the fella wanted to sell?"

Maggie grimaced. "You're right. But we can always try to change his mind. I'm determined to give it my best shot. What about you?"

Bluey merely grunted and kicked at the dirt with the toe of his boot. Then he looked up at her again. "We need you to help us, Maggie. You gotta change this bloke's mind. We got nowhere else to go."

Maggie blinked back a sudden rush of emotion. She felt for the old stockman and all the other employees who called Hetherington Station home. She wasn't at all certain she'd have any sway over the new owner, least of all convincing him to keep the place and its employees. That knowledge filled her with dread. There were a lot of people depending on her.

Bluey's expression remained solemn. In an effort to reassure him once again, she reached out and patted his weathered arm.

"It's going to be all right, Bluey. I promise I'll do everything in my power to make sure you and Daphne, along with everyone else who lives here, are well taken care of. I'll convince the new owner to keep us all on or die trying."

His pale blue eyes crinkled with good humor. "No need to get that dramatic, Maggie. I'm sure it won't come to that."

"Let's hope so."

She swallowed a sigh. At twenty-five, she'd defied all the naysayers and taken on the challenge of overseeing nearly one hundred and fifty thousand acres of prime beef cattle land in the heart of the outback. Three years later, she was still in charge, and prided herself on having done a good job. The station was thriving.

Central Queensland was famous for its heat, dust and flies and its long dry summers, but Maggie had been born on the neighboring station. Raising cattle in the outback was in her blood. She couldn't imagine being anywhere else or doing anything else. She'd loved every moment of the past three years, battling the elements, making bargains with God, and getting the most out of every acre of land and the station hands she was responsible for.

And that was the problem. There was more than just her job at stake. The station was her life, and the life of the six others who lived and worked there. The land ran in their veins. The thought of all of them losing their livelihoods, coupled with the loss of their home, filled her with dread.

As the vehicle drew closer, Bluey muttered something under his breath, dipped his hat in her direction, and bid her a hasty goodbye. She watched him head toward the stables, his bow-legged gait and slight limp a testament to the years he'd spent in the saddle and an old knee injury. It was clear he didn't want to meet the new owner. She wished she didn't have to meet him either, but she had no choice. She was the boss, after all.

Her life on the station and the bright future she'd almost taken for granted were now in jeopardy. Arthur Hetherington had died. His sole beneficiary was minutes away from arriving to claim his inheritance and likely to bring to an end her time on Hetherington Station. But she wouldn't make it easy for him. She would do all she could to have him fall in love with the station or at the very least see the value in keeping it.

A humorless smile tilted her lips upward. She didn't know what kind of man Rafael Hetherington was, but she was sure, like those before him, he wouldn't stand a chance against her. There wasn't a man within a hundred miles who would take on a determined Maggie Fairfax. When she set her mind to achieving something, nothing and no one could deter her from her goal.

Okay, so ownership of the station had passed into the hands of a city slicker who was unlikely to understand the love someone could have for the land, but she sure as hell intended to do everything in her power to make him see that selling the station would be the worst thing he could do.

Raf Hetherington kept his foot hard on the accelerator of the rented four-wheel-drive. He'd flown into Roma from Brisbane that morning and had hired the Toyota Land Cruiser from the Hertz car rental agency at the airport. Though Raf had initially enquired about something smaller, the man behind the service counter had convinced him otherwise.

"Those other cars are best kept on the bitumen," the young man behind the counter had advised. "If you're heading off-road, you'd best take a four-wheel-drive."

After bouncing around the cab for the past thirty minutes, Raf was relieved he'd taken the man's advice. According to the GPS, he was less than a mile from the station. The long, straight dirt road stretched out in front of him. Wide-open plains covered in low scrubby brushes had dominated the landscape for the past hour. An occasional tall and majestic gum tree had broken up the monotony.

Now he was almost at his destination. In fact, he could just make out the shape of outbuildings in the distance. Thank goodness. He hadn't passed a single car since he'd left the outskirts of Roma. Apart from the occasional mailbox along the side of the road, he'd seen no other signs of civilization. If he had a breakdown, the chances of him being found quickly were slim. There wasn't even decent mobile phone coverage.

"How do people live out here?" he muttered as the Toyota hit another pothole, throwing him sideways in the seat.

So much for thinking this would be a grand adventure... A week or two away from the office and the hustle and bustle of the city to unwind and relax.

If it hadn't been for the sudden passing of his uncle Arthur, Raf wouldn't be there now. Though he'd handled the financials for his uncle for years, this would be the first time he'd ventured out to the station. Now it was his. The farm had suffered financially during the drought and faced different pressures when it had flooded, but the past few seasons had been good for the station and from what he'd seen of the income receipts, it was getting back on its feet. Not that decent profits would be enough to entice him to keep it. What did he want with a cattle station a million miles from anywhere? His life was in the city.

Now and then, his uncle had issued him an invitation to visit the place, but Raf had always turned him down. He'd had no interest in spending time in the bush. His uncle had also spoken about the woman who was managing the place.

Maggie Fairfax had worked there for the past three years. Uncle Arthur had always spoken highly of her. Raf was curious about why a woman would want to live in the middle of nowhere, surrounded by nothing but thousands of cattle and a handful of mostly male employees. He pictured her as an older woman, past her prime. She was probably a spinster, as Uncle Arthur had never mentioned a husband or family.

Raf felt a twinge of guilt at the possibility that not only would the woman lose her job, but she'd also be forced to move. Though the station had been owned by his uncle for the past thirty years, Raf had no sentimental attachment to the land. In fact, the best thing to do would be to sell it. He'd said as much to the estate lawyer when the man had told Raf about his inheritance.

The lawyer had been in full agreement. Central Queensland was currently experiencing a good season. They'd had a flood not so long ago and it had filled the dams and rivers and had given the pasture a welcome boost. That meant an abundance of feed and water for the stock for some time to come.

But a good season didn't last forever, and no one wanted to buy a farm in the drought. The time to sell was now when the going was good. He could invest the proceeds in something more stable—like Brisbane real estate, the value of which wouldn't fluctuate at the whim of the weather.

Not that he needed the money. He'd graduated university nine years earlier and had landed a job in a highly respected investment banking firm. Hard work and excellent investments over the years, along with his growing expertise in the finance industry, had seen his bank balance swell to generous proportions. Coupled with the billion-dollar estate he'd just inherited from his uncle, he need never worry about money again.

But it wasn't in him to do nothing. He was only thirty, hardly retirement age. Besides, work got him out of bed each day. His mother and father were always jet-setting from one exotic international location to another. They were rarely at home long enough to unpack their bags. Good on them. They'd worked hard during their lifetime as corporate lawyers and deserved a stress-free retirement. And his only sibling was busy being a wife and raising two rambunctious boys.

Without warning, a kangaroo bounded across the road straight into his path. He slammed on the brakes and turned the wheel, narrowly avoiding the animal. With his heart pounding and adrenaline spiking, he brought the Toyota to a halt on the roadside to give himself a few moments to catch his breath. He'd come out there to rest and unwind before putting the place on the market. Almost hitting a kangaroo sure as hell wasn't what he'd had in mind.

When he felt sufficiently recovered, he checked over his shoulder out of habit and pulled the Land Cruiser back onto the road. His uncle's unexpected death at sixty had made Raf realize that life was short. There was no guarantee he'd die of old age.

That made him think about how much of his time he devoted to his work and how he could drop dead tomorrow with no one at the office missing him. Well, maybe his secretary, Jessica, but she was in love with him, and though he'd told her from the outset that he had a rule against dating women in his office, that hadn't deterred her from trying to convince him she was worth breaking the rules.

On an impulse, he'd decided to hell with it. He'd take a couple of weeks' leave to visit his uncle's outback station and get a taste of the Australian bush before it was too late. Once the property was sold, the opportunity to spend time out there would be lost.

Jessica had been amused when he'd told her where he was going. She'd been at pains to tell him the closest airport to Hetherington Station was more than an hour's drive away and that from the look of the map she'd consulted, not all the journey could be made on paved roads. But he was not to be deterred, and here he was. About to come face to face with Maggie Fairfax.

He'd had the estate lawyer phone ahead to warn her of his arrival. Given the lack of hotels in the area, he hoped she'd at least arranged for some accommodations for him. He didn't expect her to share her house, but surely on a farm that comprised more than one hundred and fifty thousand acres, there would be somewhere he could stay. It was only for a week or two, after all.

The cloud of red dust grew bigger until finally a once-white Land Cruiser emerged and came to a halt a few yards from where Maggie stood.

At least he had the sense to hire a four-wheel-drive. Not like the city lawyer who'd turned up in a Mercedes coupe a few weeks ago...

Her thoughts were interrupted when the driver's door opened and a sinfully good-looking man of about her age wearing a suit and tie climbed out. Although he was laughably overdressed for the outback, her stomach took a nosedive, and the sudden rush of awareness that pulsed through her immediately irritated her.

Of course he's good looking. No doubt he's rich and powerful too. His uncle owned one of the largest cattle stations in Central Queensland. Money likely runs in the family.

The newcomer took a moment to brush invisible dust off his suit jacket. Maggie took the time to inventory his physical appearance. Tall, well over six feet. Chocolate-brown hair that had been tended to by a barber who'd made sure the man had gotten his money's worth. Military short around the sides and back. Pretty much a buzz cut. The only glimpse of personality that remained in her unwanted visitor's hair was in the wave of fringe that had been left to fall at a rakish angle over his right eye.

Blue eyes, almost as bright as hers, framed by dark lashes, stared at her with a mixture of friendliness and wariness. It was obvious he wasn't quite certain of his welcome.

Yes, you should be nervous.

Maggie chuckled silently in anticipation and then quickly rearranged her expression into one of polite friendliness as the stranger strode up to her with a smile.

Raf's first glimpse of Maggie Fairfax took him by surprise. She stood tall and straight in the shade of an enormous gum tree that grew outside a wire fence that surrounded a large homestead. He guessed she was about his age, maybe a little younger. A long way from the aging spinster he'd envisaged. Thick blond hair that had been pulled back into a ponytail peeked out from beneath a battered Akubra hat. Bright blue eyes the color of the summer sky stared back at him with a mixture of resentment and curiosity. Her skin was tanned from hours in the sun, but still looked youthful.

As he walked toward her, he continued to catalog her appearance. Her green-colored work shirt had the long sleeves rolled up to the elbows. The ends of the shirt were tucked into a pair of worn jeans. Her slim waist was encircled by a wide leather belt. A pair of dusty, well-worn work boots completed the ensemble.

Coming to a halt a few feet in front of her, he stuck out his hand. "Hi. I'm Raf Hetherington. You must be Maggie Fairfax."

Chapter Two

♥

Maggie plastered a smile on her face and forced herself to return the handshake. "Nice to meet you," she murmured.

Her mind distantly catalogued the warmth of his skin and the rough calluses on his palm. She frowned. She'd expected him to have hands that were soft from office work.

Maybe the calluses are from lifting weights at the gym...

Yes, that was more likely. There was no way a man who looked like Raf Hetherington did manual labor for a living.

To her consternation, up close he was even better looking. Firm jaw. Straight white teeth. Laugh lines visible at the corners of his eyes. His olive skin was tanned and glowing, like he'd spent plenty of time in the sun. Either that, or he'd had a spray tan.

She'd heard there were men who liked to get a tan that way. It was safer than sun baking, but in her world, a man paying for a tan was an alien concept. She could just imagine the way her brothers would react if they heard about something like that. All six of them would be in hysterics. Her three younger sisters would be equally amused.

"My uncle always spoke highly of you," the visitor continued. "On his behalf, I'd like to thank you for everything you've done for the place. You've battled some hard years recently. Droughts and floods and fluctuating cattle prices. It must be a tough life."

She found herself reluctantly impressed by his apparent knowledge about the station. She was also quietly impressed with his good manners. She frowned. She didn't want to find anything to like about him. Right now, he was enemy number one.

"Yes, it is," she eventually responded. "But I wouldn't want to live anywhere else."

A fly buzzed around his face. He brushed it away and looked around at the red dirt and the dust that had finally settled. He grimaced. "If you say so."

Her stomach dipped with disappointment. It was obvious he had no affinity for the place, and how could he? He'd been there less than five minutes. He had no idea how beautiful the station looked during a summer storm, when blue-black clouds gathered on the horizon and the rain washed everything clean. Or how the colors of the sunset in the evening were breathtaking — all reds and oranges and purples. Or the amazing native wildlife – kangaroos, wallabies, bandicoots, emus, birds of every description.

I'll just have to show him that this place is worth keeping. I also need to convince him that no one's expecting him to stay. I'm more than capable of running this place without him. In fact, I'd prefer it that way...

Raf had made his way to the back of the Land Cruiser and now retrieved two large suitcases. Spying them, Maggie had another moment of concern.

"How long are you staying?" she asked, striving to keep her tone neutral.

"Oh, I haven't decided. A week. Maybe two. It depends."

Her stomach lurched in alarm. A week or two? "On what?"

He shrugged nonchalantly. "I don't know. I'll see how long it takes me to get bored."

His calm certainty that it was only a matter of time before he lost interest in the place irritated her no end, but she supposed she ought to be grateful that he wasn't intending to stay indefinitely. Having him around would be annoying. It would slow her down and interfere with her work. Heaven forbid if he actually expected her to babysit him.

Then again, the more time she spent with him, the greater the probability that she'd persuade him not to sell. She had to show him such a great time that he'd want to return. As the beginnings of a plan bubbled beneath the surface, she shot him a winning smile.

"Well, we're very pleased to have you here for as long as you care to stay. Two weeks won't be nearly enough to show you all the sights, but I'll ensure you experience as much of the authentic station life as you can while you're here."

He quirked a dark eyebrow upward. No doubt her sudden warming to him came as a surprise.

"That would be very nice of you," he replied. "I must admit, I didn't expect to receive quite such a hospitable welcome."

She pretended confusion. "Why ever not?"

He shrugged. "I thought you might be concerned about my plans for the place. How long I intend to keep it. That kind of thing."

She forced herself to keep her tone neutral. "You're the new owner. It's yours to do with as you please."

He picked up his suitcases and started toward her. "You're right about that."

His dismissive tone set her teeth on edge again. It was all she could do not to bark out a retort.

I must hold my tongue. I need to keep him on side, remember?

With an effort, she controlled her temper and smiled sweetly once again. "If there's anything I can do to make your stay more comfortable, just let me know."

He came to a halt beside her. "Thanks. You can start by showing me to my lodgings."

Maggie was almost overcome by a momentary stab of panic. The guest cottage had stood derelict for years and the dongas were being used by the station hands. Bluey and Daphne lived in the small worker's cottage, the only home Bluey had known. There was no way she was uprooting them for the sake of their unwelcome guest. The only available "lodgings" were in the homestead that were currently occupied by her.

"I-I'm sorry," she stammered. "There's only the homestead..."

Seemingly unaware of the turmoil inside her, he flashed her a brilliant smile. "Great. That will do nicely. This way, right?"

Without waiting for her response, he turned and strode off toward the house. Panic surged through her. She was pretty sure he didn't have a clue that she'd been living in the homestead since the time she'd arrived three years before. The former owner hadn't cared. Arthur Hetherington had rarely visited anyway, and on those few occasions when he had, he'd only been there for a few hours before flying back in his private plane to Brisbane. He'd never stayed overnight. Finding accommodations for him had never been a problem.

But Arthur's nephew had just announced he was staying a week. Maybe two. She had to let him know that he'd be sharing those lodgings. Heat flared in her cheeks. She cursed under her breath. She had nothing to be embarrassed about. She'd done nothing wrong. She had every right to live on the station. Try telling that to her conscience. She felt like a kid who'd been caught with her hand in the cookie jar.

Oh, hell. How did I get into this mess? I should have asked the lawyer if my visitor intended on spending the night. It didn't occur to me. I thought he'd be here for a few hours, a day at the most, just like his late uncle.

Her unwelcome guest was halfway across the front yard when she called out to him again.

"Ah, Mr Hetherington?"

He stopped and turned to face her. "Please, call me Raf."

"Ah, Raf. Yes. Well, see. The thing is... I live in the homestead."

Once again, he raised a single, dark brow. "You live in the homestead? The same homestead where I'm headed?"

She refused to look away. "Yes."

"I see. Was my uncle aware of that?"

Anger rushed through her at his implication. "Of course he was! What do you think? That I snuck in there and set up house without his permission?"

He gave an infuriating shrug that neither confirmed nor denied. She ground her teeth together, struggling for patience.

"My employment package included living in the homestead. It's never been a problem in the past. I hope it won't be a problem now," she said stiffly and then forced a smile.

He gazed at her a moment and then shrugged again. "Whatever. As long as I have my own bed and bathroom, we'll be fine." He turned his back on her and continued toward the house.

A fresh wave of embarrassment heated her cheeks. "Ah, Raf?"

He stopped and kept his back to her for a moment before slowly turning around. "Yes?" His voice was tinged with impatience.

"Um… There's only one bathroom."

He shook his head in disbelief. "Only one bathroom? What is this? The dark ages?"

"No. But you're staying in a homestead that's been there for more than a hundred years. It's had some updates over the years, like indoor plumbing and electricity—"

"Hallelujah for that." His voice was as dry as the adjoining paddock.

"But I'm afraid there isn't an ensuite."

He compressed his lips and slowly nodded his head. "Okay. So that means we're sharing." He gave her a quick once-over that annoyingly left a trail of heat in its wake. "I guess I can live with that."

Raf hid a smile. It was obvious the woman wasn't entirely pleased with his presence. He could tell she was working hard to be civil. Not that he blamed her. No doubt the lawyer had informed her about his intentions, and that would mean she could very well be out of a job. He could talk to the new owners about the possibility of keeping the staff on, but he had no power to force them to retain the existing employees. As much as he regretted the possibility that people might lose their job because of his actions, once the sale had gone through, that kind of detail was out of his control.

He didn't know why he'd given her a hard time about the accommodations. He already knew she lived in the homestead. Some rascal inside him had wanted to tease her, to see if he could get under her skin. It appeared he'd succeeded.

Another fly buzzed close to his face. He set down one of his suitcases and swatted at it with his hand. The midday sun bore down on his head. Sweat trickled down his back. He glanced longingly toward the homestead, hoping his erstwhile host would take the hint and lead the way out of the heat, but she gave every sign of remaining where she was.

Finally, he said, "Do you mind if we go inside? This heat's killing me."

She smirked. "In case you didn't notice, we're in January. Summers are hot, especially out here. Oh, and by the way, the air conditioning in the homestead's on the blink. I've put in a call to the local guy in Roma, but I haven't heard from him yet. Thank God for ceiling fans."

Raf swallowed a groan. The thought of spending any time in the outback without the comforts of air conditioning filled him with dread, but he sensed the woman standing in front of him would scorn any sign of weakness. For some reason, he wanted her to like him. Or at least, respect him.

Which is crazy. We've only just met and once I leave and sell the farm, we'll never see each other again. What do I care whether she likes me?

With a sigh, Maggie strode past Raf and headed toward the homestead. As she set a determined pace, she tried to ignore the man behind her, lugging his suitcases. She wished he was short and fat and ugly. Or brash and rude. That she could handle. The fact he was courteous and polite and good-looking was unsettling to her peace of mind.

She hated that he was there to divest himself of the place as quickly as he could. The best chance she had to keep her job was to try to convince him not to sell and to keep her on as manager. One of the reasons she'd told him about the air conditioning problem was so he realized she wasn't a weakling and would put up with less-than-ideal conditions.

It would be interesting to see how he coped with it. January in Central Queensland could get extremely hot. It might be a good thing he'd arrived when he did. Maybe he'd have more influence over the air conditioning mechanic than she did. Being prepared to pay over and above the call-out fee should do it. She wondered if he was the kind of man who was prepared to spend money on his comfort.

She wouldn't complain if he did. She'd put up with hot, sleepless nights for almost a week. It would be nice to find relief at last from the heat. On another sigh, she walked up the wide concrete steps that led to the front door of the homestead. She reached for the screen door and held it open for her unwanted guest.

Raf hefted his suitcases across the front yard, all the while enjoying the view of Maggie Fairfax from behind. She had a very tidy figure. Tall and lean, but with enough curves in the right places to make things interesting. He'd already checked out her ring finger. It was bare. The lawyer had told him the manager lived alone in the homestead. He assumed that meant she wasn't married, but looking at her, there could definitely be a boyfriend in the picture.

There were several other employees who lived on the station. All but one of them were male and most of them were under thirty. They were housed in worker's quarters about two hundred yards from the homestead. Close enough that spending time together outside of work hours was possible. The idea made him frown.

As he drew closer to the homestead, thoughts of Maggie and her male staff disappeared from his mind. From a distance, the sheer size of the house was impressive. Large and expansive, it was surrounded by wide verandas that were decorated with intricate lace ironwork panels from another era. She was like a majestic queen atop a high ridge, overlooking her dominion. But up close, it was clear his uncle had spent no money on the place since he'd owned it.

Dry floorboards creaked beneath Raf's feet. The external timber weatherboards were covered in cracked and peeling white paint. The louvre windows also looked original, opened to catch the slightest breeze and covered in a layer of red dust. The only thing that wasn't ancient was the corrugated iron roof. That looked new. Or at least newer than the rest of the place. He asked Maggie about it.

"Yep. We had a bad hailstorm a couple of years back. Destroyed a lot of the roofs on the outbuildings, including the homestead. As you can see, we've replaced all of them."

He turned and looked around him. The outbuildings he'd seen from the driveway were huddled together a few hundred yards away. He noticed one of them was a machinery shed that housed tractors, a loader, and various other pieces of farm equipment. Another building looked to be an accommodation block and then there were two other structures closer to the homestead whose purpose he couldn't identify.

"What are they used for?" he asked, pointing toward them.

"One's an old meat house. The other one next to it was a kitchen. Back in the old days, the kitchen was always outside the main house in case of fire. It also kept the homestead a lot cooler in the summer without a fire burning in the kitchen stove all day."

"And what about the meat house? What was it used for?"

"Funnily enough, it was used for meat," she said dryly. "You might have noticed we're a long way from town, particularly back in the days of horse and cart. Before electricity and refrigeration, people out here killed their own meat, salted it to preserve it as long as possible, and then hung it in the meat house. You'll see evidence of old mesh screens fixed to the top half of the door and across the windows. That was to keep the flies out."

"Why not just seal the building completely? Why the need for windows?" he asked without thinking.

Maggie all but rolled her eyes. "No electricity, remember? How were they going to see inside? Besides, it would have been a sauna in the summer with no ventilation."

Raf blushed and looked away. He wasn't used to feeling like an idiot. He prided himself on being reasonably intelligent and able to hold his own in most circumstances, but being out there was like arriving on another planet. The landscape was completely foreign. Large swathes of brown mountains, red dirt, and dull green paddocks for as far as the eye could see, and they were in a good season. He couldn't imagine how uninviting and desolate the place would look in the middle of a drought.

He stepped inside the homestead and was immediately enveloped in air that was at least a few degrees cooler than outside. He sighed in relief. Maggie pushed past him and led the way down a long hallway. The polished wooden floorboards that might have once been something to be seen had dulled to a low sheen, the dark patina testament to the countless pairs of shoes that had no doubt traversed it over the years.

He followed Maggie past two bedrooms, one on either side of the hallway. Next came the living room and kitchen. He managed a passing glance at both rooms before she came to a halt inside a modest guest room. The double bed took up most of the room. A couple of bedside tables and a chest of drawers completed the furniture.

The air was stifling. It felt like the room had been closed up for a long time. And maybe it had.

"Sorry about the heat," Maggie said as she crossed the room and pulled open the two windows that faced outside and then switched on the ceiling fan. It slowly creaked into life.

"Right. No air conditioner. How long's it been on the blink?"

"Nearly a week."

He gaped. "You've been without air conditioning for a week?"

"Yep. We're in the outback. Tradesmen aren't very thick on the ground out here. You have to wait in line."

"Did they say how long it'll be before they come out here?"

"No. They still haven't returned my call."

Indignation flooded through Raf. "Leave it with me. I'll make some calls. Doing without air conditioning in this heat's unacceptable. No one should have to put up with that."

"You won't get any argument from me," Maggie murmured.

She went to the chest of drawers and pulled out a towel. "The sheets are clean and here's a fresh towel. The bathroom's down the hall on the right. I'll put the kettle on. It's almost lunchtime. Are you hungry? I could fix you something to eat."

"No, I'm fine. But a coffee would be great," he replied, wheeling his suitcases into one corner.

"I can do coffee. How do you take it?"

"Black, no sugar."

Maggie offered him a brief smile. "Great. I'll leave you to settle in. You'll find me in the kitchen."

With that, she crossed the room and left, pulling the door closed behind her. A whiff of faintly cool air blew in from the open windows, lifting the leaves on an ancient gum tree that provided shade to that side of the house. Raf swiped at the sweat on his brow and sank onto the bed. Pulling out his phone from his back pocket, he checked the screen.

He'd run out of service somewhere between Roma and Hetherington Station, but right now the screen showed three bars. Enough signal to send text messages and make phone calls, at least. No doubt there were things that could be done to improve the service.

Raf had heard good things about Elon Musk's Internet service. Starlink was the new rage. Elon had seen an opportunity to connect people living in the outback with the rest of the world, something governments didn't always prioritize.

Living in Brisbane, Raf didn't have to worry about good Internet service, but it would be a big help to the people living out there, so far away from the highly populated cities. He might look into setting it up. Then again, he was only there for a week or two. He could probably manage without decent Internet in that time. In fact, it could be an excellent opportunity to disengage from technology altogether and reconnect with Raf Hetherington.

At thirty, he wasn't getting any younger. He'd always expected to be married and with a kid or two by now. The fact he'd met no one he wanted to build a future with meant that hadn't happened, but putting so many hours in at work, even on weekends, hadn't helped.

This time away from the office would give him a chance to recharge and reassess; to reflect on what he'd achieved thus far and set new goals for the future. Penciling in some "me time" would help achieve a better work/life balance. Isn't that what everyone kept going on about these days?

More free time would also increase his odds of meeting his soul mate, although parking himself for a week or two in the middle of nowhere wouldn't do much for that. He could always go into Roma and check out some bars. Surely there was some place the people around there went to socialize. And there was always the delectable Maggie Fairfax to flirt with.

He smiled. Though she was most definitely put out by his presence, it was clear she was also smart enough to realize he held her future in his hands. She likely wanted to hate him and all that he stood for, but she would also realize she needed him to keep the station in order to keep her job. On first impressions, he'd seen nothing that would persuade him to change his mind, but he suddenly found himself anticipating the lengths Maggie would go to in order to convince him otherwise.

He stood and loosened his tie and then dropped it onto the bed. He considered changing out of his business shirt and putting on something a little more casual, but then decided against it. He'd prefer to spend the time with his host.

He chuckled as he undid the top two buttons of his shirt and tried to tell himself he'd done it to feel cooler. Spending time with his beautiful station manager would definitely be a pleasant pastime, even if she didn't exactly welcome his presence. The decision to visit Hetherington Station before it was sold might just turn out to be the best he'd made in a long time.

Chapter Three

♥

While Maggie waited for the kettle to boil, she fixed the makings of coffee. She didn't own a fancy machine that spat out barista-style coffee. Raf would have to be content with the instant variety. She spooned coffee into two mugs and added a spoonful of sugar to hers. Adding the boiling water, she gave both mugs a quick stir and set them on the counter.

Crossing to the fridge, she pulled out a covered dish containing half a loaf of banana bread she'd made earlier in the week. She cut two pieces and put them under the grill to toast. She'd just finished buttering the bread when Raf walked into the room.

He had rolled up the sleeves of his business shirt to his elbows, exposing a portion of tanned and muscled forearms. Once again, the fact he wasn't pasty white surprised her. He'd also removed his tie and had undone the top two buttons of his shirt. She glimpsed curly, dark hair peeking out of the opening.

Her stomach clenched with awareness. Men with hairy chests had always attracted her. She hated that she'd noticed his. For now, he was her new boss. She needed to keep a professional distance if she had any hope of convincing him to not only keep the station, but to let her remain in his employ.

She handed him a mug of coffee in silence and then collected her own, along with the plate of freshly toasted banana bread. She set the plate down on the scarred wooden table that stood a short distance away.

"Thank you. That smells delicious," he said. He pulled out a chair and took a seat.

She swallowed a groan of frustration. He was so goddamn polite! His charming demeanor made it so much harder to dislike him. And she very much wanted to dislike him. Or at least keep up her disgruntlement over the tenuousness of her situation.

Don't be so dramatic. All I have to do is convince him to keep the station and all of its employees and everything will be dandy. He can go back to his life in the city and leave us alone. If I only see him once or twice a year, that will be fine.

She sat in her usual seat, directly across from him, and sipped her coffee in silence.

"So, I guess the lawyer told you I'm going to put this place on the market."

It was more a statement than a question and though this wasn't the first time that possibility had been put to her, Maggie's stomach sank like a stone.

Raf sipped from his coffee and watched as Maggie's expression changed. Until now, she'd vacillated between being coolly polite to cautiously friendly, but now there was a downturn to her mouth, a tightness around her jawline and her blue eyes flashed with fire.

"Yes, the lawyer mentioned that," she said tightly.

"I assume you want to stay on after it's sold. Is that right?"

She nodded. "Yes. This is my home. It's also home to six other people. We all live and work out here."

"I understand and I want you to know my decision to sell isn't personal. I'm not really sure why my uncle left this place to me. I'd never expressed the slightest bit of interest in his station and other than doing his financial books, I had nothing to do with it."

An awkward silence fell between them. Raf reached for a piece of banana bread and took a bite. It was warm and moist and delicious. Melted butter ran down his fingers. Unselfconsciously, he licked them clean. Feeling Maggie's gaze on him, he looked up mid-swipe of his tongue and raised an eyebrow in silent query.

Crimson flared across her cheeks, and she hastily averted her gaze. Appearing flustered, she brought her coffee mug up to her mouth and took a gulp.

"Ouch," she muttered.

"Too hot?" he enquired lazily, curious about her reaction. *Could it be she's as aware of me as I am of her?*

Without responding, she reached for the remaining slice of banana bread and stuffed half of it in her mouth. She started coughing almost immediately. Tears formed in her eyes. He frowned in concern and leaned across the table.

"Are you all right?"

"I'm fine," she gasped.

She reached for her coffee again. This time, she took a smaller sip. The coughing attack gradually subsided. She eventually raised her gaze to his.

"Sorry about that. The banana bread went down the wrong way."

He waved away her apology. "No need to apologize. As long as you're okay."

She managed a brief smile. "Absolutely. Now, where were we?"

"We were talking about the future of the station."

She nodded. "Right. Specifically, your intention to sell it and get rid of those of us on it."

He paused momentarily, choosing to ignore the last part of her statement. He shrugged. "I work in finance. My life's in Brisbane. I have neither the time nor the inclination to be a part of this." His hand encompassed the homestead, the outbuildings, the station.

"Right. You see this as just a pile of scrub and dirt that could be sold in the blink of an eye for a hefty amount, enabling you to go on your merry way."

Her voice vibrated with anger. He again refused to rise to the bait.

"I don't pretend to have a connection with this place," he said calmly. "The only link is that it was owned by my late uncle. As far as I know, he purchased the property about thirty years ago as an investment. Some years he gained a decent return, other years he incurred substantial losses, but I'm sure I don't need to tell you that."

Her expression remained closed. Her lips had thinned into a stubborn line. He sighed and tried again.

"What I'm trying to say is that I'm not sentimental about the place, and neither was Uncle Arthur. Remind me again how often he came out to visit."

She pursed her lips and stared at the table. Color stained her cheeks. "I'll admit he wasn't a regular visitor, but he got out here at least two or three times a year."

"In thirty years?"

She continued to focus her gaze downward. "I don't know how often he visited in the thirty years he owned the place. I've only been here for three."

He conceded her point with a brief nod and then sighed again. He didn't want to antagonize her unnecessarily. Far from it. While he wouldn't be there long enough for them to become friends, he tried to avoid deliberately courting enemies. He much preferred to go through life getting along with people. It was less stressful that way. He felt some sympathy for her plight. But that wasn't enough to change his mind about selling.

"Look, I get you live and work out here and if the new owner doesn't choose to keep you on, then you're not only out of a job, you're also out of a home. But that's not my problem. I didn't ask for my uncle to leave me this place, but now that he has, I have the right to do whatever I want with it and from where I sit, the best thing I can do is put it on the market and invest the proceeds in something a little more stable."

"Right. Of course," she sneered. "It's all about the money. You don't give a toss about the people who live and work here, some of whom have lived here all their lives. Bluey, our senior stockman, was born here. Hetherington Station's the only home he's ever known. His wife, Daphne, has been here for fifty years. To put it bluntly, they have nowhere else to go. Then there are the other employees. Good, hardworking men who dedicate themselves to this station. But none of that matters to you, does it? Your only concern is to get rid of the place as soon as possible and bank your millions so that you can buy another EV for your garage that's no doubt already full of such cars."

A spark of anger ignited at her words. He fought to hold it at bay. Gritting his teeth, he attempted to respond civilly.

"You know nothing about me. Why would you assume I drive an electric car?"

"Don't you?" she fired back.

A part of him admired her courage. She was deliberately goading him, uncaring how quick his temper might be. She was either obtuse or simply didn't care that her words might push him over the edge and into a situation that might turn violent. Of course, he'd never hurt anyone in his life, and it would never occur to him to be violent with a woman, but she didn't know that. She was in the middle of nowhere with a virtual stranger and yet, she didn't seem to have any concern for her welfare. Her recklessness concerned him.

What if I was a dangerous man? What if my temper was so volatile, I exploded? What would she do? How would she protect herself?

She continued to glare at him across the table, and he realized he hadn't responded to her question. Drawing in a deep breath, he calmly replied, "As a matter of fact, I drive a RAM. It's a 5.7 liter gas-guzzling V8 diesel."

Surprise flashed behind her eyes. Frown lines marred the smooth skin of her forehead. "Why the hell would you drive something like that around Brisbane? It must be a bitch to park."

He threw back his head and laughed. "You've got that right. I don't know what I was thinking. I wanted the storage space in the tray for when I go surfing, but it would have been much more practical to get something smaller. A modest SUV, perhaps. But there's nothing that beats the power of a RAM."

She lifted a perfectly shaped brow. "Oh, so it's all about the horsepower. You and my brothers would get on well."

"You have brothers?"

"Yes. Six of them."

He almost choked on his surprise. "You have six brothers?"

"And three sisters. There are ten of us altogether."

"Wow."

He tried to get his head around what having that many siblings would be like. At the same time, he suppressed a surge of envy. Though he loved his sister to bits, he would have also enjoyed having more than one sibling. If ever he had kids, he was determined to have a whole heap of them. Maybe not ten, but five or six, at least. He just hoped his future wife would be as keen as he was to have a large family.

"What about you?"

Maggie's question interrupted his thoughts.

"Me?"

"How many siblings do you have?"

"Um, only one."

"Wow. That sucks."

He chuckled. "I guess that depends on how much you like your siblings, but I agree. I would have loved to have been from a big family."

She smiled. Her gaze grew distant. "Yes, I wouldn't change my family for all the money in the world."

"How do they feel about you living and working out here, so far away from everything?"

She grinned wryly. "Most of my family live on the adjoining station. Marlowe Downs has been in my family since the beginning of time. Well, maybe not that long, but long enough."

"That's pretty cool. So, you were born for this kind of life. Why aren't you working on your family station?"

She chuckled. "If you knew anything about my brothers, you wouldn't ask that." She paused and then added, "I wanted to strike out on my own; get out from under their shadows; do something for me." She turned a challenging gaze on him. "And I've succeeded."

"Now I understand what draws you to such an isolated part of the world."

"It might be isolated, but it's beautiful."

He nodded abstractly. "I guess."

She laughed. "You don't sound convinced."

He shrugged. "The landscape I drove through was interesting enough, but it didn't exactly captivate me. In fact, all I saw for miles and miles were drab looking bushes and shrubs, cleared land peppered with gum trees and nothing much else. If anything, it was kind of monotonous."

She tilted her head and smiled. "I'll concede there are quite a few miles where the landscape barely changes, but you haven't seen it at its finest. Wait until you stand on the mossy rocks beneath the waterfall on the edge of our southern boundary, or swim in the natural hot springs that bubble out of the bore drain. Or watch a sunset from one of the hilltops, surrounded by nothing but the glorious Australian bush."

She stopped suddenly and averted her gaze. A becoming blush stained her cheeks.

"I'm sorry," she said. "I'm rambling. I'm sure you're not the least bit interested in listening to me talk about this place."

"I might not have any connection to this station, but that doesn't mean I don't appreciate the way you feel about it."

She looked at him, and her expression filled with curiosity. "Your uncle owned this station for many years. Why didn't you ever come out for a visit?"

"I'm a city boy, born and bred. I was never interested in Uncle Arthur's farm. From time to time, he used to invite me to come with him, but I never took him up on his offer. I was always too busy. I didn't have a lot of spare time to waste. To tell you the truth, my uncle rarely spoke about the place. In fact, he probably told me more about you than he did the livestock."

She blinked in surprise. "About me?"

"Yes. He told me you were hardworking. He admired your grit. A woman living so far from civilization and yet from all accounts, you loved it. It pleased him to know how much you enjoyed living and working out here, even if he couldn't understand the appeal."

She laughed and her eyes grew distant. "Your uncle was always happy to spend money in the right places. He might not have given much thought about making improvements to the homestead, but he never scrimped when it came to the station. He made sure we had the best equipment and that when feed was scarce, there was money to buy it in. One thing he did enjoy was the annual branding and drenching of the cattle."

She smiled as she reminisced. "He'd fly out on a chartered plane and spend all day watching the men do their thing. Mustering the herd into the yards. Pushing them into the holding pens. From his perch on top of the railing, he'd watch as the cattle went up the race and were put into the headlock, branded, and then drenched. The entire process seemed to fascinate him. I guess it wasn't every day he got to see something like that."

"You're right," Raf responded. "He spent most of his time behind a desk, like I do. He was a commercial lawyer, like my father. They were in partnership together. Uncle Arthur bought the station as an investment and to help offset other more profitable ventures. There's no better way to procure tax losses than by owning a farm."

He said the words in jest, but Maggie's expression grew serious.

"You're right about that," she said quietly. "We've had more bad years than good out here. When the seasons are good, we celebrate, but no one forgets how quickly things can change. We go from raging floods to droughts and bushfires, and hardly anything in between. One thing none of us can control is the weather."

"It's a tough life," he said softly.

She smiled grimly. "You bet. But a rewarding one. Just you wait and see. By the end of your stay, I'm sure you'll agree with me."

He silently admired her confidence, all the while doubting that anything she could show him would be enough for him to change his mind. Still, he looked forward to seeing what lengths she was prepared to go to in order to convince him otherwise.

Chapter Four

♥

Maggie tore her gaze away from Raf's. For a moment, she'd gotten lost in the brilliance of his blue eyes and the connection that had momentarily flared between them. She needed to remember who he was and his reason for being there. In fact, she needed to get on with the job of showing him around the station. He'd already made it clear that selling was on his mind, but she refused to give up so easily.

Of course, if the worst happened and she had to leave, she could always get a job at her family station, but what about the other employees? Besides, what she'd told Raf was true. She loved Hetherington Station and she enjoyed running her own show. At Marlowe Downs, she'd have to answer to her brothers, and they'd forever treat her as their younger sister, even though she was older than most of them. They wouldn't take her seriously and she'd resent that. No, it would be better for everyone if she worked elsewhere. Better still, that she be allowed to stay working right there.

At Maggie's suggestion, after helping to clean up the mugs and plates, Raf followed her outside to the stables. The sharp aromas of fresh hay and horses immediately beset him as they stepped inside. It was a good thing he didn't mind the smell. It took a moment for his eyes to adjust to the dimness. Shadows morphed into stables and dark shapes gradually transformed into horses. Though he'd only had a handful of riding lessons when he was a kid, he wasn't afraid of the enormous beasts. In fact, he welcomed the opportunity to get up close and personal with the beautiful creatures. He stepped forward and a tall chestnut stuck out his head. Doe-like dark eyes gazed at him curiously.

Raf reached out and stroked the horse's soft nose. "Hello, boy. What's your name?"

"She's a girl," Maggie corrected, coming to a halt beside him. She patted the horse fondly. "This is Lady."

"Hello, Lady," Raf said, giving the horse another pat. "Aren't you a beauty?"

"The best of Hetherington Station stock," Maggie added. "Born and bred right here, along with most of our horses."

"Who breaks them in?"

"Bluey, mostly. He's our senior stockman. You won't find a more capable, more experienced horseman. We're lucky to have him."

Giving Lady a final pat, Maggie turned and headed outside the stables to the holding yards. Raf followed quietly beside her. A lean, white-haired man wearing cowboy boots and a battered Akubra was working with a young horse. It was obvious from the horse's jitteriness and the old man's calm and gentle crooning that the horse was being broken in.

"There's Bluey. He's with one of our yearlings." She paused. "Hey, Bluey. This is Mr Hetherington. Come over and say hello."

The old man pointedly ignored them and continued patiently working with the flighty filly. Raf wasn't certain whether the man was hard of hearing, or just plain rude. Given the circumstances of his visit, Raf could understand the staff not wanting to roll out the welcome mat.

As the horse pulled back and stood on her hind legs, flailing wildly with a combination of fear and anger, the stockman tugged gently on the long rein attached to the bridle. Talking softly, calmly, tenderly without pause, slowly the horse quieted.

Raf watched, fascinated. The scene was one of mutual trust and respect. This wasn't a man exerting his will on an animal. It was clear the two had formed a pact, a mutual understanding between two minds who'd come to an unspoken agreement. While Raf watched on, the filly snorted and flung her long tail high and then stepped calmly up to the stockman and thrust her nose into his outstretched palm. Just like that, they declared a truce.

Raf turned to Maggie, filled with quiet amazement. "That was magical."

She nodded. Her blue eyes gleamed with understanding. "People sometimes get the wrong idea when they hear about horse breaking. They think it's all about someone forcing an animal to bend to their will. That's not how it is at all. The first thing that needs to happen is to establish a positive and trusting relationship between the horse and its handler. The process typically begins with introducing the horse to basic handling, grooming, and groundwork to build mutual respect and communication. Bluey's been doing this all his life. He's an expert. But even Bluey doesn't rush things."

"How long does it normally take to break in a horse?" Raf asked.

"It takes weeks to build the kind of trust that's required. No one sets out to break a horse's spirit. That's not what horse breaking's about."

Raf turned back toward the yard. Bluey continued talking quietly to and patting the horse. "How long before she'll be ready to be ridden?"

"Once trust has been established and she's responding to the bridle, she needs to get used to the sensation of having weight on her back." Bluey will gradually introduce a saddle. Then he'll work to desensitize her to various stimuli, such as noise and movement, ensuring that she remains calm and re-sponsive no matter the situation. Riding sessions commence slowly after that, with an emphasis on teaching her to respond to cues and commands not only from the reins, but from the thighs, from oral commands, shifting the rider's weight... All sorts of things."

Raf shook his head, filled with admiration. "I didn't know there was so much to it."

Maggie's soft smile lit up her face and reminded Raf of how beautiful she was.

"Oh, yes. Patience, consistency, and a gentle approach are key elements in breaking in a horse, along with fostering a bond that forms the foundation for a trusting partnership between horse and rider. As I said, Bluey's been doing this all his life. You won't find a better man around horses." Her expression darkened. "Not everyone's as gentle or patient as he."

Raf gazed at her, curious. "Are you speaking from personal experience?"

She pursed her lips and nodded. "Yes. We had a stockman employed here a few months ago. Came to us from another station. Bragged about his ability with horses, in particular his skill in breaking them in." Her expression turned grim. "I caught him beating one of our young geldings with a stick to make the horse more compliant. When I protested his methods, he told me I didn't know the first thing about breaking in horses and that I best mind my own business." Her eyes narrowed, as if recalling the conversation. When she spoke again, her tone was brusque. "Finding workers out here isn't easy, but I fired him on the spot. We don't need people like that on our station." She paused and then added, "Sorry, *your* station."

He shrugged off her comment and gazed at her with fresh admiration. It was tough being a boss anywhere, but out here, in the middle of nowhere where anything could go awry, where a disgruntled employee could turn nasty and nobody would even know about it, he couldn't imagine the extra layer of difficulty that came with having to deal with the isolation Maggie faced every day. And yet, she seemed to take it all in her stride. Loved it, even.

"How about we go on a tour?" she suggested, interrupting his thoughts. "Might as well see what you inherited before you dispose of it."

"Might as well," he murmured.

She'd already turned away from him and now strode toward the machinery shed. He hurried to catch up with her.

"Do you want to go in my rental car?" he asked. "It's four-wheel-drive."

She glanced at him and smirked. "*All* of our farm vehicles are four-wheel-drive. They're the only thing tough enough to withstand these harsh conditions."

She walked into the machinery shed, past a couple of enormous tractors, some kind of farming implement and pulled up beside a pair of quad bikes.

"Do you know how to ride one of these?" she asked.

Raf gave the bikes a dubious look. "No, but I can't imagine they're too hard. Do they have gears?"

"That one does." She tapped a lever on the left handlebar. "This is the clutch. It works just like a manual car. Put in the clutch before you change gears. This is the gearshift." She pointed toward a lever in front of the left footrest. "One click down for first, then click up for second, third and fourth." She leaned over and squeezed a lever attached to the right handlebar. "This is your brake."

"Where's the accelerator?"

She shot him a droll look. "I don't know you well enough to know if you made that comment in all seriousness, but just in case you did, on a bike, we call it a throttle. And it's here." She tapped the right handlebar. "Turn it backward to speed up. Take the pressure off if you want to slow down. Got it?"

"I think so. As long as I know how to stop, I guess I'll be fine," he quipped with a confidence he was far from feeling.

"Good." She gave him a quick once-over. "By the way, you might want to consider changing out of that suit. It's not exactly work wear for out here."

He glanced down at his clothes and shrugged. "I'll be fine."

"Suit yourself." She tossed him a helmet. "Put this on. Safety is a top priority on this station." She winked.

Raf hid his nervousness behind a smile. After securing the helmet on his head, he copied Maggie's practiced movement by placing one foot on the step and lifting his other leg over the bike. He landed a little gracelessly in the seat and was relieved when she made no comment. Instead, she pulled on her own helmet, switched on the ignition on her bike, gave him a thumbs up and then she was off.

Trying to remember what she'd told him, he started the bike and put it in gear. A few bunny hops later and he was away, grateful that she'd spared him the embarrassment of witnessing his less-than-elegant take-off. He had no idea where they were headed, but he easily followed the cloud of dust that she left behind.

He passed several more outbuildings housing more machinery and two large sheds that were full of hay. Four young stockmen hefting large hay bales gave him a friendly wave as he rode by. They appeared to be making their way to the stables. No doubt they were more of the station's employees.

A mile or so from the homestead, he spied a rudimentary airstrip built from clay. Though it looked rock hard, was flat and stretched a fair distance, he wasn't at all sure it was suitable for landing on. Then again, Maggie had mentioned his uncle had flown out there on a chartered plane several times a year. He supposed the airstrip must be up to the job after all.

As he bounced along a rutted track, following Maggie's dust, he wondered how much further they had to go to reach their destination. The sun beat down on his head. Sweat trickled down his back, pasting his shirt to his skin. He should have taken Maggie's advice and changed at least into something cooler, like a cotton T-shirt, rather than sticking with the fine Italian silk business shirt.

Thankfully, he caught up with her about ten minutes later, when she slowed and came to a halt. He eased off the throttle, tapped the brake and managed to stop beside her without stalling.

She pulled off her helmet and shook out her hair. Her ponytail had come loose, and the thick golden strands gleamed in the sunlight. He itched to run his fingers through it. In an effort to distract himself, he tugged at his own helmet and removed it.

"How're you doing?" she asked.

"Not too bad. I've made it this far without falling off, at least."

She shot him a grin. "You're not doing too bad for a bike virgin."

He flushed. At the same time, blood rushed to his groin. Her expression remained lighthearted. He couldn't tell if she was intentionally flirting with him or merely being friendly.

"Where are we going?" he asked.

"To the billabong. It's so hot today, I thought you might like a swim."

Her tone remained casual. Once again, he studied her face for a hint about whether there was more to her comment than friendly banter, but he read nothing in the innocent look on her face.

"Sounds good, but I'm rather overdressed for swimming, and I don't recall packing a pair of swimming trunks."

Her gaze raked over him, heating his blood. She grinned again. "You could always go skinny dipping."

He almost groaned aloud. God, she was killing him. She had to be flirting with him. Their conversation had gone well beyond what he'd considered friendly banter. He decided to give back as good as he got.

"I'm game if you are."

This time, it was her cheeks that turned crimson. She ducked her head and busied herself with something on her bike. He chuckled silently. *Touché*. Two could play at this game. Anticipation surged through him.

Instead of responding, she tugged her helmet back over her head and secured the strap. She flicked him a glance. "Ready?"

Without waiting for his answer, she once again took off.

By the time they arrived at the billabong, the mid-afternoon sun blazed even hotter, radiating heat and bouncing off the shiny plastic of Maggie's quad bike. She wanted to blame the residual heat in her cheeks on the hot day, but for her entire adult life she'd made it a habit not to lie to herself and she wasn't about to start now. Her body was flushed not because of the summer sun, but because of the sexy visitor riding on his bike beside her.

When the estate lawyer informed her that Arthur's nephew would be visiting the station, she felt nothing more than a slight curiosity about the man, aside from dread for the future. He obviously wasn't interested in farming life, or he would have been out there earlier, while his uncle was still alive. The fact he hadn't stepped foot on the station until now told her all she needed to know about the man. She'd figured he didn't give a toss about the station and would put it on the market as soon as he could.

And she hadn't been wrong about that. Raf had told her that's exactly what he planned. His trip from Brisbane would be nothing more than an exercise to assess the property's net worth so that he could maximize his returns when he sold it. Knowing his plans filled her with a mixture of sadness and disappointment for herself and the station's workers. Not only would they be out of work, they'd also be forced to find other homes. No straightforward task in the sparsely populated outback, where good jobs and housing were scarce.

As she brought the bike to a halt a second time and engaged the park brake, she sighed. She wasn't at all sure there was any point in trying to convince Raf to change his mind, but she wouldn't give up without a fight. Too many people relied on the station for their livelihood. She owed it to them to do whatever she could to convince him not to sell. Pulling off her helmet, she flashed him a brilliant smile.

"So, this is one of the best-kept secrets on Hetherington Station. I'm not sure even your uncle knew about it."

Raf tugged off his helmet and gazed around him at the ancient gum trees, the low scrubby bushes, and the thick tufts of native grasses that surrounded a roughly circular shaped pool of dark water. Despite the heat of the day, when his gaze landed on the billabong, his expression turned dubious.

"Are you sure it's safe to swim in there?"

"Of course it is! We swim here all the time. What are you afraid of? A billabong monster?"

He shot her an embarrassed look. "Yeah, right. I was thinking more like leeches. Or some other weird creepy crawly that likes to hang out in water so dark you can't even see the bottom. It's freaky. There could be anything in there."

"Don't tell me you're scared?" she teased.

"Of course not!" he protested. "I swim in the ocean and that's not always safe. But surfing in the waves isn't half as dangerous as that water looks."

Maggie opened her mouth to continue to give him a hard time about his limited swimming experiences, but then realized he was genuinely concerned about what might lie beneath the dark waters of the billabong. Taking pity on him, she gave him a reassuring smile.

"I promise there's nothing harmful in the water. It gets its dark color from the tannin that leaks into it from the gum leaves. They fall from the trees and end up in the water, where they slowly decompose. That's all. The water will be cool and clean, and on a hot day like this, it'll feel delicious. Hey, you've come all this way to experience the outback. Take a ride on the wild side." She winked.

He chuckled. "I thought I'd already done that by agreeing to come with you on a quad bike. That was a first for me."

"Then let's keep building on those firsts. Nothing like being pushed outside of your comfort zone to feel like you're living."

He grinned. "I guess you're right. And anyone who knows me well knows that I never back down from a challenge."

Maggie stored that bit of information away for later reflection. It gave her hope that he wasn't scared of confronting unfamiliar and challenging situations. Maybe she could convince him to keep the station. Only time would tell.

Raf climbed off the bike a little awkwardly, but stayed on his feet. He then stripped off his shirt, his shoes and socks and had started on his belt when Maggie forced her gaze away. She'd dared him to go skinny dipping. Now she couldn't help but wonder if that was just another challenge he'd decided to face head-on.

From the corner of her eye, she glimpsed smooth, toned flesh. His biceps bulged and his well-formed pectorals flexed with his movements. A pelt of thick, dark hair covered the top half of his chest. A thin line descended from his belly button, across his washboard-flat stomach, and disappeared into his boxers. As if sensing her stare, he paused in his undressing and captured her gaze. For the life of her, she couldn't look away.

As the silence lengthened between them, he raised a single, dark eyebrow in silent query. "Are you coming in?"

Her face flamed with embarrassment. She quickly lowered her gaze and got busy pulling off her boots and socks. The memory of his husky voice sent ripples of awareness coursing through her. Low and deep and sexy, as sexy as the image he presented. An almost-naked, perfectly sculptured man set against the backdrop of the glorious Carnarvon Ranges.

Her hands went to the waistband of her khaki shorts. She hesitated. She'd never stripped off for anyone, let alone a man she'd only just met. But she'd just issued him a challenge to go skinny dipping, and he'd taken her up on that. What would he think if she backed out?

Before she could change her mind, she quickly slipped the shorts off her hips and stepped out of them. She dropped them onto the back of the bike and then reached for the buttons on her shirt. Once again, she hesitated. Her shirt was long enough that it fell to mid-thigh, covering all the essentials. The thought of taking it off filled her with nerves. She snuck another look at Raf. He now strode fully naked toward the billabong. Her face burned again.

This was her fault. She was the one who'd dared him to go skinny dipping. She'd only done it because some imp inside her had wanted to get under his skin, like he'd so quickly and so easily had gotten under hers. Now she was going to pay the price. If she remained in her clothes, he'd think she was a coward. If she went in after him naked...

Heaven help me...

She was far from a prude and was comfortable with her body and the way she looked. She was taut and toned and trim from years of physical labor on the station. But Raf was an almost-stranger. Worst still, he was now her boss. At least, while ever he owned the place.

Do I really want to get buck naked with my boss? Heck, no.

Body confidence or not, they'd known each other for a matter of hours. It was crazy to have baited him that way. She'd dared him to go swimming without his clothes and he'd risen to the challenge. Failing to do the same thing would paint her a coward.

So be it. There's no way I'm going in naked. Short-less is as good as it's going to get.

Swallowing a sigh over her foolhardiness, she drew in a breath, squared her shoulders and strode toward the billabong. Raf stood on the edge of the water, watching her with unconcealed interest. His gaze raked over her in a deliberate manner, setting the blood rushing through her veins. From the gleam in his eyes, she might as well have been naked. Heat trailed in the wake of his gaze. Her nipples hardened reflexively. Her stomach clenched with nerves.

Those final few steps to the billabong seemed to take an eon, but at last she reached the water's edge. Raf's bold gaze remained on hers, but now a smile twitched at his lips.

"Chicken," he murmured.

The single word burned. She flushed with embarrassment and cast around for something to say. She was under no obligation to justify her change of mind, but it was obvious from Raf's expectant gaze he was waiting for some kind of response.

She smiled sweetly. "I never said I was going skinny dipping. It's not my fault you misunderstood."

He grinned. "Touché."

She was glad he'd responded so lightheartedly. That spoke volumes for his character. He could have easily turned sulky. After all, he'd taken her up on her challenge and she'd reneged. But it seemed he wasn't harboring any hard feelings and for that, she was pleased.

A moment later, Raf turned away and took a few tentative steps into the water.

"Oh, hell! What's that?" he yelped, kicking at the water with his foot.

Relieved that his attention had been diverted, she merely shrugged, walked into the water a little farther, and then plunged all the way in.

She swam out quickly until the water was up to her shoulders, preventing any further scrutiny and giving her a chance to calm her racing heart. The last thing she needed was to fall for the sexy owner. Her only goal was to get him to keep the station. She had to remain focused on that. When Raf swam out toward her, she barely suppressed a groan.

His arms were long and muscular as they ate up the distance between them. When he reached her side, he came upright and shook his head in a graceful arc. Water sprayed from his overlong fringe into the air and landed on her face. She sputtered with indignation. He merely grinned.

"You're right. This feels amazing."

"Worth taking on the creepy crawly creatures of the deep?" she teased.

His face lost a shade of color, and his eyes filled with concern. "You told me there weren't any creepy crawlies."

She shrugged. "Why do you think I kept my clothes on?"

He frowned. "What kind of creepy crawlies?"

"Oh, the usual kind. Leeches, water beetles, eels."

His eyes widened in alarm. His frown deepened. "*Eels?*"

As genuine fear filled his face, she took pity on him once again. She wasn't used to dealing with a city slicker.

"I'm joking, Raf. There's nothing in the water that can hurt you. Relax. Enjoy it. It's all yours, remember?"

Chapter Five

❤

Raf actually found solace in the dark-colored water that concealed his raging hard on. He didn't know what kind of reaction Maggie expected from him when she strode into the billabong, but she couldn't be surprised that she'd aroused him. Okay, so she was almost fully clothed, but that hadn't concealed the fact that her body was the stuff of fantasies. Long, toned limbs tanned by the sun. Blond hair flowing out across her shoulders. Full breasts whose rounded shape was clearly visible beneath the wet fabric of her shirt. When she turned to swim away from him, he'd glimpsed white cotton panties that covered her shapely ass. Somehow, the plain and sensible underwear was more erotic than any of the black lacy numbers he'd seen in the past.

Despite his disappointment that she hadn't stripped down like she'd intimated, he wasn't at all dissatisfied with her display. He'd called her a chicken, but that wasn't exactly fair.

It had taken guts to step out in front of him without her shorts on, no matter how long her shirt was.

It was obvious she wasn't shy about her body. Confidence in a woman was a real turn-on. For her to be brave enough to swim with him in her panties made him wonder about how confident she might be in other areas of her life. Like fucking. No matter that he was only there for a week or two. There was no harm in having fun. Especially with a stunning blond who seemed determined to show him a good time.

But just how good of a time is she willing to show me?

He was suddenly extremely curious to find out.

With that thought in mind, he swam closer, until his thigh brushed against hers beneath the water. Her eyes went wide on a little gasp, but she didn't move away. A fresh wave of desire washed over him, sending more blood straight to his groin. His cock throbbed below the water and his heavy balls reminded him it had been way too long since he'd last had sex.

"Do you come here often?" he asked.

"As often as time allows. Especially in the summer. You think it's hot today but come February, this place will be unbearable."

"So why do you stay?" he asked, suddenly curious.

A slow smile lit up her face. "I love it out here. I love the heat and the dust and the flies. I love the amazing sunsets. I love working with the cattle. I love the people out here. They're different from city folks. More down to earth. More caring.

People out here only have each other to rely on. That creates a special relationship that's hard to define."

"A bit like the relationship Bluey has with the horses he breaks in," Raf murmured. "Watching him work with that filly was something else."

Maggie's eyes widened with surprise, but she nodded. "You're right. I didn't expect you to understand."

"Because I'm from the city?" he teased.

"Yes. It usually takes time to become attuned to the unique ways of the outback. You've barely been here five minutes."

"Perhaps, but that doesn't mean I'm not observant or sensitive to things."

She regarded him. "You surprise me."

"In a good way, I hope."

Her gaze shifted to his chest, visible above the water. She looked her fill before raising her eyes back to his. Her blue eyes showed a mix of good humor and challenge as she gazed at him again.

"Absolutely."

His gut somersaulted in a flash of desire. It was obvious she liked what she saw. It was all he could do not to drag her in his arms and ravish her like his body urged him to do.

"You said you were in finance. What does that entail?" she asked.

Her question distracted him. He wondered if that was her intent.

"I invest other people's money and hopefully make them a decent return. They pay me well to do that job. On top of that, I earn a percentage of their profits."

"Sounds lucrative."

"It is. At least, it is for me. I've been lucky."

She gave him a sideways look. "We make our own luck. Then again, you got lucky with your inheritance. Being the sole beneficiary of Hetherington Station is nothing to take lightly. Why did he choose you?"

"I have no idea," Raf answered honestly. "Uncle Arthur had no wife or children, but I'm not his only living relative. I have a sister, for one. And my parents are still alive. My father and Uncle Arthur were brothers. He could have left the station to Dad."

"Is your father interested in the land?"

Raf laughed. "Not at all. Then again, neither am I."

"Curious," she stated. "Then again, I guess he had to leave it to someone. Why not you?"

"Exactly," Raf agreed. He paused and then surprised himself by saying, "There's a part of me that thinks I should keep it. For Uncle Arthur's sake. He gave his name to this station. It could be the foundation of a family dynasty, passed down to future generations."

"That's what happened with my family's station. Marlowe Downs. About fifty miles from here. It's been in my family since the mid-1800s. With a bit of luck, it'll stay in the family for another two hundred years."

Raf chuckled. "With all those siblings of yours, that surely won't be too hard."

She smiled. "You're right. Four of my brothers live there, working right alongside Dad and the other stockmen. One of my younger sisters has been studying agribusiness at university in Brisbane. I think she also has hopes of returning to the station one day."

"It's great that you can work together as a family. Not all families can do that. At least, not successfully."

"Are you speaking from experience?"

"No. In fact, my father and Uncle Arthur had a very successful partnership. Then again, I couldn't imagine sharing an office with my sister. She's very artistic. A creative type. Less inclined to work to a schedule and prefers to go with the vibe of a situation, rather than the facts. I love her to bits, but we could never work together. I certainly admire siblings who do, particularly out here where it's difficult to escape each other. After all, where is there to go?"

Maggie swirled the water with her hand and smiled. "Only about one hundred and fifty thousand acres. Surely you've noticed the wide-open spaces? That's part of what I love about the place."

"I meant escaping to another suburb, another town; being able to hang out with people who aren't related to you."

She chuckled. "I know what you meant. The truth is, I'm not sure most of us had a say in it. My brothers, like me, have this land running through their veins. They love it as much as I do.

For them, working on the station alongside their family was always something they were going to do."

"They don't have arguments?" Raf asked, curious.

Maggie laughed enthusiastically. The unfettered sound of it shimmered across Raf's veins.

"Of course they do. Occasionally it even comes to fisticuffs. But they work things out and move on. No one stays angry for very long."

"Sounds like you have a close and supportive family."

Her expression turned whimsical. "Yes, I do. They're wonderful."

"What will happen if the new owner of Hetherington Station doesn't take you on?"

She narrowed her eyes at him. "So, you've definitely decided to sell then?"

He held her gaze. "I haven't definitely decided anything. But I've been upfront about my options and, from what I can see, selling this place would be the sensible thing to do."

"Says you."

With a flick of her arm and a kick of her feet, she swam away from him.

Raf sighed and paddled over to her. Half-expecting her to move again, he was relieved when she stayed where she was, though she continued to scowl at him.

"I understand how the idea of selling is distressing for you, but look at it from my point of view. I live and work in the city. I have no need for an outback station. I don't know why my uncle left it to me because, quite frankly, handing this station onto someone who can work it and love it like you do would be the best for everyone."

"The best for you, no doubt," she retorted.

He inclined his head, holding onto his patience. He understood her anger. If he were in her position, he'd likely feel the same way.

"Don't you care about all the people who live here?" she cried. "Their lives are intimately connected to this land, and if the next owner decides not to keep them on, they'll have nowhere to go," she cried. Don't you care about that at all?"

This time, without waiting for his answer, she swam swiftly for the bank. He watched her splash in the shallows and then she was on the grass that surrounded the billabong. He cursed softly. She was mercurial. Sunny one minute and snarly the next. He thought about the long night ahead as he slowly followed her out of the water.

He wouldn't apologize for his plans, but he did want to talk to her about them. However, with the way things had just ended between them, no doubt he was in for a solitary evening. He was grateful for one thing: he no longer had to worry about concealing his erection.

Maggie did her best to ignore the man beside her. She hated the power he had in determining her future and that of the people she cared for. And while he hadn't asked to inherit the station and his reasons for selling the place on financial grounds were sound, she didn't have to like them. What she needed to do was to put forward a compelling argument for keeping the place so she could secure the future of those who loved it.

Oh, Arthur! What were you thinking? Did you not care at all for those of us who have given so much to this land?

They made it back to the homestead without incident. Maggie had been so upset, she'd struggled briefly, pulling her shorts back on and had barely registered Raf doing the same. She'd been determined to leave the billabong as quickly as possible. Which they had.

Her temper had cooled somewhat en route to the homestead, and she refocused on her surroundings. Whenever they came across a gate, Raf rode ahead and opened it for her. At one point, Maggie stopped to repair a hole in a fence with tools and wire she always kept on the back of the bike for such necessities. Raf watched her in silence, and when she'd finished, he'd returned to his bike and followed confidently beside her. He'd picked up changing the gears quickly and it irritated her that something that should have been at least a little challenging for a city slicker who'd never ridden a bike appeared to be so easy.

He's probably had everything in his life come easy... Career... Money... A multi-million-dollar cattle station... Women...

That last thought pulled her up short.

What the hell was I thinking back at the billabong? Why did I challenge him to go skinny dipping? That's not me. Thank goodness I kept most of my clothes on! Besides, we've only just met, and I need for him to take me seriously if he's to listen to my arguments against selling. Now he'll think I'm looking to persuade him in other ways. So stupid!

What irritated her the most was her reaction to him. When he'd brushed up against her in the water, her heart rate had skyrocketed. She'd never been so turned on by a mere touch. For a moment, she'd been too astonished by her reaction to respond.

So what if he was drop-dead gorgeous? So what if he made her go weak at the knees? So what if he was personable, intelligent and thoughtful? None of that counted with Raf Hetherington. That was the reason she'd picked a fight with him. It was childish and rude, but he was there to bring an end to her livelihood, her dreams of running the station for as long as she wanted. Not to mention the impact a decision to sell would have on the other employee. She needed to be more professional. She didn't know him and she needed to learn more if she was to persuade him from his current course.

She'd shown him the billabong and while he'd appeared more impressed with her body than with the natural wonder—entirely her fault—there were plenty more natural wonders on the property to see that were sure to make him think twice about disposing of his inheritance so quickly. At least, that's what she hoped.

When Raf arrived back at the homestead, he was pleasantly surprised to discover Maggie in the kitchen preparing dinner. After going through the last gate, she'd rode on ahead of him, no doubt glad to be rid of his company, at least for a short while. It had taken him another twenty minutes to make it back. He'd assumed she'd still be stewing over his likely decision to sell the station, but the brief smile and murmured greeting she shot in his direction as he entered the kitchen indicated otherwise.

While she had his head in a spin with her mercurial moods, he was glad she wasn't someone who bore a grudge. That would be unbearable. He planned to spend at least a week there, catching up on some R and R, as well as familiarizing himself with all the station had to offer in order to educate himself about its worth. Whenever it came to buying or selling real estate, he prided himself on doing his own research. This would be no different.

"Is there anything I can do to help?" he asked, feeling a little awkward about how the afternoon had played out.

"Do you know how to peel potatoes?" she asked, looking dubious.

"Of course!" he replied, slightly affronted. "What do you take me for?"

She gave him a dry look. "A city boy who eats out more than he cooks. If he cooks at all."

He opened his mouth in outrage and then caught the gleam of humor in her eyes. He settled on a non-committal grunt. The truth was, he did eat out occasionally. Most of the time, it was more convenient than grocery shopping for food and cooking for one. But that didn't mean he didn't know how or that he didn't enjoy the process. In fact, he often used cooking to relax.

"It looks like Uncle Arthur at least spent some money modernizing the kitchen," he said, looking around.

A row of sparkling stainless steel cooking pots hung from hooks along a rail that ran above the generous island bench that stood in the center of the kitchen. Other cooking implements hung beside them within easy reach. A shiny, nine-burner gas cooktop and oven took up a fair amount of the counter space on the opposite wall, along with cupboards, a fridge, a microwave, a dishwasher, and a coffee nook.

Maggie nodded. "Yes, although he didn't exactly do the upgrades voluntarily."

Raf raised an eyebrow in silent query.

"We had a small kitchen fire last year," she explained. "A dodgy electrical cord on the microwave. Thank goodness I was in the house when it happened. I put it out before it really got going. It was only the kitchen that suffered damage. Insurance covered the cost of the refurbishment."

Raf nodded. "That explains why the rest of the homestead still looks like it's in its original condition."

She chuckled. "Pretty much. As I said, your uncle made a few updates—the air conditioning, for one—but for the rest of the place, this is about how it would have looked a hundred years ago."

Raf frowned. "That reminds me. I meant to call the air conditioning mechanic and see if I could get him out here faster."

"Good luck with that. As I told you earlier, tradesmen are slim on the ground, and they're all worked off their feet. But you're welcome to try. He's Aaron Luke. Perhaps you can charm him with your big city ways."

Although Raf was pretty sure she'd meant to insult him by referring to his "big city" charm he let the comment slide. Life out there in the summer without air conditioning would be unbearable. He might only have to tolerate it for a week or so, but what about Maggie?

"Can you text me his number? I'll call him first thing in the morning."

"Sure." She sidled over to the far end of the counter where her phone was plugged into a charger. "What's your number?" she threw over her shoulder.

He gave it to her. A few moments later, his phone beeped with an incoming text. "Thanks," he said, scanning the details.

"Let's hope you have better luck than I did," she murmured and returned to the salad she'd been preparing.

"So, where are those potatoes?" he asked, getting up and washing his hands in the sink.

"In the pantry."

She indicated a door that led off the kitchen. Inside was a good-sized walk-in pantry that was well-stocked with mostly non-perishable food. He found a wooden box containing potatoes and pulled out enough for the two of them.

He brought them out and dropped them into the sink. "Where's the potato peeler?"

She chuckled as if in disbelief. "You really know how to peel potatoes?"

The challenge in her eyes sent a surge of blood straight to his groin. It was all he could do not to groan. But he kept his gaze steady on hers and nodded.

"Just watch me."

Chapter Six

♥

While Raf washed and peeled the potatoes over the sink, Maggie focused her attention on a salad. She kept herself busy slicing tomatoes, snapping peas and julienning carrots, but her gaze kept drifting toward him. His overlong fringe was still damp from their swim, and it now curled enticingly at the ends. His earlier clean-shaven look now sported a dark stubble, making him look even more desirable. He also had nice hands. Long fingers that ended in clean and tidy fingernails, muscular forearms covered in a light sprinkling of dark hair.

She snuck another glance and realized his fingers were bare. No rings of any kind. When they'd talked earlier about his family, he'd made no mention of a wife. Did that mean he was single? The thought caused her heart to somersault.

Stop it! Who cares whether he's single? He's here to sell the station, and that's bad news for me and for the others. I need to focus on what's important and stop getting distracted by pointless things. Besides, lots of married men don't wear rings...

"I know it's a bit early for dinner, but seeing as we skipped lunch, I thought you might be hungry," she said.

He looked across at her and grinned. "You're right. I'm famished. It feels like a lifetime since that banana bread."

She smiled. "I think I recall offering you lunch. You turned me down."

He chuckled. "So you did. My bad. Now that I know you don't eat too often, I won't make the same mistake again."

"Sorry. Sometimes I skip lunch, especially if I'm working away from the homestead. Unless I've actually planned to be away for the whole day, I rarely take a packed lunch with me. After you told me you didn't want to eat, I didn't think about it again."

"That's okay. I'll survive. But I'm most definitely looking forward to dinner. What are we having?"

"Steak and salad with mashed potato. Is that all right?"

"Sounds great."

"Are you allergic to anything?"

"Only iodine."

"Well, I'll be sure not to serve up any of that...yet."

He laughed.

"How do you take your steak?"

"Medium rare. But I'm hungry enough and polite enough to eat whatever you plate up."

"That's fine. I can do medium rare."

He kept his gaze on her. "I really admire how self-sufficient you are, Maggie. Living way out here in the middle of nowhere with very little support."

She shrugged and kept her gaze on the bowl of lettuce she'd just washed. "Everyone's self-sufficient out here. There's no choice."

"True, but not everyone's as adaptable to that as you seem to be. A lot of the women I know wouldn't have a clue how to go about mending a fence, let alone running a cattle station."

"No doubt they have other strengths," she murmured, keen to get the attention off her.

"No doubt they do," Raf agreed and returned his focus back to the potatoes. "But just so you know, the kind of confidence and adaptability you have is a real turn on for me."

She closed her eyes against a wave of heat that threatened to engulf her face. If she wasn't already so aware of him, his frank comment might not have had any effect. As it was, she'd been fighting her attraction to him almost from the first moment she'd set eyes on him.

"Please don't say things like that," she said through gritted teeth.

"Why not?"

Another wave of embarrassment washed over her. "Because... Because it isn't appropriate. We hardly know each other and until you sell this place, you're my boss."

His eyes glittered with good humor. It was obvious he wasn't taking her request seriously. "I think we passed "appropriate" when you took your shorts off for me."

She gasped in outrage. Her face flamed. "I didn't take them off for you! I...I..."

He held his hands up in a sign of surrender. "Okay, okay. I withdraw that. You took them off because...?"

"If you must know, I took them off because it would have been darn uncomfortable riding back on the bike with wet shorts," she lied.

"Ah. I see. Now I understand. Glad you cleared that up. I'd hate for there to be any more *misunderstandings.*"

She ducked her head to hide the fresh wave of heat that blasted her cheeks and focused on the salad, all the time wishing that the floor would open up and swallow her.

As if oblivious to her discomfort, Raf continued. "So, have you ever dated your boss?"

She groaned aloud her frustration. "You're kidding me! Are you referring to Arthur?"

He chuckled. "Of course not. You must have had other bosses."

"Yes, but I never dated any of them."

"There's always a first time," he quipped.

She groaned loudly again, making it clear from her tone and from the stern look she gave him that she'd had enough of the conversation. Raf merely shrugged. She turned away and busied herself with the thawed-out steak she'd taken from the freezer earlier.

"Can I use one of these pots?" Raf asked, reaching for one overheard.

She half-turned toward him. "Sure."

He filled a pot with water and then dropped the potatoes in. Without asking for help, he worked out how to switch on the cooktop and set the potatoes to boil. Then he wiped his hands on a tea towel and smiled. "Right, then. What's next?"

"I'm going to cook the steak outside on the barbeque." She picked up the plate of meat and headed across the room.

"Great. I'll come and keep you company."

"There's no need. I don't need help."

"I didn't say I was going to help. Just keep you company."

Maggie bit back a protest. The last thing she wanted was to extend their time together, but that's exactly what she needed to do. Convincing him to keep the station was going to take time. For that reason, the more time she spent with him, the better. It was too bad his nearness, coupled with his flirty comments, filled her stomach with butterflies and sent her pulse rate soaring. But arguing with him would be churlish and besides, what was she going to do? Order him to stay in the kitchen? *His* kitchen?

"Sure. Come then. It's this way."

"Do you mind if I grab a drink first?" he asked.

Maggie shrugged. "Suit yourself."

"Do you have any beer?"

"Yes. Bottom shelf of the fridge."

"Do you want one?"

A beer before dinner was one of her favorite ways to relax. Raf's presence had disrupted her usual schedule. She realized now a beer was exactly what she needed to take the edge off.

"Sure. Thanks. I'll be out the back."

With that, she walked through the opening between the double doors that led to the back veranda, crossed over it, opened the screen door and went down the concrete steps. The barbeque was set up in a small, cleared area, close enough to the house that the outside light shining from the back veranda provided sufficient illumination in the winter months. Right now, in January, even though it was after six in the evening, with daylight saving time in full swing, it was still light enough that they didn't need any additional help to see.

She passed by four old wooden chairs arranged around a weathered timber table. Though she didn't entertain often, every now and then one of her brothers or some friends from an adjoining station would drop in and stay for dinner. If it was a pleasant evening, they'd eat outside. She thought about suggesting it to Raf and then decided against it. Safer for her libido if she met with him in a well-lit area.

Quickly and efficiently, she lit the barbeque and waited for the plate to heat. Cooking the perfect steak was all about the temperature of the cooking surface. Too hot and the meat burned on the outside and wasn't cooked on the inside. Too cold and the entire process went south.

Raf reappeared with two beers in his hands just as she dropped the steaks onto the hotplate.

"Here you go," he said, offering her one of the bottles.

"Thanks."

He'd already opened the bottle. She lifted it to her lips and took a sip. "Ah. That's just what I needed."

Raf nodded and sipped from his beer. "Nothing like a cold beer after a hot day in the sun."

He looked around him at the gardens. Though she didn't sense any judgement in his bearing, she flushed. The beds of flowers were overrun with weeds and the hedges needed pruning. With so few people on the station, taking time out from stock work to tend to the gardens just didn't happen. The only place she and Daphne put real time into was the vegetable garden. They needed that to survive.

"Who tends the gardens?" Raf asked.

"Nobody. Me. Daphne. Sometimes. Whenever I can spare the time. As you can see, that's not often," she said stiffly.

"Hey, don't get defensive. I'm not giving you a hard time. Just curious."

"The station comes first, no matter what. The cattle are what make us money. Pretty gardens are nice, but they do nothing for the bank balance."

"Of course."

Maggie turned away from his gaze and busied herself with the steaks.

Raf sipped again from his beer and sidled closer to the barbeque. "So, where did this meat come from?"

Maggie shot him a look of disbelief. "You have to ask? This is prime Hetherington steak, raised right here on the station."

Raf grinned. "Good to know. I wouldn't expect anything else."

"Then why did you ask?"

He shrugged and grinned again. "Just making conversation."

Irritation coursed through her. She ought to be grateful his inane chatter had meant that her persistent feelings of attraction had finally disappeared. That was a good thing. But her annoyance with him only made her job harder. She needed to use this opportunity to regale him with the benefits of keeping the place. To put it frankly, she needed to play nice.

She forced a smile. "Sorry, that was harsher than I intended. Of course, you're curious about this place. After all, you now own it. Ask as many questions as you like."

He took another sip of his beer. "How do you go with fresh produce, living so far from town?"

"Most of the produce is grown right here, including the salad we're eating tonight. The only thing we didn't grow are the potatoes. Daphne does most of the work in the vegetable garden. Her people are from the Mandandanji mob. She's lived here or around these parts all her life. According to Daphne, when she was a kid, there were nearly fifty of her people living and working right here on the station."

Raf's eyes brightened with interest. "What happened to them all?"

"Most of them moved into town. A lot of these stations are now owned by big corporations. They're not the family-run enterprises of the past. Big corporations are all about the bottom line. They're not interested in the lives of the people who rely on the station for their living, or the traditional custodians who might still be here."

From the guilt that flashed briefly across Raf's face, Maggie could tell her barb had hit its mark. Not that he'd had anything to do with the decisions of the past, but he also seemed disinclined to become involved with the people who worked there or be informed about what his decision to sell would mean to the people who called the station home.

"What else does Daphne do around here?" he asked.

"She cooks for the other employees and does other odd jobs. Milks the cow. Feeds the chickens. She runs into town for spare parts and groceries. She has more time on her hands now her youngest child's left the station for the bright city lights."

Raf took another sip of his beer. "How many kids does she have?"

"Eleven"

He grinned. "Wow. That's even more than your family."

She chuckled. "Yep. And all but three of Daphne's kids have up and left to live in the city. Go figure. I mean, who'd swap this kind of life for one among the rat race?"

Raf gave her a pointed look. "The city has its appeal."

Maggie scoffed. "To someone who's never been to the outback, perhaps."

"You said three of Daphne's children hung around. Where did they go?"

Maggie checked the steaks before replying. "One of her sons works on a cattle station in far north Queensland and two daughters married station hands from nearby farms. The closest one is a hundred miles away."

"A hundred miles? They might as well be in Brisbane," Raf said dryly.

"That's not so far out here. It's a hundred miles to Roma and back and we go there for anything from cattle drench to a night out on the town."

A teasing light filled his eyes. An inviting smile curved his lips. "A night out on the town? That sounds interesting. Maybe you could find time to take me barhopping while I'm here. I'd love to see what the Roma night life has to offer."

Maggie kept her gaze fixed firmly on the barbeque and did her best to ignore the sudden surge of butterflies that swarmed in her stomach. "That wouldn't take long," she murmured.

"What's the population of Roma?"

She glanced at him briefly. "Less than seven thousand. A thriving metropolis."

He laughed. "There must be somewhere we could go out."

Her stomach clenched again. This damnable attraction to him was beyond annoying. She gave a noncommittal shrug. "I guess."

"Where do you go to have a good time?" he persisted.

The thought of going out on the town with Raf filled her with all sorts of dangerous yearnings. She ruthlessly ignored them. "I rarely leave the farm. I'm too busy working." Before he could respond, she spoke again.

"These are done." She pulled the steaks off the barbeque. Not waiting for him, she collected her beer and the meat and headed back inside.

Chapter Seven

♥

Raf cut into his perfectly cooked steak and took his first bite of Hetherington beef. "*Mm.* This is delicious," he said, chewing the tender morsel.

Maggie made a noncommittal sound in the back of her throat and continued eating. She'd been quiet since his remark about checking out the Roma night life. There had been an edge to her voice when she'd responded to his questions. He wasn't sure if the idea of going out with him was repulsive, or whether it was the risk he posed to her future that had caused the air of tension that now surrounded them.

No, it couldn't be the former. It was only a matter of hours ago that she'd gone swimming with him in a shirt and panties and her attitude had been flirty and fun. She'd openly ogled him when he'd stripped down. It was only after their conversation had turned to his plans for the station that her mood had soured. He'd bet money that it was his purpose for being there that once again hung heavily on her mind and had reduced her to near silence.

"How many cattle do you run here?" he asked in an effort to restart the conversation.

She swallowed the food in her mouth and then replied. "It depends on the season. When there's plenty of water and pasture, we run about five thousand. In a poor season, we sell off everything but our prime breeding stock. That's about five hundred cattle."

"Wow. It's hard to imagine the weather can have that much of an impact on your carrying rates. I've never thought about the reality of a drought on stock numbers. I guess that's because I buy all of my steak from a butcher."

"Surely you notice when the price goes up," she said dryly.

"Yes, I guess. But only in an abstract way. Everyone knows that extreme weather events affect food supply, but making that specific connection doesn't always occur."

She rolled her eyes. "That's the problem. You city slickers think all your food comes from a supermarket."

He tamped down a spurt of irritation. "Not quite, but I take your point."

He sliced off another piece of steak and forked it in his mouth. The rich taste and the tenderness of the meat was impressive, along with the fact it had been cooked to perfection. It was clear Maggie was a competent cook, especially with steak. He liked that about her. He liked a lot of things about her. It was too bad they'd met in such difficult circumstances and that they were on opposite sides of the fence. No matter what the station had to offer, he was yet to be convinced his best option would be to keep the place. And therein lay the problem.

He didn't deliberately want to destroy Maggie's future, nor the livelihood of the other farm employees. But neither did he want to make a decision based on emotion. The sensible thing would be to sell the station and invest the proceeds into something with a more reliable return. Something that wasn't at the behest of the weather. Something like Brisbane real estate.

He'd always been a sensible man, with a cool head for business. And that's what this was. A business transaction. No matter how alluring the station manager or the fact she wanted things to remain the same. He'd take no pleasure from evicting her and the other employees from the station, but if that's what had to happen in order to broker the best deal, then so be it.

Maggie picked at her food. Her appetite had vanished with Raf's teasing words about checking out the Roma night life. He was only there for a short time. She was sure he didn't have any real interest in what Roma had to offer. Perhaps he merely wanted to break up the boredom of living on the station or was humoring her. Both possibilities were irritating, but she couldn't afford to let those feelings show.

She needed him to want to keep the station. The only way he'd do that is if he felt some kind of connection to the place, along with some sense of responsibility toward her and the other employees. Getting him to feel that way about complete strangers who were living in what was to him a completely foreign land was going to be challenging, but she had no choice. Too many people were relying on her.

The sound of Raf's chair scraping on the timber floor dragged her from her thoughts. She looked up in time to see him stand and collect his plate and take it to the sink. In a panic, she realized the opportunity to engage him in further conversation that evening was slipping through her fingers. She had to act fast.

Climbing to her feet, she took her dirty plate and cutlery into the kitchen. Raf stood at the sink, rinsing the dishes.

"You don't have to do that," she protested. "You're a guest."

"I don't mind. Besides, you cooked dinner. Where I come from, the cook never has to wash up."

"When you live on your own, you cook and clean and do everything in between," she replied with a slight grin.

He laughed. "Don't I know it."

She looked at him, curious. She hadn't asked him about his marital status or whether he lived alone. The fact he wore no wedding room didn't necessarily mean he was on his own. It was on the tip of her tongue to ask him about it, but something held her back. Whatever his situation, it was none of her business. Better to put her energies into the task at hand.

"What would you like to do tomorrow?" she asked as she put the leftover food away.

He looked up briefly from where he stood over the sink and smiled. "I'm easy. Everything out here is new to me, but I understand you might have work to do. I'm happy to fit in with your schedule."

"Good. There are a few chores that need to be attended to, but I'm sure I can make time to show you around. There's still plenty to see. You've inherited one hundred and fifty thousand acres. That covers a fair amount of ground."

Raf whistled and shook his head. "That kind of area blows my mind. It's hard to imagine one person owning all that land."

She shrugged. "You're seeing the place in a good season. We have more bad than good. When the water storages run low and fodder is scarce, we need every acre we have to keep the station viable. As your late uncle's bookkeeper, you know that better than most."

He nodded. "Yes. There have been more lean years than fat, that's for sure." He paused and then added, "How do you do it? How do you stay so committed? So determined to make things work, when all around you everything's going to hell? You don't have any control over the weather and that's what mostly determines whether you're going to make money or not."

She compressed her lips. "I don't know. You just do. You get up every day determined to make the best of it. If we need to cart water, we do. If we need to buy in feed, we do. If we need to sell off stock, we do that too. We do whatever it takes to survive so we can flourish again in prosperous times. That's all we can do."

She saw admiration in his gaze.

"You're a special breed of people who call this land home, that's for sure," he said. "The kind of resilience and mental fortitude it must take to keep getting up in the morning when you're in the middle of a severe drought is mind blowing. I have nothing but admiration for you and for all the people who live and work out here. It makes my job behind a desk, kicking back in an air-conditioned office, look easy."

"I'm sure it isn't easy doing what you do. It must be stressful having responsibility for other people's money, knowing they're expecting you to make them a decent return; blaming you if things don't work out that way."

"I guess."

Suds covered his arms, right up to his elbows, as he finished the last of the dishes. Seeing him slaving over the sink was so at odds with the image she had of him as a high powered, successful investment banker, rubbing shoulders with high rollers and playing for the kind of stakes that would make her eyes water. It was nice to discover he could be as normal as anyone else and wasn't above helping to prepare a meal or to clean up afterwards. It gave her hope that she might be able to appeal to a softer side of him; a more humane side.

"Would you like coffee?" she asked.

Drying his hands on a tea towel, he turned to her and smiled. "That would be great, thanks."

She filled the kettle and set it to boil and went about making coffee. She remembered how he liked it and made them each a cup. Glancing through the kitchen window, she could see the sun hanging low in the sky. Soon it would disappear altogether.

Dusk was her favorite time of day. It came much later in the summer. It was already after eight and the sun hadn't completely disappeared yet. Usually, this time of year, she took her coffee and sat out the back after dinner to watch the sunset. It was one of her favorite ways to relax and unwind. Doing so this evening would also give her the chance to speak further with Raf.

Pouring hot water into both cups, she handed one to him. "I like to sit out the back this time of night and watch the sun go down. It never fails to put on a wonderful display. You're welcome to join me."

"Thank you," he murmured and followed her outside.

As they settled into the matching cane wicker chairs that faced out into the backyard, he asked her about the history of the station.

Maggie smiled. She loved history. It had been her favorite subject at school. She'd always made a point of learning the history about a place wherever she went. Hetherington Station was no different, and she'd done her research within the first few months of moving there.

"The station had been in the same family for many generations before your uncle bought it," she said.

"Who were they?"

"Angus and Eliza McGregor. They emigrated from Scotland in the 1800s. They were pioneers. They built this house with their bare hands."

"How do you know this stuff?" Raf asked.

"I stumbled across some old journals in the back of a cupboard when I first moved into the homestead. I'm not sure your uncle even knew they were there."

"What happened to the family? Did they die without offspring?"

"No. In fact, they had four children. Hamish, Hugh, Freya, and Bridie. The two boys lived and worked on the station until they died. They married and had families and some of those children stayed on, but as the years went on and the cities and towns popped up, many of the younger family members drifted away. The best I can work out is that by the time your uncle came along, none of the current generation of McGregors were interested in the station. When their parents died, they sold the place to your uncle."

Raf smiled. "I guess you can be thankful they didn't sell it to one of those big corporates."

"True. I guess I can only hope that if you do decide to sell that it won't be to one of them either. They don't have a connection to the land. It's only an entry on a balance sheet to them. They know nothing about the people who make their lives out here, the pain and heartbreak, the joys and triumphs. The *living* that goes on out here."

When she finished, her face was flushed and her breath came fast. She dipped her head, a little embarrassed by her outburst.

"I'm sorry," she mumbled. "That was a bit over the top. You have the right to sell to whomever you want."

He nodded, his expression thoughtful. "True. But that doesn't mean I don't appreciate where you're coming from, or the love you have for this place. This is more than just a station to you. More than a tract of land. It's a way of life; *your* way of life. That I feel so out of place, like I'm in a foreign country, has no bearing on the way you feel about it."

He continued to regard her in the dimness. "I admire your passion. No wonder you're such a fine manager. You love this place as if it were your own. My late uncle couldn't have asked for anyone better qualified to take care of his holdings."

"You're right. I do love this place. But it's more than Hetherington Station. I love the entire area. Living in the outback. The remoteness, the wide-open spaces, the natural beauty that takes your breath away."

She glanced at him and gave an embarrassed chuckle. "Sorry, I'm getting carried away again."

"Don't be sorry. You're just being honest, and I admire that."

His gaze captured hers in a long and searching look. With an effort, she found the strength to look away. She took refuge in her coffee. The sound of the cicadas in the nearby gum trees filled the silence that fell between them. A horse neighed in the distance.

"Tell me about your life in the city," she asked quietly.

He drew in a deep breath and eased it out. "What do you want to know?"

"I don't know. What do you love about it?"

He was silent a moment, as if gathering his thoughts. "I grew up there. I've lived there all my life. I've done some traveling overseas—Europe, the US—but I keep returning home. For me, Brisbane is the best of both worlds. Part city, part country."

She snorted with disbelief. "Part country? Purlease! I'm dying to hear which part you'd describe as "country"."

He chuckled. "Have you ever been to Sydney?"

"Yes. Only once. I hated every minute. Too much traffic, too much noise, too many people." She gave an exaggerated shudder. "I don't know what it is about Sydney that everyone raves about."

Raf grinned. "It has its appeal. The harbor, the Opera House, the beaches. The restaurants, the live music, the culture. What's not to like?"

Maggie grimaced. "You can have all that. Give me wide-open spaces, absolute silence, and nothing and no one for miles around and I'm happy. I couldn't bear to live in such close quarters with other people. And the buildings and houses all squashed so closely together... The very thought gives me claustrophobia."

He quirked an eyebrow. "Really?"

"No, not really. But I don't enjoy my time spent in the city. Especially not Sydney."

"But see, that's where Brisbane's different. Okay, it isn't wide-open spaces where silence is a given, but neither is it the hustle and bustle of Sydney. Brisbane has all the delights and conveniences of a city without the crowds and noise. There are nightclubs, bars and theaters, fine dining, art galleries and shopping. Everything you could want and yet it doesn't have the frantic pace of a city like Sydney. Like I said, the best of both worlds."

Maggie shook her head. "It's still far too crowded and far too noisy for my liking."

"So, what do you do for fun?" Raf asked.

Maggie bit her lip in thought. She couldn't remember the last time she'd had fun. The station normally consumed her time. Besides, there weren't that many places to go and not that many people to hang with. Not that she'd tell him that.

"We have our local watering holes," she managed. "As you know, Roma's only an hour up the road. Then there are the social outings on other stations. Tennis matches, barbeques, that kind of thing. Now and then we go into Rockhampton for a weekend of R and R. That's always fun," she said lamely.

Raf eyed her steadily. "What kind of things do you do for R and R?"

She flushed under his curious gaze. The truth was, it had been three years since she'd had a weekend in Rockhampton. Not since she'd taken on the manager's role at Hetherington Station. There hadn't been the time to go. With a population of a little over eighty thousand, Rockhampton was their nearest rural city and offered a greater variety of fun and activities than Roma did.

"Well, there's the annual Brahman bull sale in Rockhampton," she said. "It runs over three days and attracts thousands of people from all over the state and beyond."

"How often do you go?"

She flushed again. "Not in recent times, but I've attended in the past with my family. It's a fun few days and gives me the opportunity to catch up with breeders from all over the country."

"When was the last time you went?"

"At least three years ago. Ever since taking on the job here, I haven't had enough time to get away."

He shook his head. "My uncle worked you to the bone," he muttered.

"No, he didn't. It was my choice not to go. We were so busy, but it was also because I wasn't all that keen to go. When I've been in the past, I've always returned home exhausted, and to tell you the truth, I'm always glad to be away from the noise and the crowds."

"So, what else do you do for entertainment?"

She thought for a moment. "Well, if you're talking about Rockhampton, there's also the annual beef city rodeo. Broncs, bull riding, barrel racing. There's something for everyone if you're into that kind of thing. Sometimes they even held the national finals there."

He quirked an eyebrow. "Have you ever ridden a bronc?"

She laughed and shook her head. "No. I might be up for a challenge now and then, but I'm not stupid."

He chuckled. "The men who ride those beasts have to have rocks in their head, don't you think?"

She laughed again and agreed, saying, "I bet their chiropractors are kept busy afterwards."

He grinned. "For sure. So, you're not into bronc riding even though you could if you wanted. What else does Rockhampton have to offer?"

She thought again. "Well, there are the magnificent Capricorn Caves, numerous heritage walks, the zoo, the Botanical Garden. There's quite a lot to choose from. It depends what you're interested in."

"What are *you* interested in?" he asked lazily.

She blushed at the avid interest in his gaze. "To tell you the truth, I rarely venture off the station. Not because your uncle never gave me leave, but this is my favorite place in the world. I try to spend as little time as possible away from here and I'm perfectly happy with that."

With a start, she realized she'd inadvertently become an introvert. She was twenty-eight years of age and living like a hermit. How did she ever hope to meet a prospective husband and raise all those children she dreamed about if she kept herself hidden away on the farm?

Raf's gaze remained steady on hers. Unable to maintain eye contact, she averted her gaze.

"What about those nights out in Roma? Don't you like going out to bars?"

She shrugged. "Sure. Sometimes, I guess. Occasionally I'll go to Roma with some of my men and go drinking. Sometimes we even dance."

His eyebrows rose. "You like to dance?"

She ducked her head. "Not really," she muttered. The truth was, she hated dancing. In fact, her definition of a perfect night out was to stay home, tucked up in bed with hot chocolate in one hand and a good book in the other. She swallowed a sigh.

When did I become so boring? I really do need to get out more...

Seemingly undeterred by her lack of enthusiasm, Raf's eyes gleamed.

"I love dancing," he said. "Hip hop, jazz, rock and roll. My mother made me take lessons when I was a kid. Back then, I used to hate being the only kid in my class who danced. Now I'm glad she insisted on getting me taught. I usually go out dancing at least once a week. It's a lot of fun."

"If you say so," she mumbled, glad for the deepening shadows that hid her expression from his view.

They were from different worlds. No matter that she found him wildly attractive, they had nothing in common. He liked the city life and all it had to offer. He enjoyed being around people. Heaven help her, he even liked to dance! The best thing she could do was to keep her distance. Treat him with courtesy and respect. Persuade him to keep the station and then urge him to return to his city life and all that it offered. This wasn't the first time she'd given herself a lecture about staying the hell away from him, but this time, she was determined to follow through. It was the best thing for both of them.

Chapter Eight

♥

Raf finished the rest of his coffee and sat back in his chair with a sigh, feeling relaxed and replete. He was glad Maggie appeared to have set aside her hostility, at least for the time being.

She'd been right about the sunset. It had been beautiful. All crimson reds, oranges, purples and finally, a velvety-black. Now there were stars that twinkled overhead, blanketing them with diamonds. It was so quiet, so peaceful, especially now the cicadas had called it a night. He heard the faintest hoot of an owl in the distance and smiled.

He couldn't remember the last occasion he'd taken time out to enjoy the sunset. Usually, he was still behind his desk at that time of the evening. With no one to come home to and with always plenty of work to be done, he'd never felt the need.

But out there it was different. He was on vacation, for one. There was also no doubt life ran at a much slower pace on the station. Not that he'd seen it in full swing. Perhaps tomorrow he'd get to see more of the action. It would be interesting to at least get up close and personal with some cattle. After all, this was a cattle station.

Maggie's love for the land was obvious. He understood why she wanted to stay. She'd been born and raised in the outback. This was home. It was no different to the way he felt about Brisbane. Familiar, a safe and secure environment that simply felt right. She couldn't help that her life was in the outback any more than he could change the way he felt about the city.

It surprised him to discover he hadn't been bored since he'd arrived. He realized he hadn't once gone looking for his phone to check his social pages or missed texts or missed calls. Of course, he'd only spent half a day there. It would be interesting to see how he felt by the end of the first week.

It was very possible he'd be climbing the walls by then. After all, that would be the longest time he'd spent away from civilization. Then again, there was every chance the magnetic attraction between him and Maggie would be enough to stave off boredom. She certainly posed a challenge that kept things interesting and not only because they were in conflict about what should happen to the station. He looked forward to finding out the end result.

He sighed quietly again and glanced in her direction. She sat beside him, her face in profile as she stared out across the back lawn. Her face was in shadows. The only illumination came from the light in the kitchen behind them. A little frown line appeared between her eyes. He wondered what she was thinking. Then she stood abruptly, empty coffee mug in hand.

"I've had a long day. I'm going to turn in."

He looked up at her and nodded. It wasn't that late—maybe nine o'clock. But for all he knew, she'd been up at the crack of dawn. Either that or she was using it as an excuse to put some distance between them.

"Sure. Have a good sleep. I'll see you in the morning," he said.

With that, she was gone, leaving him alone with his thoughts.

Maggie turned over in bed for the umpteenth time, dragging the sheet with her. It had been a big day, both physically and emotionally. Attending to the usual chores on the station, along with meeting Raf and mentally battling the near certainty his next move would be to sell the place. She'd promised Bluey she'd do everything in her power to keep his livelihood safe, but she wasn't sure if she'd be successful, and it was that knowledge that now kept her awake.

That wasn't the only thing keeping her from sleep. She was acutely aware of Raf right across the hall. She'd turned in before him, but she'd still been wide awake when she'd heard his footsteps on the timber floor. She'd heard his door open and close and then open again. A few minutes later, she'd heard water running in the bathroom. After that, the house had fallen silent. She assumed he was in bed. No doubt sound asleep. After all, what did he have on his mind to keep him awake? He held all the cards.

A squeak of bedsprings from the room opposite snagged her attention.

He must be turning over in his sleep. Lucky for him to have found respite.

An image of him dark and slumbering filled her mind. There was no doubt he was an exemplary physical specimen. Tall and broad and muscular. Just the kind of physique that turned her on. And that hairy chest! Superb! She longed to tangle her fingers in its softness.

Desire flickered to life inside her. Her hand stole beneath the covers. She flicked at her nipples and then slid her hand further to settle comfortably against her mound.

She'd been in a state of arousal almost from the moment Raf had first spoken. Things hadn't improved as the day wore on. Seeing him naked in the billabong had only increased the yearning. No wonder she was restless and jittery. She needed to relieve the tension that had been building inside her all day.

Her fingers applied the right kind of pressure to her pleasure spot, and she sighed and let her legs fall open. As she worked herself up to an orgasm, her traitorous thoughts centered on the man who slept across the hall. She wondered if he wore pajamas, or if he slept naked, like she did. She wondered if the perfectly sculptured pectorals were as firm to the touch as they looked.

In her mind's eye, she traced the trail of dark hair that led from his belly button to beneath the waistband of his shorts and pictured his erection: thick and hard and impressive. He had a confidence, an air of authority that was appealing, even more so when that confidence followed him into the bedroom.

Her fingers worked faster as she neared the peak. Rolling over onto her stomach, she buried her face against the pillow to smother her sounds of fulfilment. She was pretty sure her house guest was asleep, but just in case...

As the last ripples of her climax subsided, she sighed quietly in satisfaction. She was relaxed and replete. Hopefully, that meant she'd soon fall asleep. To that end, she breathed in deeply and eased the air out between her lips. She didn't feel good knowing that it was thoughts of Raf that had gotten her off, but she accepted that what was done was done. She couldn't help her attraction to him, no matter how much she might wish differently.

She sighed again. It wasn't fair that he kept dominating her thoughts. It was none of her business what he wore to bed. Her sole focus had to be on convincing him to keep the station. It was the only thing that mattered. To that end, she needed to keep her temper in check, forget about her wayward fantasies, and do everything in her power to show him what a wonderful part of the world this was and how honored he should feel to own a small part of it. So honored that he wouldn't ever want to sell it.

No biggie. She should be able to do that with one hand tied behind her back. Too bad her awareness of him kept getting in the way. Her attraction to him was making a difficult situation even more complicated. But she was done with that now.

So what if he was the sexiest man she'd ever met? So what if he set her heart thumping so hard whenever he was near, she was concerned it might beat right out of her chest? None of that mattered. She could conquer her physical attraction to him, especially when the station was on the line.

Physical attraction came and went. Everyone knew that. The station and the people who depended upon it would be enduring. She wouldn't let a diversion in the form of Raf Hetherington distract her from getting what she wanted. All she needed to do was to convince him to keep the place and then he could leave. There was no need for him to hang around after that. She had everything in hand. She always did.

Raf turned over in bed and willed himself to sleep. He'd been lying there for the best part of an hour and was still wide awake. It wasn't just the utter silence outside his window. Or the foreign sounds of night animals. Or the unfamiliar bed. Or the heat that lingered on the night air. No, it was Maggie Fairfax. She was the main reason he couldn't sleep.

She was right across the hall. So close, but so far away. He hadn't expected to be attracted to the station manager. No doubt the fact he hadn't had sex for weeks was another reason he'd had a perpetual hard-on almost from the moment he'd set eyes on her. Their frolic in the billabong hadn't helped, despite its abrupt end.

He'd been disappointed, but not surprised, when she'd kept most of her clothes on. He hadn't really expected her to strip down in front of him. After all, they were almost-strangers. Not only that, for the moment at least, he was her boss.

Still, he wasn't complaining, and he'd looked his fill as she'd walked into the water. Even when she'd dived in and had swum out to where the water lapped her shoulders, the pool hadn't been dark enough to disguise her shapely body.

Her wet shirt had clung to her, clearly outlining her bountiful breasts. Long, graceful limbs with well-defined muscles only served to turn him on. Every time she kicked her legs, her shirt rode high, giving him a tantalizing glimpse of her white panties. His cock had throbbed almost painfully at the sight of her and hours later, his erection had barely subsided. No wonder he couldn't fall asleep.

With a sigh of defeat, he kicked off the sheet and reached down to encircle his cock. It was thick and hard and demanding attention. His balls were heavy and full. With long, sure strokes, he worked himself up to a climax. The whole time, he pictured Maggie. With a muffled oath, he orgasmed and then looked around for some tissues. Finding none, he leaned over and picked up the boxer shorts he'd discarded on his way into bed. Cleaning himself up, he tossed the underwear aside and then rolled over and fell instantly asleep.

Maggie woke early the next day feeling torn between wanting to keep her distance from Raf, but also needing to convince him to keep the station. By the time he appeared in the kitchen dressed in a casual shirt, jeans and expensive loafers, she'd gotten to where she wished Arthur had never put her in this position.

Raf appeared rested and refreshed. "Morning," he said, smiling pleasantly.

"Morning," she mumbled.

"Something smells delicious. What's for breakfast?"

"Bacon and eggs. There's also toast, and I've just boiled the kettle for coffee."

"Sounds great. You must have been up early?"

"Yes. I normally rise at six. There are always chores to be done before the real work starts."

He took a seat at the breakfast bar. "Such as?"

"Feeding the horses, chickens, and dogs. Mucking out the stables. Just because you get to sleep in past eight doesn't mean the rest of us do."

He inclined his head. "Point noted. You should have woken me. I'd have been happy to give you a hand."

"Why? So you can go back to Brisbane and brag to your friends about what's it's like to be a farmer?"

Despite her caustic comment, his tone remained neutral. "No, so I could help you out. Lighten your load."

As quickly as her anger had ignited, it deflated. She bit her lip and then mumbled an apology. It wasn't Raf she was upset about, per se. It was the entire situation. The fact she'd fantasized about him the night before had also contributed to her bad mood.

So much for my vow to control my temper...

In silence, he helped himself to the cooked breakfast and then returned to his seat to eat. The kettle boiled, and she made them both coffee. She set a cup down in front of him.

"Thank you. Are you joining me for breakfast?"

"I ate earlier," she replied.

He grimaced. "Now I really wish you'd woken me."

As he filled his mouth with egg and chewed on the crispy bacon, she sipped from her coffee and tried to work out how best to get what she wanted without having to spend too much time with him. Being up close and personal to him wasn't good for her equilibrium. Nor did it help with keeping her head clear. Or sleeping.

"You talked about a waterfall yesterday. Standing on mossy rocks? Do you think we could go and see that?" he asked around a mouthful.

She blinked, surprised he remembered. He'd obviously been paying attention. "That's on our southern border. It'll take us most of the day to get there and back."

He quirked a single dark eyebrow. "Do you have somewhere else to be?"

She raised a single blond eyebrow.

He flushed. "Sorry, of course you do. This is a working station and you're in charge. You mentioned last night about having to do chores."

She grimaced. "Yes. But I also agreed to show you around. I want you to see your station. I want you to see it through my eyes. I'm doing my best to convince you to keep it, remember?"

"Great. I'd love for you to be my tour guide."

The accompanying smile he gave her warmed her all the way through. She was once again reminded of how good looking he was. With a determined effort, she ignored the feelings coursing through her and steadfastly forced the thought from her mind.

"I'm happy to take you to see the waterfall, but we might check in on the cattle along the way and if I see something else that needs to be done, I'll have to attend to that too. Is that okay?"

"Sounds okay to me."

"Good. We'll need to pack food and water." She glanced at his leather loafers. "You might also want to change out of those shoes. They're not exactly practical for where we're going."

"That's okay. They're sturdier than they look," he replied cheerfully.

She shrugged. "Suit yourself."

It meant nothing to her if he destroyed an expensive pair of shoes. She opened a cupboard and retrieved a couple of empty water bottles and began filling them.

"Do you need any help?"

"No, thanks. This won't take long. I'll pack some of the leftovers in the fridge for lunch. Cold meat. Some salad stuff. Bread. Fruit. Is that okay?"

"Of course."

She glanced at his bare head. "You'll also need a hat. One with a decent brim. It's going to be a hot day."

He grimaced. "I don't have one."

Of course you don't. You're a city boy. It wouldn't have occurred to you to bring a hat...

With another sigh, she stopped what she was doing and walked over to where several battered Akubras hung from ancient hooks that were fixed to the wall. She reached for one of the hats and tossed it toward him. He caught it easily.

"You can use that one."

"Thanks," he replied and slipped it on his head. He gave it a slight adjustment. "How do I look?"

Maggie compressed her lips with a groan. He looked even more sexy than usual. Not that she'd tell him that. He wore the hat so naturally, like he'd been born to be a cowboy. The angle he'd set it gave him a rakish air that made her stomach dip on a surge of desire. With an edge of desperation, she fought off the unwelcome feeling.

Oblivious to her inner turmoil, Raf flashed her a wide, white smile and followed through with a cheeky wink. "Well?" he asked expectantly.

Her stomach dipped again. "You look fine," she mumbled, and beat a hasty retreat out of the kitchen. She'd come back and finish packing for their journey just as soon as she had her heart rate back under control. She swallowed another sigh and silently cursed Raf Hetherington.

It was going to be a long day.

Chapter Nine

♥

Raf bounced along in one of the station's four-wheel-drive utes, with Maggie at the wheel. She handled the road well. No surprise. But road was an understatement. More like a rutted hint of a dirt track that reminded him of just how far away they were from his city life. They'd been driving for more than an hour and were still on Hetherington land. He wasn't sure he would ever get his head around the vastness of his inheritance—if he decided to keep it. The feeling of his comparative insignificance was a little overwhelming. But the thrill of the challenge before him was—he thought somewhat reluctantly—tantalizing ... promising. A little like the competent woman beside him, whose attention was riveted on avoiding potential hazards ahead.

They drove through several paddocks. Most of them held cattle. The big red beasts were even bigger up close. Not that they got out of the ute. Maggie cast her eyes over the animals as they drove by and seemed satisfied by what she saw. He had yet to catch sight of anything that vaguely resembled the topography he expected surrounding a waterfall.

So far, the landscape had been a dominated by wide-open plains dotted with gum trees, scrubby bushes and various native grasses. He only knew they were native because Maggie had told him. They'd seen two kangaroos and a mob of emus, but that had been the extent of the fauna. Still, for all its sameness, the landscape held a strange kind of beauty and he found himself enjoying the ride, not the least because of his companion.

He glanced across at her. She held the steering wheel with a casual confidence, turning this way and that to avoid the un-seen—at least to him—holes and jutting stones. She'd rolled up the long sleeves of her pink cotton shirt to her elbows, and he watched the muscles in her slim, tanned forearms respond to the steering of the ute. She wore another pair of khaki work shorts that finished mid-thigh. They emphasized her long toned legs, particularly when they hitched slightly, like they had when she'd slid in behind the wheel. Her hair, pulled back into its customary ponytail, bounced around her head in rhythm with the vehicle.

"I almost hit a kangaroo on my way out here yesterday."

She flicked him a glance. "Really?"

"Yes. It came out of nowhere."

She gave him a brief grin. "That's what it's like out here. You have to be on the lookout. They're even worse first thing in the morning or just on dusk. That's feeding and watering time for most animals. You're lucky there's still plenty of both around. They don't have to travel too far. When the grasses die and the watering holes dry up, they're forced to go farther afield. That's when you must be really careful. You'll see them everywhere."

"Have you ever hit one?"

She grimaced. "Unfortunately, yes. It happens to most locals, eventually. No matter how observant you are, there's always one you overlook."

Raf thought back to the kangaroo he'd narrowly avoided the day before and nodded. "I know what you mean."

He turned and gazed out of the window, taking in the mountain range in the distance. "That's the Carnarvon Range, right?"

Maggie nodded. "Yes. They form part of the Great Dividing Range. They're renowned for their spectacular natural beauty and significant cultural heritage. Have you ever been to Carnarvon Gorge?"

He shook his head. "No. Is it nearby?"

She chuckled. "If you call a three-and-a-half-hour drive nearby. It's north of Roma, in the Carnarvon National Park. The gorge is famous for its steep sandstone walls, indigenous rock art, and diverse habitats. Water erosion has shaped it over millions of years. It's home to numerous plants and animals, some of which are unique to the area. You really ought to make time to see it."

He shot her a doubtful look. He hadn't been planning on staying long enough to take all-day excursions to far-flung places up north.

"You don't have to do it this trip. There's always next time." She winked.

He laughed. "You sound so confident there'll be a next time."

"Hey, I haven't given up yet that I'll change your mind about selling. Who knows? There might be plenty of 'next times'."

Her confidence was alluring. He even allowed himself a few moments to imagine what it might be like to spend more time discovering the outback, particularly with the very desirable Maggie Fairfax along for the ride. A few moments of fantasy, but only a few. His life was in the city. Life in the outback would never be for him, no matter how alluring the woman who sat beside him.

Oblivious to his thoughts, Maggie continued.

"The park's vegetation varies from eucalypt forests and lush fern-filled gorges to dry rainforests, providing habitats for a wide range of wildlife. Aboriginal people have lived in the Carnarvon Range for thousands of years, and the area contains many sites of cultural significance, including some amazing rock art galleries. They're considered some of the finest in Australia and offer a glimpse into the rich cultural history of the indigenous peoples of the region. Tourists come from all over the world to experience them."

As if suddenly aware of her rambling monologue, she flushed and stopped speaking. "I'm sorry. I sound like a tour guide. You probably know this."

He smiled teasingly. "To the contrary, I'm fascinated. It makes me ashamed to admit I know very little about the tourist attractions my home state has to offer."

She frowned. "I thought you'd lived in Queensland all your life?"

"I have. That's what makes it even more shameful. I haven't even made time to explore my own city let alone the region. I get up, go to work. Come home. Go out. Come home. Rinse and repeat, week after week."

"Sounds exciting," she said dryly. "But you forgot about the dancing."

He laughed. "You're right. I do like to dance. But that's about it most weeks. Until now, I've never given it any thought. It's just what I do. What most of my friends do. Now I feel like I've robbed myself of something; like I've been missing out."

"When's the last time you took a vacation?"

He paused to think. "I don't know. Define the word "vacation.""

She laughed. "You're as bad as me." She paused. "When was the last time you took time off work?"

"Nearly a year ago. I was the best man at my friend's wedding in Melbourne. I took a couple of days off on either side of the weekend to help him celebrate. Does that count?"

She shook her head. "A couple of days off on either side of a weekend? That's not a vacation. When was the last time you took two or three weeks off, went somewhere new and exciting, stayed up late, slept in, drank too much, did things you'd never done?"

He stared at her in consternation. "I've never taken that much time off work. I can't imagine being away from my clients for that long. I'm not exactly the adventurous type. Nor am I spontaneous. In fact, my EA thought it hysterical when I told her I was coming out here."

"So, your planned two-week visit to the station will be the longest time you've ever been away from your office?" Maggie asked, her eyes wide with astonishment.

He nodded. "Yep. I guess you could say we have that in common, at least. You don't enjoy being away from your work, either."

She acknowledged his comment with a nod.

"In fact," he continued, "you're the first woman I've met who understands my commitment to my job. You feel the same way about yours. Believe me, the only thing that's kept me from being glued to my laptop since I've arrived has been the intermittent Internet service. If I was staying out here longer, we'd definitely have to do something about that."

Her eyes suddenly shone with hope, and he cursed silently. He didn't want to give her reason to think his visit would be any longer than he'd planned, and he certainly didn't want to give her false expectations as far as the future of the station went.

Before he could correct her misunderstanding, she turned off the track and slowed to a crawl over even rougher terrain. If there was a road, he couldn't imagine it, let alone see it. They slowly climbed over rocks and around anthills and over logs until finally Maggie brought the ute to a stop. He realized that at some point the elevation of the landscape had inclined.

"Is this it?" he asked, looking around him cautiously at the rugged landscape. "I thought we were going to a waterfall?"

She switched off the ignition and grinned. "We are. Unfortunately, we have to hike the rest of the way." She looked pointedly down at his loafers. "I warned you about those shoes."

Without waiting for him to respond, she climbed out of the vehicle and went around the back. Raf stepped out, closing the door behind him. A slight breeze tugged at the brim of his Akubra and he planted it more firmly on his head before joining her. She had the ute tailgate down and was already adjusting one backpack across her shoulders where they'd stowed their lunch.

Raf reached for the other one and shrugged it onto his back. "By the way, the reason I didn't change my shoes wasn't because I doubted what you'd said. I didn't bring any proper walking shoes." He gave her a sheepish look. "The truth is, I wasn't expecting to get up close and personal with the station. I thought I could see everything I needed to from the comfort of a vehicle. My bad." He glanced dubiously down at his loafers. "Just how far do we have to walk?"

Maggie barely suppressed a groan. If there wasn't so much riding on the need to convince Raf to change his mind about selling, she would have left him to his own devices and simply gotten on with her day. There was always so much to do on the station and the last thing she wanted was to waste time keeping him amused.

She tamped down on her annoyance and the low hum of irritation of physical attraction. She'd agreed to show him the waterfall because she believed the power of persuasion lay in the station's natural beauty. It had the power to change his mind. As the caretaker, she desperately wanted him to embrace the wonder of what he'd been gifted.

She vowed silently to renew her efforts in that regard. The length of his stay was tenuous at best. This was the longest vacation he'd ever taken. There was no guarantee he'd see out the expected week or two. Particularly if he started suffering Internet withdrawal.

Giving him a moment to adjust his backpack to a more comfortable position, Maggie settled her hat more firmly on her head, lifted and locked the tailgate, and then headed off toward the waterfall. It nestled among a tall stand of granite rocks surrounded by ancient gums. It had always been one of her favorite spots to sit and think, though it had been months since she'd been there. The constant demands of station life, along with the travel time to get there, had kept her away for far too long.

As they trekked toward their destination, Maggie regaled Raf with stories from the past about the station. If she couldn't impress him with its beauty, perhaps history would be the key.

"They used to drive cattle from here to the Roma sale yards. It would take them more than a week. They couldn't drive the cattle too hard or else they'd lose too much condition before they arrived, and that meant lower prices. They'd drive more than a thousand head at a time."

"All on horseback," Raf mused. "Talk about doing it tough."

"Right. But they didn't know any different. There weren't any trucks out here then."

"Of course not. Trucks weren't widely used in Australia for transporting livestock until after the Second World War."

Maggie looked at him in surprise. "Impressive."

He smiled disarmingly. "I'm a bit of a history buff. The first trucks were steam driven. They were used at copper mines in South Australia from 1863. It wasn't until 1912 that the first internal-combustion engine was introduced."

She stared at him with an unreadable expression. He dropped his gaze and gave a self-deprecating chuckle. "Sorry. I don't want to bore you."

"No, not at all. I love history, too. Please, go on."

He grinned. "Okay, but don't forget, you encouraged this. In the 1920s, growth in the trucking industry stalled when state governments focused their attention on expanding the rail lines, but after the War, shipping was in short supply and the trains were bearing way too much of the burden of moving freight. That's when trucks were brought in to make up for the shortfall and the trucking industry was born," he finished triumphantly.

Though fascinated by his recount, Maggie found herself surprised. Raf had made no mention of his love of history when she'd been telling him, albeit briefly, about the history of the station the previous night. A warm feeling washed over her at the realization they had that in common, at least. She thought about the journals. If he read them, there was a chance he might develop a connection with the station; a sense of belonging that might give him pause before putting the station on the market. It was worth a shot.

"Given your love of history, you might be interested in reading the McGregor family journals that I told you about last night."

He nodded. "Sure."

She smiled, suddenly filled with renewed hope. "Great. Now, let's go find us that waterfall."

The night before, Raf had been intrigued by the pioneering family who'd originally settled on Hetherington Station, and he was looking forward to reading the journals. He could tell from Maggie's expression that she hoped the journals might bring about a change of heart. His gut clenched at the likelihood of letting her down. He loved his life in Brisbane. The idea of uprooting it for the vastness of the unknown was daunting, to say the least.

A dull roar of water in the distance broke through his thoughts, signaling they were getting closer to their destination. He sighed, glancing wryly at his feet. While his expensive loafers were completely at home in the boardroom, they were not serving him well in the great outdoors.

He had blisters on both heels, and he swore every rock he stepped on left its imprint on his foot. The thin rubber soles were no match for the rugged terrain Maggie led him through. He was just grateful they were nearly at the end. He refused to even think about the journey back. But the possibility of seeing Maggie strip down again? That was a thought he relished.

His gut clenched with desire and blood rushed to his groin, distracting him from the pain in his feet. Just the thought of getting up close and personal to a wet and willing Maggie had his body poised for action.

Of course, there was no guarantee she'd be willing. Their conversations had see-sawed between fun and lighthearted, to rather tense. There was every chance she wouldn't even be up for a swim today.

Maybe this time she's brought a bathing suit? After all, this little excursion's been planned...

He experienced a sharp stab of anticipation at the thought. Maggie, in a bikini, would be well worth the arduous trek. As for him, he was more than happy to strip off once again. Especially if it drew her appreciative gaze. He hadn't missed the flare of interest in her eyes at the billabong. He had no hangups about his body and prided himself on keeping in shape. He went to the gym most days and worked hard to keep fit. Though he was far from an exhibitionist, neither was he a prude.

The roar of the waterfall grew louder, making conversation impossible, reducing communication to hand signals. Maggie pointed in the direction they needed to go and went ahead. The rocks surrounding the canyon were higher and finding finger holds proved to be a challenge. He watched her unerringly cling to nooks and crannies and set her feet on almost invisible ledges. Raf followed more cautiously behind her, finding the same finger holds and ledges for his feet. One foot forward, one finger hold and then another step forward, another finger hold until finally he followed her around the corner of a large rock. Raf pulled up with a gasp.

High above them, a tremendous stream of water pounded over a rocky riverbed and dropped into the foam below. They were perched about halfway between the waterfall and the top of the range from where it flowed. Maggie turned toward him, her face alight with wonder.

Raf basked in it for a moment, understanding how she felt. The view was spectacular. The spray saturated them in minutes. The sound was absolutely deafening. The combination of natural wonders assaulting his senses was uplifting. He returned her enthusiastic grin and gave her two thumbs up.

Still smiling, she led the way down, picking her way carefully between the rocks. Raf paid extra attention. The grip on his loafers was as good as non-existent and the closer they got to the bottom, the wetter and more slippery the rocks became. At one point, his foot slid out from beneath him on a thick patch of moss, and it was all he could do to keep his balance. Maggie immediately swung around. Her expression made it clear she wanted to know if he was okay. He glanced wryly at his shoes and gave her a thumbs up and a reassuring grin.

She made it to the bottom first and dropped her backpack onto a natural sandy beach that had formed along the riverbank a little further downstream. Raf joined her a few moments later.

"What do you think?" she yelled, pointing toward the waterfall. "Was it worth the effort?"

"You bet," he shouted back. He shucked off his backpack and dropped it on the ground near hers.

"Ready for a swim?" she yelled.

He couldn't contain a wide grin. "Absolutely!" He shucked off his clothes.

From the corner of his eye, he saw Maggie stripping down to a tiny yellow bikini that was somehow even more alluring than bare skin. He made no bones about looking his fill, giving her a slow once-over and though she couldn't have possibly heard his fox whistle, he could tell from the glint in her eye that she'd seen him do it. The smile of encouragement as she turned and sauntered toward the water told him she was more than happy to be there with him.

Making quick work of his shoes and clothes, out of deference to her bikini, he left his boxers on, but it would have taken only a passing glance for her to notice his raging hard-on. He followed quickly on her heels and plunged in just as she came up for air.

"Oh, that feels good!" she exclaimed. Her ponytail had come loose. She swiped the hair out of her eyes and grinned.

Raf grinned back. The water was up to their necks and was cool and clear and sweet. He'd expected river water to be murky and muddy, but not here. As if reading his mind, Maggie spoke.

"It's because the water's running," she explained. "It's filtered by the rocks. This water runs through sandstone. That's why it's so clean and clear."

"It's wonderful. I had no idea things like this existed in the outback."

"You city folks don't have a monopoly on wonderful," she gently chided.

He flushed but took her teasing gibe in the way it appeared intended. "You're right. How come you're not inundated with tourists? I'd pay good money to visit this."

She held a finger up to her lips. "*Shh.* It's a secret. This is private property. Not many people know about its existence, and we'd like it to stay that way."

He nodded sagely, all the time working to keep the smile off his face. "Well, as it's currently *my* private property, my lips are sealed."

They trod water, slowly circling one another. As their conversation ceased, Raf's heart rate sped up with every beat. He felt the pull drawing them inexorably together. Whether it was the water or some other force, they circled closer and closer. So close, he could see tiny dark flecks in Maggie's blue eyes and could almost count the freckles on her nose. When her arm brushed against his, electricity arced through him.

His gaze locked on hers. His heart hammered. The roar of the waterfall behind them became nothing but a dull sound. As he watched, her gaze went wide. She looked away. Then her tongue sneaked out to nervously lick her bottom lip. It was all he could do to hold back a groan.

Desire raged through him. Despite the coldness of the water, his body was on fire. All he wanted was to close the distance between them and press himself against her and kiss her until they were both breathless.

But is that what she wants?

She was certainly giving him plenty of signs she was interested but was it wise to break his rule and indulge with this employee, particularly given the circumstances? Would it be fair?

Hey, if she's willing, why not?

He frowned at the thought, hearing his cock talk. Still, they were both adults and if she wanted to go for it, who was he to argue?

Chapter Ten

♥

Maggie saw the desire flaring hotly in Raf's eyes, and it turned her insides to mush. Her nipples hardened, her stomach clenched, and heat centered in her core. She wished she could gain some self-control over her body's response to him, but in reality, she struggled to resist the urge to reach out and pull him towards her, their lips and bodies merging.

The carnality of her thoughts should have shocked her. She wasn't the kind of girl who indulged in casual affairs. In fact, she'd never engaged in casual sex. She'd never had sex, period. She'd had a boyfriend briefly in high school, and another one a couple of years ago, but in both instances, she'd done nothing more than fool around. Kissing and fondling through their clothing was about as far as things had gone.

She'd spent most of her adult life living in the outback where eligible bachelors were few and far between and though there had been a few jackaroos over the years who were keen to get to know her better, none of them had interested her enough to sleep with.

Until now.

Not that Raf was a jackaroo. In fact, he was the last type of man she would have ever expected to be attracted to. He was city born and bred. The two of them had nothing in common, other than a love of history and a piece of land and even that was a source of conflict.

And that's the number one reason it's probably not a wise idea to sleep with him...

Until she knew whether he was going to hang around, she'd be crazy to have sex with him. Already, he made her feel things she hadn't felt before, and that was stupid enough. To complicate matters by sleeping with him when it was highly likely he'd be gone before the end of the month would be more than stupid.

She wasn't a young girl at the mercy of her hormones. She thought things through. She knew better than to base decisions on nothing more than what felt good in the moment. If she'd been that way inclined, she'd have had sex years ago. But that wasn't the way she lived her life. She'd never made impulsive decisions before over serious matters and she wouldn't start now. But boy, was it hard. Raf had her body humming and yearning for things she could barely describe.

Slowly, regretfully, she pushed away until there was a decent amount of water between them. Realization dawned in Raf's expression, followed by disappointment and finally resignation, but to her relief, he didn't comment. Instead, he sent a wave of water surging in her direction, hitting her full in the face. She gasped and sputtered in outrage and looked at him in shock. But instead of getting angry, she heaved an arm back and returned fire, finding herself in a full-on water fight.

She gave as good as she got and kept at it until her arms ached. Seeing her flagging spirits, Raf dived under the water and came up beside her, grabbing her around the waist.

"Hey!" she shrieked as he drew her in close against him.

He merely grinned. "Are you ready to surrender?"

The warmth of his hard body against her near-naked skin did strange things to her equilibrium. It took all her effort to extricate herself from his embrace and swim away.

"Let's get something to eat."

Not waiting for his response, she swam quickly toward the bank. As the water turned shallow, she stood and stepped out of the river. She walked to the sandy beach where they'd left their backpacks.

"We forgot to pack towels," Raf said, coming up behind her.

She shrugged. The sun had enough heat in it that it wouldn't be long before they were dry. She opened the first backpack and pulled out a picnic rug. She spread it out on the sand. Leftover cold meat, a dish of sliced tomatoes, cheese, pickles, and a loaf of sliced bread followed.

She set the food out on the blanket. "Make yourself a sandwich. There's a thermos of coffee in your backpack, along with a couple of mugs. I even packed some sugar."

He raised a single dark eyebrow. "I don't take sugar."

"No, but I do," she quipped and then followed it with a grin.

He smiled back, that nice easy smile that made her want to kiss him and do other things she had no business thinking about. In an effort to distract herself, she busied herself making a sandwich.

"Did you bring any mayonnaise? Napkins? What about a plate?" he asked.

She'd already started sputtering in outrage before she noticed the teasing glint in his eyes. She punched him lightly on the shoulder.

Raf burst into laughter. "You should have seen your face!"

Maggie poked her tongue out at him, only increasing his hilarity. Her pique eased, and she offered him a reluctant grin.

"You don't play fair," she moaned.

Slowly, his expression sobered. His eyes filled with determination. "You're right. I don't play fair. I play to win."

The sun was low in the sky when Maggie and Raf made their way back to the homestead. She drove the ute over the rutted track, keeping a close eye out for kangaroos and other local fauna. It had been a nice day. Too nice. Raf was a decent guy, easy to be around, despite his intention to uproot her life and the lives of the other station employees. A part of her wished they'd met in different circumstances.

Why does he have to be a city slicker? Why can't he be a new farmhand looking for work? Why can't he be someone who actually wants to live in the outback?

She swallowed a sigh.

Back at the homestead, she was grateful to find a note taped to the fridge.

Dinner is in the oven.

Maggie had caught up with Daphne before they'd left and asked if she could put together the evening meal. Now she was glad she had. Their day out in the sun and the water had drained them both of energy. Having dinner already prepared was a godsend.

Opening the oven, Maggie found a beef roast and baked vegetables. Her mouth watered. It had been a long time since their simple meal of sandwiches and fruit.

"Something smells good."

She turned as Raf walked into the kitchen. "Roast meat and vegetables, courtesy of Daphne. She's worth her weight in gold. Are you hungry?"

"Starving."

"Good. I'll set the table. Do you mind going into the wine cellar and choosing a bottle of red?"

A single dark eyebrow quirked upward. "A wine cellar? My, that sounds very sophisticated."

She laughed. "Don't get too excited. It's nothing more than a roughhewn space carved out of the ground below the house. I believe it was used to store preserves and other vegetables back before there was electricity. It's pretty dark and dingy down there. Better watch out for creepy crawlies. I know how much you love them."

His expression became alarmed. "Like snakes?"

"No, not snakes. There's no way for them to get in there, but there might be a few spiders."

He shuddered. "I hate spiders."

She rolled her eyes. "You're a big boy. You'll be fine."

With that, Maggie crossed the kitchen and lifted a trapdoor that formed part of the kitchen floor. Tugging on the handle, she lifted the door and set it aside, revealing a set of wooden stairs that disappeared into the darkness.

"Where's the light switch?" Raf asked.

Maggie shook her head. "There's no light switch, I'm afraid. Remember that this building was constructed before electricity was invented.

A flash of panic filled Raf's gaze. "Then how do you see down there?"

Maggie smiled and handed him a torch. "Here. This will do just fine."

Raf took the torch from her and switched it on, angling the bright beam of light in the direction of the stairs.

"This seems to be a lot of trouble just to fetch a bottle of wine," he mumbled.

"True. But it gets so hot out here in the summer, it's hard to keep red wine cool. It tastes better if it's been cellared. Trust me." She gave him another reassuring smile.

With a sigh, Raf made his way cautiously down the stairs. Maggie waited close by.

"Any preference?" he shouted up a few moments later.

"I tend to favor a Merlot or a Cabernet Sauvignon, but you're the one who's gone to all the trouble to fetch it. You get to choose."

A few minutes later, Raf reappeared brandishing two bottles. "I got one of each. I hope that's okay."

Maggie shrugged. "Sure. A glass or two is about my limit most nights. I have a station to run and that doesn't make allowances for a hangover, but you're welcome to indulge."

He brought the bottles over to the counter and set them down. On impulse, Maggie reached over and pretended to brush cobwebs off his hair. Raf frowned.

"What is it?" he asked, uncertainty and suspicion warring on his face.

"Just a few cobwebs. Nothing to worry about."

His eyes went wide. "Cobwebs? You mean I could have a spider in my hair?"

She chuckled. "Just because you have cobwebs doesn't mean there's a spider."

Raf scratched frantically at his hair with his fingers. Maggie doubled over with laughter.

"You should see your face," she gasped.

Raf's expression was somber. "I could be bitten by a venomous spider any moment, and we're at least an hour from any medical service. Doesn't that concern you?"

"No," she managed, trying hard to contain her mirth.

Raf's eyes suddenly narrowed. "You were joking, right? There weren't any cobwebs in my hair."

She nodded. "You're right. I'm sorry, but I couldn't resist. You seemed so hung up about the thought of encountering a spider. You're a big strong man and you're afraid of an itsy-bitsy spider."

"We weren't all raised in the outback, coming into contact with dangerous creatures every day," he muttered. "And just because I'm a man doesn't mean I can't be afraid of spiders."

She felt an immediate sense of remorse. "True. That was insensitive of me. Anyone can be afraid of spiders. It doesn't make them weak." She paused. "Thank you for the wine."

"You're welcome," he replied in a mollified tone. "By the way, you're right about the cellar. It's at least ten degrees cooler down there."

"Yep."

With that, she busied herself removing the pan of roast meat and vegetables from the oven and serving out two plates. Grabbing cutlery and napkins, she set the table. Raf fetched two wine glasses from a cupboard he'd noticed her fetch them from before and opened the bottle of Merlot. He let the wine rest for a few minutes while Maggie set the plates on the table. As she took a seat, Raf set a glass of wine down in front of her.

"Thank you."

He took the seat next to hers, which brought him closer. Raising his glass, he gave a toast.

"To outback cellars and the people who built them."

They clinked glasses and sipped at their wine.

"*Mm*, that's delicious," Maggie murmured.

Raf picked up the bottle and read the label. "A 2018 vintage. Nice."

"The wine collection belonged to your uncle. I guess it now belongs to you. Arthur loved the idea of the cellar. He brought several cases of wine here and asked me to store them. He gave me liberty to drink what I wanted."

"Very generous of him. He must have known you weren't a soak." Raf gave her a teasing wink.

Maggie's stomach took a nosedive. Flustered by the sudden rush of feelings, she took refuge in her wine. She took a big gulp and instantly regretted it when it went down the wrong way, and she broke into a coughing fit.

"Are you all right?"

When she continued to gasp and cough, he pushed away from the table and stood and thumped her twice between the shoulder blades.

She gasped again but dragged in enough oxygen to fill her lungs and slow the irritation. After a while, the coughing stopped altogether.

"Thank you," she said as Raf returned to his seat. "That was totally embarrassing."

"Think nothing of it. I'm just glad I was around to help. Can't have you dropping dead on me. Who'd step in and manage my farm?"

There was a teasing tone to his comment and Maggie was pretty sure he'd made the comment in jest, but it reminded her once again that everything had changed. People were relying on her to convince Raf to keep the place. Though she was trying, it seemed she wasn't making much progress. She needed to focus on her strategy. He'd previously expressed an interest in reading the journals. Maybe that would do the trick. She'd make sure she got them to him that very night while his interest was fresh.

"Have you always wanted to spend your life in the outback?" Raf asked, slicing into a baked potato.

She smiled wryly. "Yes. Even during my years in Brisbane attending boarding school, I yearned to be back home. My fondest memories were of the school holidays, when my brothers and sisters and I got to hang out watching the jackaroos and jillaroos in action at our family station. As we got older, we joined in."

He gave her a look filled with curiosity. "You didn't enjoy living in Brisbane?"

She shrugged and popped a piece of tender beef into her mouth. She took the time to chew and swallow before she responded.

"I didn't *not* enjoy it, but it never felt like home. It was nice to have shops right down the street and open all hours. It was lovely to spend a day on the river or drive south to the Gold Coast and spend a day on the beach, but the city never took hold of me like it has you. I guess that has something to do with the fact you were born there. For you, the city's home. It makes sense to you."

Raf nodded thoughtfully. "Yeah. I've never spent much time thinking about it, but it is home. The only place I've lived. And of course, you can't beat the Brisbane weather."

She chuckled. "You're right about that. I could do with a few less days of forty-plus degrees Celsius out here at the height of summer."

"At least it's a dry heat. Brisbane can get awfully humid. Which isn't fun."

"There is that." She smiled. "I guess that's why they invented air conditioning."

Raf laughed. "Speaking of air conditioning. I got onto someone in Roma this morning. They've promised to be here within the next few days."

Maggie blinked in surprise. "Wow. That soon? You have the magic touch."

He flushed. "I think it had more to do with my promise to pay double what they wanted to get the job done."

Maggie shook her head. "Money talks."

"Every time."

She frowned. "Doesn't that bother you? That he who has the gold never waits in line?"

Raf shrugged. "I can't say it bothers me. That's just the way the world works. I'm just glad I'm able to help."

"Don't get me wrong," she said hurriedly. "I'm pleased as anyone that the AC might finally be fixed. It'll certainly make things more comfortable around here. But what about all those people who can't afford to have people come running at the click of their fingers? What about those who haven't got the kind of money it takes to get things done in an instant?"

Raf compressed his lips. "I've never said life is fair. It isn't. There are always people who are going to have more than others. That's the way it is. But apart from my recent inheritance, I've worked hard for everything I have. No one gave me anything. I got my first job when I turned fifteen and I've been working ever since. That's how you get ahead. I won't apologize for having more than some because I've been prepared to get off my butt and work for it."

"I didn't mean to imply that someone handed your life on a silver platter," she said. "There are plenty of people who start with nothing and end up successful beyond their wildest dreams because they've been prepared to work hard, make sacrifices, and take risks. Make their own luck. I applaud those people. It's the ones who haven't had to work and yet still cruise the highways of life without a care in the world, at least as far as money is concerned. They're the ones who upset me. They're also often the ones who are oblivious to how most of us live. From paycheck to paycheck, praying nothing serious goes wrong in between, which will leave us short."

Raf eyed her with compassion. "You're right. There are plenty of people out there working their butts off and not getting anywhere. They're the ones I feel sorry for. It's like they can never catch a break. I guess all we can do is give where we can, help out when it's possible, and hope they get lucky."

She glanced at him in surprise. "So, you're a philanthropist?"

He shook his head. "I'm not wealthy enough to take on that handle, but I give where I can. At my suggestion, the company I work for set up a charitable foundation supporting homeless youth. We run regular sessions with them in a local hall, provide food, shelter and mentoring. We've got a whole heap of other businesses on board who do what they can to help. So far, we've had some pretty good successes."

She gazed at him with admiration, seeing him in a different light. "That's so wonderful. I'd love to be in a position like that one day to give something back to young people who don't get the best start in life and struggle into adulthood, or who haven't been able to get things together for whatever reason. So many of them have no real clue about what they want out of life and no plan for getting there. I've often thought about setting up a program that invites young people to give farm work a try. It can be very rewarding, even in the middle of nowhere." She gave him a pointed look.

He chuckled. "Touché. For the record, I never said a life out here couldn't be rewarding. Just different. Not what I'm used to."

"Do you think you could ever get used to it?"

The words came out before she could stop them. Heat erupted in her face and spread across her cheeks. She averted her gaze.

"I'm sorry, Raf. I don't know why I asked you that. You've made it clear your heart belongs to the city."

His expression turned thoughtful. "Before I came here, I never gave a thought to living elsewhere. Even though I've traveled the world, Brisbane has always been my home. But being here, seeing what it has to offer..." His voice drifted off, and then his gaze met hers. "This place has taken me by surprise."

They continued to stare at each other. Maggie couldn't look away. Her heart somersaulted in her chest and then took off at a gallop. She didn't want to read anything into Raf's words, but it was hard not to take hope.

"Does that mean you're reconsidering your decision to sell?" she asked, unable to stop herself.

He grimaced. "Probably not."

Her shoulders slumped, and her spirits deflated. She should have known better than to think she'd changed his mind in so little time. Still, it was obvious the place had touched him in ways he wouldn't or couldn't yet acknowledge. She could only hope that over the coming week or two, the connection that he couldn't verbalize right now might turn into something more lasting.

She didn't need him to fall in love with the place and declare he'd stay there forever. All she needed was for him to retain ownership. An absentee owner was just fine. She'd already learned to deal successfully with one of those.

The fact that this owner made her heart thump faster and yearn for wicked things was neither here nor there. That was only a fleeting attraction. As soon as he returned to the city and her life returned to normal, she'd forget all about him.

Chapter Eleven

♥

Raf was in an introspective mood by the time he helped Maggie clean up after dinner. The bottle of wine they'd shared had helped soften the mood between them. They'd spent the rest of the evening talking about their high school days. Raf admitted he'd been captain of the rugby union football team and that he'd had plenty of friends. Maggie confessed she was a book nerd and had spent a lot of her time in the library. He found it surprising that a woman who made her living in the great outdoors also enjoyed solitary, indoor pursuits such as reading, but that only reinforced his growing belief that she was a fascinating contradiction.

On the one hand, she lived so successfully in what was traditionally a man's world. Hell, out there in the outback, it was still a man's world. Take the air conditioning mechanic, Aaron Luke. Though it was true, that Raf had made it worth the man's time, he'd happily agreed to take on the job and head out there before the end of the week. Raf was pretty sure it was the fact Aaron had been dealing with another man that he'd been so affable about the job.

That kind of sexism really pissed Raf off. Surely, they'd come far enough that women were no longer treated like second-class citizens. But time moved slower in the outback, and it was clear that out there, men still got away with crap. Raf would make sure to draw the man's attention to it when he caught up with him and make it clear that he wouldn't tolerate that kind of treatment.

As Maggie wiped the counters and returned her cloth to the kitchen sink, Raf put away the last of the dishes. The second bottle of wine stood unopened where he'd left it.

"Would you like another glass of wine?" he asked.

She gave a brief shake of her head. "No, thanks. I'm not much of a drinker. Your wine collection's safe with me."

"You're welcome to help yourself any time the mood strikes you."

"Thank you. I appreciate that."

Their gazes locked briefly before Maggie looked away. An awkward silence fell between them. Raf cast around for something to say. Before he could think of anything, Maggie spoke again.

"Are you still interested in reading those journals?"

He seized on the distraction. "Yes. Very much so."

"Good. I'll go and get them for you."

She returned a few moments later carrying a pile of leather-bound books. She held them out toward him.

"Here you go. I put them in chronological order. It's a bit pedantic of me, but I like to read that way. Of course, you can read them in whatever order you like."

"I like to read that way, too. If I come across a book that's part of a series, I have to buy all the ones before it and make sure I start with the first one. That's the only thing that makes sense to me."

She grinned. "Me, too!"

As he reached for the dusty pile of journals, their fingers brushed. A frisson of awareness tingled up his arm. He resolutely ignored it.

"Thanks," he said, taking the journals from her. "I really appreciate you letting me read them."

Her sudden smile lit up her face, reminding him of her beauty. Reflexively, his body stirred. With a determined effort, he steadfastly ignored the rush of blood and smiled briefly in return.

"Looks like I'm going to be busy. Do you mind if I call it a night? I'm keen to get started."

She took a step back. "Of course not. Go for it. I look forward to hearing your thoughts about them tomorrow."

"For sure," he agreed.

She opened her mouth as if to say something else, but then closed it. Before things got awkward again, he slipped past her and headed down the hallway toward the guest bedroom. The room was still uncomfortably warm, although some of that could be attributed to the heat that still flooded his body. On impulse, he dropped the journals onto the bed and then stripped off his clothes. A cold shower was just what he needed.

Draping a towel around his waist, he opened the door and padded barefoot down the hallway to the bathroom. He tapped on the closed door to make sure the room was empty before slipping inside.

Like the rest of the homestead, it looked like it had been many decades since it had been renovated. Seventies-styled lime-green penny tiles lined the floor. An avocado-colored pedestal sink stood against one wall, a matching bathtub on another. In the far corner was the shower. A simple shower-head and a striped shower curtain that matched the rest of the décor in age and style. Maggie hadn't exaggerated when she'd said his uncle had opted to spend his money on the station. Raf wondered if Uncle Arthur had even stepped foot in the homestead.

Probably not. After all, Maggie said he'd never spent the night here. There's no reason for him to have come inside.

Hanging the towel up on a rack beside Maggie's, Raf pushed the curtain aside and stepped into the modest shower recep-tacle. Opening up the taps, he gasped as a sluice of cold water gushed over his head. It didn't take long for goosebumps to form on his flesh.

Adjusting the water to a slightly warmer temperature, he sighed in satisfaction and enjoyed the rest of his shower.

Though he wasn't particularly dirty after his swim, it still felt good to lather his skin and wash it clean.

Mindful that it was likely the homestead ran on rainwater, he didn't spend as long as he usually did under the deluge. Turning off the taps, he shook the water from his hair and then stepped out and toweled off before tying it around his waist and heading back out to his room.

Noises coming from the direction of the kitchen tempted him to return there and spend more time with Maggie, but common sense prevailed. While there was most definitely physical attraction simmering between them, a fling probably wasn't the wisest thing for him to engage in. And that's all it would be. Even if he decided against selling the place, there was no way he was going to live there. There was no point in starting something with his delectable station manager in those circumstances. Maggie deserved better, and she obviously knew that, too. After all, she'd been the one to pull back at the waterfall.

Raf ignored a stab of disappointment at the memory and stepped back inside his bedroom. He'd left the windows open to catch whatever breeze they could. Refreshed from the shower, he was ready to spend an hour or two reading about the lives of the McGregor family. Maggie had told him those early pioneers had built the homestead. He looked forward to reading about that. It was mind-boggling to think they'd built such a grand place without the use of modern technology and power tools. Raf wondered how long it had taken to complete the place.

With a renewed sense of enthusiasm, he shifted the pile of journals to the bedside table so that they were within easy reach. Then he flung the towel over a chair and climbed naked onto the bed. Stacking the pillows behind his head and making himself comfortable, he reached for the journal on the top of the pile and opened it.

The pages had yellowed with age, and the ink had faded. In some places, it was barely legible. The flowing, flowery style of handwriting led him to believe it was the matriarch of the family who'd taken the time to commit their lives to paper. Upon glancing inside the front cover, he confirmed his suspicions by seeing the words "Eliza Mary McGregor" inscribed on the page, along with the years 1862-1870.

He turned his attention to the first entry.

It's taken us more than a month to journey across land, but we've finally made it. We've arrived at our new home. A settler's block issued by the Australian government. How lucky we are to be able to come here and start a new life! The trek has been arduous on all of us, especially me. I'm six months along in my first pregnancy. The heat has been the worst. Even the oxen have felt it, pulling our belongings along on hired wagons so rickety I was afraid they would fail to make the distance.

But we're here now, and all is good. My husband, Angus, has found us a pleasant spot near a waterhole to make our camp. He's pitched our tent and gathered firewood. I've cleared a spot to set up the cooking pot. It's still unbearably hot, but now that we've arrived, I can focus on doing what I need to do to survive. We brought rations with us from Rockhampton, a thriving gold mining town, but they won't last forever. I plan to start a vegetable garden. I hope the waterhole proves to be a reliable water source.

Water is one thing that's been scarce. Though we crossed a river and a few creeks, a lot of them were dry. I hope that's not a permanent situation. If it is, we'll be in deep trouble.

But enough of that negativity. This is the start of our new life. We finally have a place to call our own. McGregor Downs. This is where we will live for as long as the good Lord chooses. This is where we will raise our babies. This is where we'll die. It's a little daunting to think we'll likely never see Scotland again.

It's a strange and unfamiliar land. So wide, so dry, so barren. Unrelenting heat. Wide blue skies. Scrubby, dull-green vegetation. So different from Scotland. Different even from Rockhampton. Then again, what did I expect? We're at the bottom of the world. At least, that's how Angus describes it.

Raf flipped over a few more pages.

It's been a while since I last put ink to paper. I've been terribly sad about losing our first baby. She was born too early. There was nothing either of us could do. The nearest doctor's more than a day's ride away. He wouldn't have made it in time. Angus blames himself. He said it wouldn't have happened if we'd stayed in Scotland.

Maybe that's true.

But what's done is done and though it tears me apart to think of my infant daughter lying in her grave, I don't regret following my husband out here. To be sure, this place is a harsh and rugged land, but it also has a strange beauty among the red and golds and browns. I'm still not used to the heat, but it's beginning to feel more like home.

Angus has built a hut from timber that he's cut from the gum trees that are in plentiful supply nearby. It's not much, but it keeps us dry during the infrequent periods of rain and is more comfortable than the canvas tent.

I console Angus with the knowledge there'll be other babies and they'll survive. I'm sure of it. He and I grow more resilient every day and our children will be the same. They'll learn to live in this harsh brown land like we have, and they'll love it as I do.

Shifting his position on the bed, Raf kept reading.

I met some of the native Aboriginals the other day. Angus was in the field, tending to his crops. I was drawing water from the waterhole for my struggling vegetable garden. The natives appeared from nowhere. So silent on their bare feet! Three men about my age, tall and well-built, holding spears.

It was a little disconcerting, but they were more curious than anything. We communicated mostly using hand signs. I'm not sure what language they speak, but it definitely isn't Scottish! They left as silently as they arrived. It's nice to know there are others living out here. I hope to see them again sometime.

Flipping over a few more pages, Raf kept reading. The date on the top of the page was February 1865.

Angus has finally given up on his crops. Three years of droughts. He's convinced this land isn't a place for growing anything other than cattle. He says they're the only beasts who can survive out here. He's gone to Rockhampton to buy some stock. I stayed behind with our son, Hamish. He's barely a year old. Too young to make the arduous journey.

I don't mind being out here. I'm not on my own. I have Hamish and I have Mary. She's a young Aboriginal girl from a local tribe. That's not her real name. I couldn't understand the name she gave me, so I named her after one of my sisters. Mary turned up out of the blue right when I was in the middle of giving birth to Hamish. Somehow, she could tell I was in trouble. He was taking far too long to be born. She helped me deliver him and she's been with me ever since. It's too bad she wasn't around to help when I birthed my daughter. She might have survived then. Mary helps with Hamish and with the cooking and housecleaning.

Angus has built us a bigger house. This one has four rooms. It's so much grander than our hut. Angus tells me one day he'll build me the grandest house I've ever seen. That'll be nice, but I'm content with what I have. Sometimes I miss my homeland, especially the family I left behind. But my life's here now, with my husband and my baby, and I wouldn't have it any other way.

Raf heard the sound of Maggie's footsteps as she walked down the hallway. No doubt she'd notice the light seeping from beneath his door and realize he was still awake. He wondered if she'd pop her head in and wish him goodnight. His gut clenched in anticipation at the thought.

But her footsteps made no pause as they continued passed his room and onto hers. He swallowed a sigh of disappointment and returned to Eliza's journals. The date on the top of the page was October 1870.

Angus was right. The cattle are flourishing. We started with fifty head. At last count, we had nearly three hundred. I love them. Their dark red hides, all glossy and soft. Their soulful brown eyes. Their gentle natures. Angus tells me not to get too close, but I don't care. They need love like everyone else.

We have added to our little family. Another son, Hugh, and a daughter, Freya. She's the spitting image of her daddy and we all love her so. It's been another dry summer and we're worried about our water supply. It's a constant challenge and we do all that we can to preserve every drop. Angus has devised a system of water tanks and other contraptions to catch whatever falls from the sky. It all helps.

In some sad news, we have lost a cherished member of our extended family. Mary's husband, Roderick (his Anglicized name!) has died from a snake bite. Roderick came to us shortly after Mary arrived. He's been a valuable member of our family, helping Angus with stock work and other jobs on the farm. Mary's understandably devastated. They have three children. He'll be sorely missed by us all.

It was the last entry in that journal. Setting it aside, Raf picked up the next one from the pile. Beneath Eliza McGregor's name, the dates inscribed in the front cover were 1871-1885. The first entry was dated June 1871.

One thing I'll never get used to is winter without snow. Though it's cold enough, with thick frost on the ground, it's nothing like the cold winters of Scotland. And there's more than mild winters to be thankful for.

We've had some good years, with abundant feed and water for the cattle. Decent and frequent rainfall has seen to that. We thank God every day for his bounty.

The children are flourishing. Hamish turned seven back in January. Our little Bridie was born last month. She has black curly hair and eyes as blue as the summer sky. She looks a lot like me. Her brothers and sister adore her. So do her daddy and me.

Mary was with me during my labor. She's been there for all my births. She's a godsend. My angel. I love my husband very much, but it's nice to have female companionship. Our journeys into Rockhampton are infrequent and there are long spans of time between visits. Mail is also infrequent. I haven't heard from my family in Scotland for more than a year.

Angus has come through on his promise to build me a beautiful home. It's the grandest home I've ever seen. It's taken him nearly three years to build it, but now it's finished and I couldn't be happier! Six bedrooms, a large and airy kitchen and two sitting rooms! Two! One bedroom would have thrilled me! I don't know if we'll have enough children to fill the bedrooms. I lost another baby before Bridie. Who knows if it will happen again?

After all these years, you'd think I'd be used to the heat, but it's something that always creeps up on me and takes me by surprise.

One day the weather will be wonderfully mild days, cool nights. The next, it's hot. And it stays hot for months and months.

Even so, I've grown to love this place. The red and purple and orange sunsets that are so beautiful they take your breath away. The wide-open spaces. The horizon that goes on forever. The vast blue sky. I've never seen a sky so blue! Certainly not in Scotland. This wide brown land is home. I can't imagine living anywhere else now.

Raf wondered what it would be like to have that kind of connection to a place. He loved Brisbane. It was home. But he wasn't sure if he had a spiritual connection to the place, like Eliza McGregor obviously had with the outback. And to think she'd emigrated from Scotland.

Perhaps it's time to explore more of the world? Discover where my soul feels a kinship? If such a thing exists…

The sound of the shower interrupted his musings. Images of Maggie at the waterfall immediately flooded his mind. He pictured her naked. Full breasts, taut nipples, skin all wet and slippery. His cock stirred for the umpteenth time that day.

With a sigh of resignation, he set aside the journal he'd been reading and reached over and switched off the bedside lamp. Re-adjusting his pillows, he shifted down lower in the bed. His cock was already standing to attention in anticipation of what was to come. With the sound of the shower filling his ears, he closed his eyes and began stroking himself.

It didn't take long to orgasm. Maggie seemed to have that effect on him. Whenever he was around her, all he could think about was sex. He could sense her attraction toward him. That knowledge kept his desire at fever pitch. It was only the fact she hadn't yet made a move on him that held him back.

He was used to modern women. Women who went after what they wanted. Whether that was a job, a promotion, a new car, or a man. Confident women didn't threaten him. In fact, they were a turn-on. Maggie was plenty confident, especially in her role as station manager.

So, what's holding her back from propositioning me?

Perhaps it was the same reasons he hadn't yet made a move. He was there for such a short time, and then he'd return to his life in Brisbane. He'd been very clear about that. A fling would get messy, as he was still technically her boss. That was something they could definitely do without.

As he rolled over onto his side, feeling mostly relaxed and replete, he tamped down on an unexpected surge of disappointment. He cursed quietly and closed his eyes, determined to find refuge in sleep.

Chapter Twelve

♥

Maggie jumped out of bed the next morning later than usual, but still determined to take Raf on another adventure. Her usual chores around the station were building up, but she had only a limited amount of time to impress him with what the place had to offer, and that meant spending more time with him.

With that thought in mind, she showered and dressed and then reached for her phone and texted four of her employees, delegating them with tasks that would help to keep the station functioning as it should while she was otherwise engaged. She'd catch up with them later and thank them for picking up the slack while she was busy with Raf.

Then she made a call to one of her neighbors. Todd Whittaker hadn't always gotten on with the other farmers. In fact, most of them regarded him with suspicion and disdain, and those feelings were well-placed. A year earlier, Todd and his father had been involved in a scandal of mammoth proportions. Falsifying records, lying to government officials and even switching biosecurity samples during an outbreak of tuberculosis were just a few of their crimes.

While no charges had been laid and as far as Maggie knew, they'd suffered no more repercussions past considerable fines levied by Biosecurity Queensland and a quarantine period for their stock, their reputations had been deservedly trashed, and it would take a long time for anyone around the district to trust them again.

But old man Alistair Whittaker had dropped dead of a heart attack a few weeks ago and since then, Todd appeared to be making more of an effort to right some wrongs. She'd heard that he'd visited with all his neighbors and had apologized for everything that had gone on in the past, including with Maggie's own family. Todd had even called a truce with her father and had apologized for the feud that had been ongoing between her father and Todd's since the time both men were boys.

Maggie was both surprised and pleased that Todd appeared to be doing what he could to make amends. It seemed he was genuinely trying to turn over a new leaf and shed his asshole tendencies. Even her older brother, Brock, had expressed his surprise at the change in his former enemy. Perhaps, for Todd, being out from under his father's nasty influence had turned into a good thing.

Whatever had brought about the transformation, Maggie was glad. It meant that she was on speaking terms with her neighbor, including feeling comfortable enough to request a favor from him. And a favor was what she needed today if the plan she'd hatched while she'd lain awake last night was to come to fruition.

She dialed his number and was pleased when he answered on the second ring. "Hi, Todd. It's Maggie."

"Hi, Maggie. How are things?"

"Great. We could do with some rain, of course. No doubt you're the same."

"Yeah. There's actually a bit forecast in the next little while. We'll have to wait and see."

"Yes. Fingers crossed."

"What can I do for you?"

"Actually, I need a favor."

"What is it?"

"You wouldn't have a spare hour or so to take me and a guest up in your helicopter?"

"Sure. I only had it serviced the other day. It's good to go. When do you want to take off?"

"Today would be great. I'm happy to fit in with you about the timing."

"What about straight after breakfast? Would that work for you?"

She smiled. "Absolutely. That sounds great. Thank you."

"No problem. I'll drop in around nine."

"We'll be ready."

She ended the call and then leaped out of bed. She'd formulated the plan to show Raf around his property from the air, but until now, she wasn't sure she could pull it off. Now, thanks to Todd, it was going to happen. She couldn't wait to tell Raf.

She'd had an aerial tour of Hetherington Station the first year she'd been there. Arthur had taken her up in his chartered plane and they'd flown over the entire area. It had been amazing to see the land stretched out beneath her for as far as she could see and know that she had a part to play in its success. At the time, she'd experienced a visceral reaction and an indescribable feeling of belonging. She hoped Raf might experience the same reaction.

Dressing quickly in shorts and a work shirt, she ran a brush through her hair and then pulled it back into the usual ponytail. After brushing her teeth and applying sunscreen, she strode out of the bathroom and back down the hallway to knock on Raf's door.

"Come in."

She hesitated a moment.

Surely he wouldn't invite me in if he wasn't decent?

Drawing in a breath, she opened the door. He was propped up against the pillows, one of Eliza's journals lay open in his hands. She was both relieved and disappointed to notice the sheet had been pulled up over his hips. Even so, the wide expanse of naked chest covered in springy dark hair did all sorts of things to her equilibrium. Deliberately averting her gaze, she greeted him with a smile.

"Good morning. I hope you slept well."

He smiled back at her. "I did, thank you. Even after spending way too much time last night reading these." He indicated the pile of journals. "They're a fascinating glimpse into the past, aren't they?"

"Absolutely. I'm glad you're enjoying them."

He shook his head slowly back and forth as he mused. "We think we have it so tough these days. We complain when the Internet goes down. To think of the things these early pioneers went through just to survive!"

"I agree," she said, coming farther into the room. "It puts my gripe about the broken air conditioning into perspective, doesn't it?"

He chuckled. "I don't know. I think a gripe about broken air conditioning is justified this day and age."

"Thanks. You're very understanding."

He gave her a once-over. "You're already up and dressed. Are you going somewhere?"

"Actually, yes. I've arranged for us to take a helicopter ride over the station. I thought you might like to see what you own from the air."

He looked immediately interested. "That sounds great."

He set the journal aside and sat up straighter in the bed. The sheet slipped and Maggie's heart lurched as the thick nest of curls between his legs was half-exposed. With face flaming, she averted her gaze.

"I'll meet you outside. We're leaving in twenty-five minutes."

With that, she escaped the room and hurried off to fix breakfast.

Raf got dressed in record time and found Maggie in the kitchen. She was serving up two plates of bacon and eggs, along with a pile of buttered toast.

"This looks great. Thank you," he said.

"You're welcome."

He was excited about taking a helicopter ride. Though he wasn't exactly the adventurous type, he had no fear of heights, and flying was one of his favorite things to do. He was curious about Maggie's motivation for arranging it. When he put the question to her, she murmured something about it being the best way to view the station and then busied herself with making coffee.

He wondered if the excursion had anything to do with her attempt to convince him not to sell, and silently concluded that it did. He had to admire her determination. Once she'd set her mind to something, she certainly wasn't easily deterred. That was just another thing he liked about her, even though he was still doubtful her strategy would work. He hadn't made a successful career for himself in the cutthroat world of finance without being able to hold his own course free from outside influence.

They sat and ate together in companionable silence and had just enough time to down a cup of coffee before they heard an approaching helicopter.

"That would be him," Maggie murmured.

She stood and gathered their plates, quickly rinsing them in the sink and leaving them to dry. Raf did the same with their coffee cups.

"Who's the pilot?" he asked, drying his hands on a tea towel.

"Todd Whittaker. He's one of my neighbors."

"Nice of him to offer to take us up for a ride. How much is he charging?"

Maggie shook her head. "No charge. That's not how we do things out here. We help each other out whenever we can. He's doing me a favor today. Tomorrow he might need one from me. It all works out in the end."

"That's very generous of him. The running costs of those birds don't come cheap."

"That's true."

Raf silently marveled at the way things worked in the out-back. No money changing hands for services between neighbors. Just a promise to help someone out and the knowledge that the favor would be returned in the future. He couldn't imagine such an arrangement ever working in the city. It was rather refreshing.

"We'd better go," Maggie said. "We don't want to keep Todd waiting. He might be doing us a favor, but it goes without saying no one takes advantage."

"Of course."

Raf followed her outside. The sound of the chopper as it came into land in an open paddock not far from the homestead was deafening. They walked toward it and then waited for the pilot to cut the engine before proceeding closer. As the noise receded, the pilot emerged and strode toward them.

He was about their age, tall, broad-shouldered and good looking. Raf took an instant dislike to him. And then he made a sound of disgust in the back of his throat.

Get over yourself. It's only because this walking runway model is living next door to Maggie that you're so antsy.

It didn't seem to matter that was true. Raf couldn't help the stab of jealousy that went through him when Maggie greeted the pilot with a brief hug.

"Todd. It's good to see you again. Thank you for doing this. I really appreciate it."

"No problem, Maggie. To tell you the truth, I was surprised to get your call. I wasn't sure whether I was back in your good books."

She shrugged. "We all make mistakes. I hear you're doing your best to make up for them now your father's gone. My condolences again for your loss," she added.

"Thanks. But we all know he was a prick. As far as I'm concerned, we're all better off now he's gone."

She made a non-committal sound in the back of her throat before turning toward Raf. "This is Raf Hetherington. He just inherited Hetherington station. Raf, meet Todd Whittaker."

Raf held out his hand, and Todd shook it. "Nice to meet you," Raf said.

"You, too." Todd regarded him curiously. "So, you're Arthur's son?"

"His nephew," Raf corrected. "Arthur didn't have any kids."

"Oh, I see. Well, welcome to the outback. We're glad to have you here."

"Thanks."

"It's great to have someone young enough to put down roots and make a real contribution to the local community," Todd continued. He stretched an arm out wide to indicate the expanse of landscape. "As you can see, we're not exactly overrun with people out here. If anyone wants to stay and make a life out here, we'll welcome them with open arms."

Maggie ducked her head, as if embarrassed. Raf quickly set the record straight.

"Oh, I'm afraid you've misunderstood. I'm not staying. I'm just out here to look around before I put the place on the market. My life's in Brisbane."

Todd flushed. Some of his enthusiasm dimmed. "Oh. Sorry, I just thought..."

"That's okay," Raf replied.

"I'm hoping to convince him to change his mind," Maggie said in a rush. "That's why I wanted you to give him an aerial tour of his inheritance. See what he's giving up if he sells."

Todd nodded and then grinned. "Right. Well, I guess it's up to both of us to show him such a good time he'll want to stay."

With that, they walked to the helicopter. At Maggie's insistence, Raf sat in the cockpit with Todd. They all donned headsets so they could communicate. As the helicopter gained altitude, both Todd and Maggie entertained him with stories of the land below, pointing out special landmarks and other interesting places of note.

"If you look over to the left, that's the waterfall where we were yesterday," Maggie said.

Raf looked in the direction she'd indicated. "Wow! What a sight! It looks just as spectacular from the air," he said.

"Yes," she agreed. "And further over there is your southern boundary. You can just see the outline of the fence."

Raf was impressed. "It's amazing," he murmured, taking in the vastness before him dotted with trees and cattle.

While he'd known how big the station was on paper, viewing it from the air laid out the true scale of the property for all to see. Knowing it was his filled him with an unexpected sense of pride.

At Todd's suggestion, they flew over and along parts of the Carnarvon Range. Taking in the ancient land below, Raf had to admit, the scenery was breathtaking. The soaring sandstone cliffs, the unique rock formations which Maggie had told him contained ancient Aboriginal artwork had him wanting to explore and marvel at the way such paintings had withstood the test of time, and how the power of nature had carved out such incredible geological features. And all of it was within tantalizing reach of his property. The thought gave him pause as realization dawned.

He'd been kidding himself when he'd thought the sheer magnitude and uniqueness of the land he now owned at Hetherington Station could compare with anything he owned in Brisbane. How did a block of modern, glass-and-steel townhouses stack up against the natural wonders of the outback?

But my life's in Brisbane. That's where I want to spend the rest of my days... Isn't it?

It was disquieting to discover that for the first time in his life he didn't know the answer to that.

Chapter Thirteen

♥

From her position behind Todd, Maggie snuck a look at Raf. He appeared engrossed in the scenery outside his window. They weren't that far from her family's station. As an idea formed in her mind, on impulse, she asked Todd if he wouldn't mind flying them over to Marlowe Downs and landing there. To her relief, he readily agreed.

She called ahead and spoke to her mother on the phone to let her know they were on their way. Although it was at least an hour's drive from Hetherington Station, the chopper covered the distance in no time. They arrived just as her family were sitting down for an early lunch.

All six of her brothers, along with her three sisters-in-law, crowded around the long table. Her parents were also there. Maggie made the introductions.

"Raf, this is my mum and dad, Ellen and Bob Fairfax. And my brothers in order of age from oldest to youngest are Raine, Brock, Cayd, Lachlan, Justin, and Aiden."

"Wow," Raf exclaimed. "Maggie warned me there were a few of you. She wasn't kidding!"

Everyone laughed. Maggie continued with the introductions. "The lovely ladies seated next to Raine, Brock and Cayd are my sisters-in-law. Isabella, Kelsey, and Lily. Mum, Dad, everyone. This is Raf Hetherington. He's Arthur's nephew and the new owner of Hetherington Station. And of course, you all know Todd Whittaker."

There were murmured greetings and plenty of curious sideways glances as people shuffled their chairs over to make room for the new arrivals. The three of them took their places at the table. Maggie understood her family's curiosity. They knew all about the sudden passing of her boss and that a city slicker had inherited the station. Only a couple of months earlier she'd been bemoaning that fact to Cayd, along with voicing her fears that her life as manager of the property was now under threat. And now those fears could easily become a reality. Coupled with that, she'd also invited in a man who in the not-too-distant past had been a sworn enemy.

Maggie knew well that her spontaneous decision to drop in with Raf and Todd would spark her family's interest and if she'd had the choice, she would have left Todd out of it, but she couldn't afford to give up the opportunity for Raf to spend some time with her brothers.

Raine and Brock now called Brisbane home and ran a successful business together, but the other four lived and worked on the station. If anyone could give Raf a male's perspective on the pros and cons of life in the outback, it was them.

Okay, so they had all grown up on the station and their strong connection to the place no doubt influenced their perspective, but she hoped they might assist Raf in realizing it was possible to make a good life out there, or at the least, that selling the station might not be his best option. Her family was aware of how much she loved working on Hetherington Station. She was counting on them going into bat for her and doing what they could to convince Raf not to sell.

Raf looked around him at the large and airy country-style open-concept kitchen and dining area. Though conversation had resumed around the crowded table as platters of food were passed around and plates were filled, Raf felt keenly aware of the curious glances in his direction. Silverware clattered against crockery and glasses tinkled as they were raised and clinked. The noise level was bordering on loud, but nobody seemed to mind. Raf wondered if this was what it was like around every mealtime in the Fairfax household.

Maggie's resemblance to at least some of her brothers was startling. Though Cayd and Justin were dark-haired, Brock, Lachlan, and Aiden were particularly like her, with the same thick blond hair, light eyes, and olive skin coloring. Raine was the only one whose auburn hair didn't quite match the others, but he certainly resembled his siblings in other ways, not the least in his confident, wide, white grin.

Blue and green eyes seemed to dominate the male Fairfax genes, along with broad shoulders, firm jawlines and strong opinions. As Raf helped himself to cold slices of roast beef and green salad, a disagreement broke out between Lachlan and Justin about the best time to apply fertilizer on one of their paddocks of pasture.

"It's meant to rain next week," Lachlan argued. "Better to wait until then."

"Ha," Justin scoffed. "Since when have we been able to rely on the weather predictions? I say we do it tomorrow and then it's done. We'll be busy branding those new calves next week."

Lachlan opened his mouth to respond, but Aiden beat him to it. "What do you think, Dad?"

Conversation at the table ceased, and all eyes turned toward the patriarch of the family, who sat at the head of the table. Maggie's mother sat on Bob's left and Raine was on his right.

"What odds are the weather guys giving for the rain?" Bob Fairfax asked.

Justin made a sound of disgust at the back of his throat. "Around seventy percent chance, but when have they gotten that right recently? The last few times, their predictions have been wildly off. I've lost all confidence in our so-called weather forecasters."

"Still, seventy percent chance of rain can't be dismissed," Bob replied. "If it does fall, it'll increase the effectiveness of that fertilizer considerably. How about we bring the branding forward instead? The calves won't mind if we do it this week. What do you think, boys?"

There were murmurs of agreement, and the conversation moved in another direction. Raf was impressed. The love and respect the Fairfax brothers had for their father was obvious, and how easily they accepted he had the final word.

"So, Raf. Maggie tells us you're from Brisbane. How are you finding the outback?"

The question came from Cayd, who sat directly across from him. Raf smiled. "From what I've seen so far, it's beautiful. Very different to what I'm used to, though."

Cayd laughed. "Yes. We're a long way from the shops."

"Not just the shops," Raf replied. "The beach, the nightlife, the crowds."

Cayd gave a mock shudder. "That's one thing I hate. Crowds. Give me wide-open spaces any day."

Raf chuckled. "You sound just like Maggie."

"I guess it runs in the family." Cayd grinned. "When you live out here, in the middle of nowhere, you get used to the peace and quiet. In fact, you yearn for it. Whenever I visit the city, I get claustrophobic. A day or two is all I can cope with, and then I have to get out."

"You obviously don't mind the isolation," Raf said.

"Not at all," Cayd replied. "But it's not all isolation. Roma's only a couple of hours' drive. Closer from Hetherington. And the station owners and workers in the district are a social lot. We get together whenever we can."

Raf nodded and glanced at Lily, who sat beside Cayd. "What about you, Lily? Are you a country girl?"

Lily laughed. "Not at all. I relocated out here from Sydney."

"Wow. A city girl. How long ago did you move?"

"About two months ago."

Raf stared at her in surprise. "And how are you finding it? You're a long way from the bright lights of the city."

Lily glanced at her husband. The look that passed between them was so tender, so loving, it stole Raf's breath.

"I love it," she confessed. "I didn't think I would, given that I've spent all of my life in the city, but the country's captured my heart."

"Hey," Cayd chided gently. "I thought I was the one who'd captured your heart."

The couple shared another intimate smile. Raf couldn't help but feel a stab of longing at their closeness. Though he'd dated plenty of women, he'd never felt the kind of connection the two people across from him obviously shared. He recognized special. It was something worth waiting for. Something he hoped he'd eventually find.

"What are your plans for Hetherington Station?"

This time, the question came from Justin, but as the conversation around him dwindled, Raf could see the keen interest in several pairs of eyes that turned his way, including Maggie's.

He deliberately forked a piece of beef into his mouth and chewed slowly, buying himself some time. He understood the significance of his response to Maggie and it seemed that most of her family was also interested in his answer.

"To tell you the truth, I'm not sure. When I first learned I'd inherited a cattle station in the middle of nowhere, I was of a mind straight away to put it on the market. After all, what do I need with a cattle station? But after coming out here..."

He blew his breath out on a soft sigh. "There's no doubt it's an extraordinary place. I've only seen a small part of it, but it's special knowing I own even a slice of it. And I can't help but wonder why my uncle left it to me; whether he knew something I don't. Then again, I have a great life in Brisbane. My family is there and I have a job that I love."

"What do you do?" Raine asked.

"I'm in finance. Investments, mainly."

Brock sat forward. "Really? Raine and I are in that industry, too."

Raf's eyes widened in surprise. "Really?"

"Yes," Raine added. "We have our own business. Fairfax Investments. You might have heard of it."

"Absolutely," Raf replied. "You boys are rocking it. Sorry I didn't make the connection."

Both Raine and Brock merely shrugged, and then Raine frowned.

"Hell, you're not Raphael Hetherington, are you?"

Raf nodded. "Yes. But I prefer Raf."

"I was only reading about you the other day in *Money Magazine*. It was an article on people to watch on the investment scene. I can't believe that's you!" Raine exclaimed.

"Thanks," Raf said simply.

"Have you ever thought about going out on your own?" Raine asked.

"Not seriously, but yes, the thought's crossed my mind."

"You should do it," Brock encouraged. "No doubt you're making millions for your bosses. Why not pocket some of that money yourself?"

"Of course, running your own business comes with risk," Raine warned, "but I wouldn't let that hold you back. If we can believe that magazine article, you're obviously good at what you do."

"I do all right," Raf replied.

"Then you should go for it," Raine said.

Raf grimaced. "But what about the station? If I set up my own business in Brisbane, I'd have to sell it."

"Not necessarily," Brock said. "Most of our work is done remotely. All we need is a good Internet connection. Now and then we'll have a face-to-face meeting with a client, but we organize that ahead of time. Raine spends a lot of time in Sydney. He works just as well from there."

"My family is all in Sydney," Isabella explained. "Since the birth of our son, Colton, it seems we're always on a plane. My mother's afraid her grandson will grow up not knowing her if we don't try to see her as often as possible."

"She could always hop a plane to Brisbane," Raine grumbled. "Why are we always the ones having to travel?"

Isabella squeezed her husband's arm. "Yes, she could, and she does. But she also has at least half a dozen other grandchildren she wants to spend time with. It's easier if we go to her."

"Anyway," Brock said, bringing the discussion back to Raf. "The point is your job's very mobile. You could do it from anywhere. Including right here, in the outback."

Raf nodded. "Yes. You're right. It's definitely food for thought, but I'm still not sure I could live out here. The peace and quiet's a plus, for a while anyway, but what about everything else? What is it that keeps you here?"

He directed the question to the room. It was Lily who responded.

"I guess you have to find a good enough reason to want to be here. For me, it was Cayd. He's a cattle farmer, and this is where he lives. It's not like he could up and move his herd to Sydney. Or anywhere else. So, I had to decide how much he meant to me. Whether I loved him enough to leave my family, my familiar life behind me and move." She leaned over and pressed a tender kiss against Cayd's lips before turning back to Raf. "As you can see, I did. And I haven't regretted my decision for a second."

Raf looked across at the loved-up pair and suppressed an unexpected surge of yearning. Raf couldn't help but look at Maggie. His heart skipped a beat when he found her staring at him. He wasn't sure how he felt about her. Sizzling attraction, that was a given, but they hadn't known each other long enough for him to know whether that attraction could develop into something more.

She definitely dominated his thoughts, and he was intrigued to get to know her better, but could it develop into something worth pursuing? Something worth turning his life upside down for? Perhaps he owed it to both of them to find out.

He directed his gaze toward the patriarch of the family. "Maggie tells me Marlowe Downs has been in your family for a long time."

Pride filled Bob Fairfax's face. He smiled and nodded. "Yes. Since the mid-1800s. My grandfather emigrated from England in the 1840s. He spent some time in Sydney working on farms before heading north. He was an early pioneer and established one of the first cattle stations in Central Queensland. He and some of his immediate family rest in peace on Fairfax ground. His descendants have been grazing it ever since."

"What a remarkable piece of history," Raf remarked. He looked around him at the occupants of the table. "I understand why you're all so connected to the place. The outback's been running in your veins for generations."

"That's right," Lachlan said, joining the conversation. "I spent three years at a university in Brisbane and six years before that at boarding school. I had fun living in the city, but I missed home every single day I was away." He shrugged and said simply, "This is home."

Lachlan's voice had turned husky with emotion. It was obvious to Raf how much the family station meant to him. Raf liked the idea of feeling that kind of connection to a place. He loved Brisbane, but if someone were to ask him whether he had a deep emotional connection to the place, he would honestly have to say no.

Once again, his gaze flicked to Maggie. She was now engrossed in conversation with Aiden. They were talking about cattle and pasture and other farm-related issues Raf couldn't quite follow. There was no doubt she knew what she was doing. Despite enduring extreme weather events during the three years, the station was turning a decent profit. After the past few days, he now had a better appreciation for how difficult that was to achieve.

Plentiful pasture was not a given. When the rain dried up, so did the grass. Feed had to be bought in and that put an extra strain on the budget. He'd seen the figures. Floods had their own challenges and Maggie had faced both head-on in recent times. And she hadn't given up. He wondered if his late uncle had fully appreciated just how hard his station manager worked.

She must really love the place... Why else would she give so much of herself to see it succeed?

The only thing in it for her was her salary, and that paled in comparison to the kind of profit the station could make in a good season. He tried to recall whether Uncle Arthur had ever paid her a bonus, but he thought not. He couldn't recall having to account for one in the books. That made her commitment to the station even more admirable.

Knowing how much the property meant to her made his decision about its future even more difficult. It was one thing to sell a property he'd never seen and disrupt the lives of people he'd never met. But he now knew Maggie, and he'd watched Bluey and some of the other employees at work. They were real people with real lives that his decision to sell would affect.

What was supposed to have been a quick trip to the outback for some R and R and to cast his eyes over his inheritance before putting it on the market had turned into so much more. His life was becoming entangled with Maggie's. He cared about what she thought. He cared about her.

No, that couldn't be right. He'd barely known her for three days. That wasn't long enough to care about someone.

Was it?

Chapter Fourteen

♥

The sudden sound of a baby crying caught everyone's attention. Maggie couldn't help but smile. Though she'd met her little nephew several times in the couple of months since he'd been born, she never failed to get excited at the thought of seeing him again.

"Sounds like Colton's awake. He's due for a feed," Isabella said, excusing herself from the table.

Maggie swallowed a sigh and tamped down a rush of yearning. She was acutely aware that her biological clock was ticking. She might only be twenty-eight, but she wanted a whole heap of kids. Six or seven, maybe eight. That many kids took time. A lot of time. Time she was fast using up.

She hazarded a glance in Raf's direction. She'd been listening intently to the answers he'd given her brothers. Unsurprisingly, he'd remained noncommittal about the future of the station, although she'd taken some hope that he hadn't definitively said he would be selling.

As if sensing her attention, he looked up. For long moments, their gazes caught and held. Maggie's heart skipped a beat and then began to pound in earnest. Raf's expression was unreadable, filled with conflicting emotions, but for the life of her, she couldn't look away. And then Lily said something to him and the moment between them was gone.

Trembling with emotion, Maggie's only thought was to escape. Murmuring an excuse, she stood abruptly and left the room, intent on finding the bathroom where she could take a moment to restore her equilibrium and come to terms with the fact that no matter what lectures she gave herself, she was falling for a man who was a real threat to the life she loved.

Raf stared after Maggie as she disappeared through the kitchen doorway and wondered if he should go after her. But then he caught her mother's eye. Ellen frowned at him and shook her head. Whatever troubled Maggie, it was best if he stayed out of it. He sighed quietly and returned to his meal.

The conversation around him had resumed. The noisy chatter of a large family catching up over a mealtime surrounded him. The room was full to bursting with every seat filled. Six brothers, Maggie's parents, and three sisters-in-law. Well, two sisters-in-law now that Isabella had left to tend to her baby. Then there was Todd, who seemed out of place, perched at one corner of the table.

It was quite the crowd and something he wasn't used to. He had his parents and one sister. During his growing-up years, mealtimes had been quiet and tranquil affairs. Swapping idle anecdotes. Sharing conversation about whatever stories had hit the news. A tidbit of gossip here and there. All very civilized. All very calm. Nothing like the organized mayhem of a Fairfax meal. It was a little overwhelming.

As if sensing his thoughts, Brock's wife, Kelsey, who sat beside him, lightly touched his arm.

"How're you doing?"

He managed a smile. "Okay."

"They can be overwhelming at first," she confided.

Raf's eyes widened in a grin. "I won't argue with that."

She chuckled. "I assume you don't come from a big family?"

"Right. One sister. That's it as far as siblings go."

"You have one more than me. I'm an only child."

"Wow. No wonder you know how this feels." He indicated the crowded room. "I don't think I've ever eaten a meal with so many people at the same table. The fact that they're all related... It blows my mind."

Kelsey laughed. "I know what you mean."

"Do I detect an American accent?" he asked.

She nodded. "I spent most of my life in Florida."

"Whereabouts?"

"Tampa."

"I've been to Tampa. It's a beautiful part of the world."

"It sure is."

He smiled. "I can't imagine a place on earth more different from the Australian outback."

She laughed again. "I know what you mean. It was definitely a culture shock at first. Fortunately, I'd spent a bit of time in Brisbane before I met Brock."

"How did you adjust?" he asked, curious.

"It wasn't easy, and it didn't happen overnight. In fact, Brock and I lived in Florida for the first several months of our marriage. But I always knew his heart was here, and it came down to how much I loved him. If he was happy, then I was happy, and this is his happy place. It was as simple as that."

"You look happy too," Raf commented.

Her smile was luminous. "I am."

"Don't you miss Tampa? The hustle and bustle? The beach? You had a life there. Your family."

"Of course. I was lucky that my mother agreed to emigrate with us. She now lives in Brisbane. I visit her whenever I can, but this is my home now, and it's the only place I want to be."

Raf pondered her words. It sounded so simple. It also helped that she and Brock were obviously deeply in love. Just like Cayd and Lily. It appeared love made all the difference. He suddenly wanted to know what it felt like to feel that strongly about someone that he'd be willing to completely upend his life.

Unable to stop himself, his thoughts once again turned to Maggie. He'd been drawn to her instantly and she most certainly was attracted to him. If they'd met in the city, he'd have already made a move on her to see where things might lead. The only thing that held him back now was their seemingly incompatible positions about where they wanted to live and the lives they wanted to lead. He kept coming back to that, and there was no easy way to move forward. The truth was, their differences seemed insurmountable. That wasn't something he could easily dismiss, no matter how much he might want to.

Sighing quietly, he once again took refuge in his meal.

It was late in the afternoon by the time Maggie finally farewelled her family and boarded the helicopter again. She'd checked in with Todd earlier to make sure he was okay about spending so much time away from his place. He'd assured her he had nothing pressing to do that day and was happy to stay as long as she wanted.

Raf was quiet on the flight back. Though Todd kept up a running commentary about their visit to the Fairfax family and in particular, how good the station looked, Raf responded in monosyllables that eventually forced Todd to give up. They landed in silence near the homestead. Maggie once again offered her thanks and urged Todd to visit soon.

As they walked back to the homestead, she threw Raf a sideways glance. He looked deep in thought.

"Is everything okay?" she asked.

"I guess. It was nice to meet some of your family. They're nice people."

"Thank you. My parents are the best. It can't have been easy raising ten children, especially through the uncertainties of floods and droughts when livelihoods were threatened, and money was scarce. Despite all that, we had a great childhood."

"I can tell. You and your brothers have such a great bond, which is a testament to how well you were raised.

She chuckled. "Just because we know how to behave in public doesn't mean we don't disagree. We disagree plenty, especially when it comes to the running of the station, but we also love and respect one another to mend fences when the dust has settled. Everyone's entitled to their opinion. We don't all have to agree. As long as the disagreeing's done respectfully, we're all good with that."

"It's a good way to approach life," Raf mused. "We city folk could do with a bit more of that way of thinking." He paused and then added, "I was surprised to discover that both Kelsey and Lily were once city girls. Hell, Kelsey's even switched countries! Now, they've made the outback their home. It's interesting."

Maggie eyed him quizzically. She took heart from the fact he'd paid attention to her sisters-in-law and was quite possibly even applying their situation to his own experience.

"I guess when you have the right motivation, anything's possible," she said lightly.

He nodded thoughtfully. "I guess."

Raf walked along beside Maggie toward the homestead. His thoughts kept circling around what her sisters-in-law had said. He couldn't stop thinking about whether he'd ever come to care for Maggie—or anyone—enough to make the same sacrifice. Not that it would be so difficult to live in such a beautiful part of the world. Seeing it from the air had been an experience he'd never forget.

Knowing he owned the land for as far as he could see had been exhilarating and had filled him with a sense of pride. Listening to Maggie's brothers talk about life in the outback and witnessing their obvious love for the land had been inspiring. He realized with a jolt that he wanted to feel that way about the place where he lived, too.

To be stirred by such emotions took him by surprise. He'd never felt that way before. Brisbane had always been his home, but he'd never thought much past that. He certainly had spent no time analyzing how he felt about it. But if anyone asked him if he felt a strong connection to the place, the answer would probably be "no" and that too was surprising.

As they drew closer to the homestead, he spied the same four young stockmen he'd passed by on his first day leaning against the fence. It appeared they were waiting to speak with Maggie. Raf eyed them with interest. All four of them were strapping fit men. Broad of shoulder and narrow of hip. They all had that wiry athletic build that exuded confidence and strength. Like they could wrestle a bull with their bare hands if needed.

It was obvious how keen they were on their boss. Though they took care to hide it, Raf was acutely aware of the way their gazes lingered on Maggie's face and slid over her body when they thought she wasn't looking. The spike of jealousy surprised him, even though Maggie appeared oblivious to their interest. He had no right to feel jealous over her. He had no right to feel anything at all. She deserved a man who was prepared to commit to her one hundred percent, and that wasn't him.

Unaware of his thoughts, Maggie made the introductions.

"Jack, Tom, Cody, Sam. This is Raf Hetherington. He's Arthur's nephew and the new owner of the station."

Almost immediately, their expressions closed.

"Ah. So, you're the new boss," the one named Jack said.

"Yes. I guess."

"What are your plans for the place?" Sam asked, his gaze narrowed on Raf's.

Raf did his best not to squirm under the forthright stare. "I'm not exactly sure right now. That's why I'm here. To check the place out. See if there are good reasons for me to keep it."

"How long are you here for?" Tom asked, looking him squarely in the eye.

"A week. Maybe two."

"And then what?" Jack asked. "Back to the city again?"

Raf flushed. "What makes you think I'm from the city?"

"No one who comes from the country gets around in shoes like that."

With a disparaging grin, Jack pointed toward Raf's loafers. After his travels to the waterfall the day before, they were looking seriously the worse for wear. Once again, Raf fought back a blush.

"That's enough guys," Maggie said. "No need to get personal. Yes, Raf's from the city, but that doesn't mean we show him disrespect. That's not how we treat our guests, is it?"

She looked hard at each of the young men. They mumbled their agreement amidst their apologies and lowered their eyes.

"What did you need to see me about?" Maggie asked, her tone now all business.

Jack cleared his throat. "We found three dead cattle. It looks like a wild dog attack."

"What makes you think that?" Maggie asked.

"They had their throats ripped out. There were two others we had to put down. They were still alive when we found them, but they were too badly injured to save," Cody added.

"Where did you find them?"

"Not far from the billabong," Tom said. "We were out there checking fences and came across them."

"They weren't there a couple of days ago," Maggie murmured. "Raf and I were out that way. I would have seen them."

"You're right," Jack agreed. "The corpses were fresh, and the wounds sustained by those we found alive were severe enough to have killed them if they'd been attacked two days ago. I'd say it happened last night."

"Do you get these kinds of attacks often?" Raf asked, curious.

Maggie compressed her lips. Her expression turned grim. "No, thank goodness. Wild dogs are always a threat to cattle in the outback. Most of the time, they're too cowardly to attack the herd. It seems this time they've found their courage. It's important to find the culprits and dispose of them before they can attack again."

She turned back to the men. "Go out and patrol the entire area and see if you can hunt them down. Now they've had a taste of our cattle, they'll be keen to attack again. Do whatever's necessary to eradicate the problem. Understand?"

"Do you mean they're going to shoot them?" Raf asked.

Once again, Maggie turned her attention on him. "Yes. That's exactly what they're going to do."

Raf frowned. "Is that really necessary? Perhaps they can just scare them off?"

She looked at him, incredulous. "Scare them off? They're wild dogs who've just attacked our stock. *Your* stock. Now that they've had a taste of Hetherington beef, you can bet your bottom dollar they'll be back. Who knows how many more will be attacked the second time?" She turned back to the men. "Were they heifers or steers?"

Jack grimaced. "Unfortunately, all five of them were heifers."

She looked at Raf. "Five heifers mean five less breeding stock. That's a loss of thousands of dollars, even more when you consider the calves they're no longer going to have. You're a numbers guy. Do the math. I'm not sure where your priorities lie, but mine are with the cattle."

Raf held her gaze for a little while longer and then nodded. "You're right. I'm being stupid. Showing up my city credentials, no doubt. We have to do what we can to save the cattle. The dogs can go to hell."

The young men sent up a cheer, filling Raf with a sense of satisfaction and comradery. He smiled. "Do you think I could ride along with you?"

"No way," Maggie said immediately.

Raf frowned. "Why not?"

"Because you know nothing about guns and wild dogs, or even cattle, for that matter. They're going out after dark. That's when the dogs come out. It could put the men in danger if you did something stupid."

Raf tensed, affronted. "I'm not going to do anything stupid."

"I'm not saying you'd do it on purpose. That doesn't make it any less dangerous. I'm responsible for these men and I won't put their safety at risk, all so that you can have a real outback experience you can brag about to your mates."

Anger ignited. He glared at her. "Take that back. That's not fair."

She blew out her breath on a sigh and scrubbed a hand through her hair. "You're right. I'm sorry. I shouldn't have said that. In fact, I have no right to pull rank on you at all. You're the boss. You get to say what happens tonight."

Raf took a moment to let his anger dissipate. He understood where Maggie was coming from. And she was right. He knew nothing about guns, wild dogs, or even the layout of the station. He'd been to the billabong only once and that had been in broad daylight. Besides, he'd never been hunting in his life. Why would he want to start now?

It was just that he'd gotten carried away with feeling a part of the team; one of the boys. It had been nice to feel included, even for a little while. It was the first time since he'd arrived that he felt like he belonged.

Still, that was no reason to insist on tagging along on what could be a dangerous mission. He had no intention of making it harder on the men or putting lives at risk.

He looked at Maggie. "You're right. I'm sorry. I'm being an asshole. I just thought it might be interesting to see some of the challenges of managing the cattle up close, but I don't want to get in the way or inadvertently put lives at risk through my naivety."

Maggie nodded slowly, her gaze steady on his. "Thank you for being reasonable. I appreciate it. There will be other opportunities for you to engage with the cattle over the next few days. Opportunities that don't involve firearms."

He smiled. "Right. I'm going to hold you to that."

She smiled back. "There are always the stables that need mucking out if you're looking for something interesting!"

He laughed, feeling better than he had for a long time.

After giving final instructions to the men, Maggie thanked them for their vigilance.

"We'll report back to you in the morning," Jack said.

"Thanks. I'll see you after breakfast. Good luck tonight. I hope it's a success."

Chapter Fifteen

♥

Maggie set about preparing dinner. Though Daphne cooked for the men, her role rarely extended to cooking for Maggie, unless Maggie asked. That only happened on rare occasions, when Maggie was going to be home late, like the previous night. Most of the time, Maggie was happy enough to cook for herself.

"What are we having?" Raf asked as he entered the kitchen.

He'd taken the time to shower and change into fresh clothes. He still had damp hair and had freshly shaved cheeks. The smell of his woodsy cologne as he moved closer created havoc with her senses. With a determined effort, she ignored the butterflies fluttering in her stomach and responded to his question.

"We're having grilled chicken breasts in mushroom sauce with mashed potato and another green salad. Does that sound all right?"

He grinned. "Sounds great to me. What can I do to help?"

Her belly somersaulted under the full wattage of his brilliant white smile. Once again, she pushed the tumultuous feelings aside.

"You did a fair job on those potatoes the other night. Perhaps you could start there."

He gave her a look of mock outrage. "Only a fair job? Just so you know, those potatoes were up there with the best I've ever had!"

She chuckled. "Okay, okay. They were all right. But I'm sure you can do better. I dare you to do better."

His eyes gleamed with humor. "Challenge accepted."

In companionable silence, they worked side by side in the kitchen, putting together the meal. Raf appeared happy and relaxed. Maggie was relieved he'd seen sense about joining the hunting party and had accepted her decision about it without too much fuss. She was so used to taking charge and making all the decisions. She was so used to being the boss. It was going to take some getting used to, having an owner underfoot.

That's if he stays. There's no guarantee of that.

Regardless, all she needed was for him to retain ownership. It didn't matter if he was an absentee landlord. She'd already had plenty of practice coping with that, and things had been working fine. The station was once again turning a profit and their stock rates were increasing all the time. They were almost back to pre-flood levels of stocking, and that was no easy feat.

But it had been nice to have some company these past few days. Though she often worked alongside the other men and occasionally caught up with Daphne, they gave each other space after hours. That's the way it had to be when they worked together all day.

Having Raf around at night, sharing a meal, had been something she hadn't realized she'd missed. More than that, he was good company. Although her staff were all good people, she didn't find any of them attractive. That made a vast difference. Raf was always in her thoughts. Hell, the night before, he'd also invaded her dreams.

The memory of the vivid fantasy she'd had sent heat creeping up her neck. She was sure it had everything to do with the fact she'd spent the day with him cavorting almost naked at the waterfall. He'd been on her mind. That's all.

She ignored her inner voice that told her she was lying. Her dream about Raf had nothing to do with the day they'd spent together and everything to do with her reaction to him as a man. Despite the conflict between them over the future of the station, there was an indefinable frisson of awareness that had been there from the start that drew her. Like a moth to a flame.

Her past relationships had been few and far between. Eligible men in the outback were thin on the ground. She'd had only one serious boyfriend since leaving high school and even that hadn't lasted beyond a few months. Brad had been a city boy who'd arrived in the outback on a quest for adventure.

Long and lean and with a perpetual grin on his face she'd found adorable, he'd secured work on a neighboring station.

They'd met at a cut-out party and had immediately clicked. Brad was cute and funny and eager to learn all there was to know about living and working at a cattle station. His enthusiasm was endearing. He was a sweet and considerate boyfriend, finding time for her whenever he could, but his love affair with the outback hadn't lasted long.

That hadn't come as a surprise. Life out there was tough. Long hours in the scorching sun surrounded by cattle and dust and heat and flies and not much else. Not too many people who weren't born out there lasted long. Brad had called it quits a few months in and had headed back to the city. That had been two years ago. She hadn't been heartbroken. They'd never been that serious, and she hadn't heard from him since. Neither had she had another boyfriend. Or even a one-night stand. It was likely why she found Raf so attractive!

Liar.

Once again, that annoying voice in her head called her out. She grudgingly accepted the truth. Her reaction toward Raf had nothing to do with her prolonged man-drought and everything to do with the man himself.

He was even more attractive with his sleeves rolled up and working hard in her kitchen.

Heaven help me!

"So, are you really going to make me muck out the stables?" Raf asked as he peeled another potato.

Maggie looked up from where she was cooking two chicken breasts in a pan on the stove. The smell of butter and garlic filled the air.

"Of course. That's a job we all have to do."

He frowned. "But I'm the boss."

"So?"

Her tone indicated that she couldn't see why that would make any difference. He grinned. He liked that she didn't treat him differently to anyone else. That was refreshing. He'd reached a point in his career where many people in the industry knew him. He wasn't surprised when Raine made the connection. But with that kind of profile came a certain deference from those around him, particularly those who were hoping to work with him, or become his next client. But Maggie didn't give a toss about who he was or what he might have achieved. He liked her attitude, among other things.

She still wore the shorts and work shirt she'd worn earlier that day. The soft lighting in the kitchen glinted off her shining hair, turning it gold. It was still in its customary ponytail, but a few strands had escaped and were now curled enticingly around her ears. Her olive skin glowed with health and vitality.

Her full lips invited kisses. He could still picture clearly the way she'd looked in her tiny yellow bikini.

His cock stirred, and he cursed silently. What was it about this woman that had him in an almost-constant state of arousal? It wasn't like he hadn't had his fair share of beautiful women. Take Stephanie Marshall. They'd dated on and off for the past year. She was glamorous, sophisticated, intelligent, and beautiful. She commandeered a corner office in one of the city skyscrapers and managed nearly a billion dollars' worth of hedge fund accounts. Of course, she'd never deign to do any manual work. The most physical she got was when she put herself through a grueling workout at the gym, or during an enthusiastic bout of sex.

Not that he'd minded. She'd been exactly like all the other women he'd dated. He'd never had cause to criticize them in the past. It was only since meeting Maggie that thoughts of beautiful women from his past failed to measure up.

Damn her! She's ruined me for anyone else.

The thought was alarming. He'd always planned on getting married, having a family of his own. A heap of kids. He wanted a houseful of love and laughter, noise and chaos. Just like it had been at Maggie's childhood home that afternoon.

But he'd always imagined his life in the city, in partnership with a gorgeous and glamorous city wife who loved him unconditionally, who was determined, ambitious and capable. Who was independent enough that she didn't need him to give her purpose, but who could support him and accept his support whenever it was required. Someone like Maggie.

What if I can't find that kind of woman in Brisbane?

Once again, panic nipped at his gut. He didn't want to think about the possibility that a city version of Maggie Fairfax didn't exist. That would ruin everything. It would certainly put a spanner in his plans to marry before he got too old. He'd turned thirty last birthday. That wasn't exactly young. He didn't want to be old raising a family. He wanted to be fit and energetic enough to play football with them, take them for bike rides, playdates in the park.

In fact, he probably needed to give the whole wife and kids thing a bit more serious consideration. Time waited for no man. His uncle's untimely death was a testament to that.

"Is everything all right?"

Maggie's concerned question broke into his thoughts. Forcing a smile, he responded.

"Of course."

Making a conscious effort to push the troubling thoughts aside, he cut up the potatoes and dropped them into a saucepan full of salted water. Maggie moved away from the stove, allowing him room to set the pot onto one of the hotplates and set it to boil. The smell of the frying chicken filled his nostrils.

"That smells great," he said.

"This dish is one of my favorites. I've used a frozen chicken from the supermarket. At the moment, we only have laying chickens, but I'd like to raise meat chickens right here on the station one day. That way we could have chicken on the table whenever we want.

"I'd also like to run some pigs that we can slaughter and eat. My family runs pigs. It supplements the beef. They live mostly off kitchen scraps, so they don't cost anything to feed. When we get floods out here, we're often cut off from town. Having extra food sources always makes sense. Apart from that, there's nothing like home-grown food."

"Anything else? Now's your time to put forward your case. I'm all ears."

She smiled. "In that case, I'd also like to investigate the possibility of sinking some bores. At the moment, we rely on creeks and dams and the billabong. It's fed from a natural underground spring, so it never goes dry, but that's not enough to sustain us in a drought. Last time, we had to buy in thousands of gallons of water just to keep the stock alive. That's incredibly costly, as I'm sure you know. If we had a more permanent water supply, like a bore, water scarcity wouldn't be such an issue."

Raf marveled at her ideas. It was obvious she had plenty of future plans for the station.

And I'm in a position to make them happen...

He could always keep the place. Owning the station didn't have to mean he had to live out there. His late uncle had proven that. Raf could fly out anytime the urge struck him and catch up with Maggie and the goings on around the station and then return to Brisbane.

The thought of not seeing her every day caused a sudden pang of distress. He couldn't believe how quickly he'd gotten used to her company. Hell, it had only been three days. Nowhere near long enough to have formed such an attachment. But the timing didn't seem to matter. He couldn't help how he felt. His head might scoff at such notions, but his emotions were all over the place.

For Pete's sake, I'm being ridiculous. It's lust that I'm feeling. That's all this is. A week or two back in Brisbane and I'll have forgotten all about her. Just wait and see.

Over dinner, Maggie entertained him with stories about the station. She talked about branding, drenching, calving, fencing and everything in between. There was so much to do and experience. Her daily routine involved doing things he'd barely heard of, let alone knew what they entailed.

"I'm eager to experience station life in all its glory," he surprised himself by admitting. "Do you think we could do some of those things while I'm here?"

Maggie smiled and sliced off a piece of tender chicken. "Of course. If you're game, so am I." She popped the morsel of meat into her mouth, chewed and swallowed before adding, "But I warn you, I'm a hard taskmaster. I have high standards and I don't tolerate anyone slouching off."

He grinned and saluted her. "Aye, aye, Captain. I hear you loud and clear."

Inwardly, Raf shook his head. He'd held down an office job his entire adult life and here he was, voluntarily signing up for manual labor. His family wouldn't recognize him. He barely recognized himself. What he couldn't deny was how much he looked forward to getting down and dirty on the station with Maggie in the morning.

The next six days passed in a blur of fun and laughter for Maggie. True to his word, Raf helped muck out the stables, filled the laying boxes with fresh hay for the chickens, rubbed down horses after being put through their paces by Bluey, and generally made himself useful. He'd even tried his hand at branding cattle.

Maggie found it surprising how handy he could be. For a city slicker, he'd taken to station life easier than she'd expected and was prepared to meet any challenge head-on. He'd told her that when they'd first met, but now he'd proven that by following through.

Discovering he was so capable was bittersweet. Working side by side with him over the past week or so had made her realize how well they could work together and how nice it would be to have a life partner, someone to share her hopes and dreams, to work toward a shared future. Of course, fitting Raf into that future appeared impossible.

Though he appeared to enjoy his time and had embraced even the most mundane of the daily chores, she was acutely aware that his visit was nearing its end. He'd told her one week, maybe two. Already he'd been there for nine days. Any day now he'd announce he was returning to Brisbane, back to his old life, and there would be nothing she could do to change his mind.

There had been no further talk of his plans for the future of the station. Though she could tell the place had changed him in ways even he probably didn't realize, she wasn't sure it would be enough for him to change his mind about selling. The truth was, she was out of options. She'd done all she could to show him the rewards of station life and the possibilities of building something lasting for future generations. If she hadn't managed to convince him to keep it, then so be it. She'd have to take her chances with the next owner and hope they wanted to retain her and the other employees. It was the best she could hope.

From the corner of her eye, she saw Raf approaching her where she'd taken refuge in the vegetable garden. The late-afternoon sun was behind him, silhouetting him in an orange glow. His face was cast in shadow, obscuring his expression from her gaze. She wondered at his mood.

She'd left him outside the stables where he'd been quizzing Bluey about breaking in the horses. Raf had shown interest in that on his very first day. It didn't surprise her that he'd returned to question the old stockman further.

"There you are," he said, closing the distance between them. "I've been looking for you everywhere."

"I thought I'd come out and pick some fresh greens for a salad."

"Sounds good. Talking about dinner, how about I cook tonight? You've cooked all but one meal since I got here. It's only fair I take a turn."

She blinked at him in surprise. Though he'd told her he could cook and he'd proved a capable kitchen assistant, this was the first time he'd offered to run the show.

"Are you sure?"

"Yes. Do you trust me to whip up something magnificent?"

She chuckled. "Before you get too carried away, have you checked out the contents of the pantry? I haven't been into town for a while. Some of our supplies are running low."

"Already done that. Provided there's nothing you're keeping for a special occasion, we should be good to go."

She smiled in surprise. "Help yourself to whatever you need. I look forward to seeing the finished product. Am I allowed to know ahead of time what you're cooking?"

He mock-frowned. "No way! It's going to be a surprise! You aren't allergic to anything?"

"No. But what if I don't like it?"

"You will."

"You sound terribly confident," she teased.

"Oh, I'm confident all right. This is my specialty dish."

She laughed. "I'm intrigued. Please, do tell."

"Nope. Not until it's ready to serve. My lips are sealed."

Chapter Sixteen

♥

Cooking was one of Raf's favorite pastimes. Though sometimes he took the easy way and ordered takeaway or ate out, he enjoyed creating something from nothing, even if he was only cooking for one.

Cooking also helped him to relax. After a long day at the office, there was nothing he enjoyed more than kicking back with a beer or a glass of wine and working on his next masterpiece. He'd scour his mother's old cookbooks, or scan recipes on the Internet, all the time putting together lists of ingredients to use the next time he got the urge to create.

For days, he'd been wanting to repay Maggie for all the meals she'd cooked by returning the favor, but the past six days had been hectic, filled with a wide variety of chores and other tasks that needed to be done.

It was his own fault he'd been so busy. He'd insisted on Maggie letting him tag along. He hadn't regretted his decision to get his hands dirty. Though it hadn't been without its challenges, particularly when it had come to helping with branding the cattle, it was the most fun he'd had for a long time, despite the heat and flies.

The newness of being at a cattle station. Seeing and hearing and experiencing things he'd never done before. The sheer adrenaline of being in unfamiliar surroundings, not knowing what to expect and spending it in the company of a beautiful and capable woman who intrigued him, made him laugh, and who turned him on like he'd never been turned on before made it even more enjoyable.

It had surprised him how much he'd liked the work. It was so different from his day job. He'd never imagined he was cut out to be a cattleman, and no doubt Maggie and the other workers would agree that was still the case. He conceded that he still wasn't very good at it, but it gave him a sense of accomplishment that was different from the satisfaction he felt from his usual work.

It's just that it's different, something unique. That's why it's been so much fun. And freeing myself from technology—the endless emails and telephone calls. That's been amazing. This feeling of lightness, of happiness has nothing to do with the outback or the people who live out here... Or Maggie.

Liar.

His sense of peace and relaxation and excitement came from being around her. Without her, he'd probably be on his way back to Brisbane. The station was interesting, exciting, exhilarating even, but she was the draw card that had him rethinking his position and there was no point kidding himself otherwise.

Without Maggie there guiding him, teaching him, showing him around, the place would be just another outback station where people bred cattle, tolerated the seasons, and did their best to survive. If she told him she was leaving, he wouldn't hesitate to put the station on the market. And therein lay the problem.

She loved the place with a passion that was undeniable. She didn't want to leave. If he sold the place, there was no guarantee the new owner would want her to stay, and she'd be forced to set aside her dreams for the property and start her life somewhere else, along with the other employees.

That's not my problem, no matter how much I want to help her. I must do what's right for me.

No matter how beautiful and how peaceful and how fun it was out here, or how alluring its manager, his life was in the city. It always had been. He didn't see that changing.

Raf went all out with their meal. He hadn't been exaggerating when he'd said she'd enjoy his specialty dish. The tantalizing aromas coming from the kitchen had teased Maggie all afternoon, increasing her eagerness to discover what was on the menu. When she'd tried to sneak a look, Raf had banned her from the house, handing her a glass of red wine and ushering her toward the back veranda, insisting she put her feet up while he took care of dinner.

It was nice to be waited on for a change. She couldn't remember the last time that had happened. Even when she visited with her family, she inevitably helped with the meal preparation. That's just the way things had always been done.

But knowing that Raf was going to the effort just for her filled her with warmth. She didn't want to read too much into it, but she'd be lying if she said she wasn't thrilled. Despite her best efforts, her feelings for Raf had continued to blossom. No matter how many times she told herself that there was a good chance he'd be gone soon, her heart didn't seem to care.

She was already well past a crush. It had already gone beyond mere physical attraction. His willingness to throw himself into any task on the station had impressed her, no matter how menial or mundane or messy. She'd dismissed him as a city slicker, but he was so much more than that. Yes, he lived in the city, but he was warm and funny and genuine and smart, and up for any challenge. How could she not fall for such a man?

It was going on for seven when Raf appeared in the doorway to the back veranda. He was still wearing her apron. The frilly pink accessory looked so incongruous on him, but she loved that he was brave enough to wear it.

He bowed with a flourish. "Dinner is served."

Her heart clenched. He looked so sexy in a fitted white T-shirt, jeans, the silly apron, and sporting a five o'clock shadow. She got to her feet and smiled.

"It smells good. I can't wait to see what you've come up with."

He ushered her ahead of him into the kitchen. The table had been set with a white linen tablecloth she only used when she had guests, the best silverware and crockery on offer, crystal wine glasses, as well as two antique silver candlesticks, complete with lighted candles. A bottle of red wine stood open beside them.

"Where did you find those?" she asked, pointing toward the candlesticks. "I've never seen them before."

"On a shelf in the cellar, way in the back." Raf gave an exaggerated shrug. "Please don't ask me to go back down there again. Way too scary."

She laughed. "But what if we need more red wine?"

"That's okay," he blurted. "I got extra bottles the first time I went. I needed them for my recipe, anyway."

"Ah. Red wine in our dinner. Great. Now I *am* intrigued."

Raf smiled. He waited for her to be seated and then returned to the kitchen. He came back wearing oven mitts and carrying a large baking dish. He set the dish down on the wooden board that was placed in the middle of the table. Her eyes widened in delight.

"Beef Wellington!" She grinned up at him. "How did you know that's one of my favorite dishes?"

He shrugged. "A lucky guess. I did an inventory of your pantry, fridge and freezer a couple of nights ago and discovered the makings for it. The only thing I couldn't find was the liver pâté, so I'm afraid we're doing without that tonight. But I found some mushrooms in the fridge, and I sautéed those with onion and garlic for added flavor."

"I'm sure it'll taste delicious," she assured him. "It certainly smells good. What are we having with it?"

"Baby roast potatoes and a garden salad, of course. What else goes best with Beef Wellington?"

"Nothing. You're right. It all sounds perfect."

Raf disappeared again and returned carrying a dish of roast potatoes and a bowl containing the salad. When he left for a third time, Maggie wondered what he'd forgotten. He returned a short time later, brandishing a gravy jug.

"And now, the pièce de résistance," he exclaimed. "The red wine sauce."

She chuckled, enjoying his performance. "Ah, I was wondering where the red wine came into it."

He set the jug on the table beside the rest of the food. "I used the pan juices from the meat and added it to the wine. It makes the perfect sauce for this dish. Full of flavor."

"I can't wait to try it."

Raf took the seat opposite her. He reached for the bottle of red wine and filled their glasses and then lifted his in a toast.

"Here's to friendships, uncles, and Hetherington Station."

She clinked her glass with his and took a sip of her wine. The rich and fruity Merlot went down smoothly. "*Mm*, that's very nice."

"Yes. A vintage drop I had time to decant. So glad I'm here to enjoy it with you."

Maggie regarded him solemnly. "I'm glad you're here too. This past week's been... Wow, where do I start?"

"Like being on an out-of-control rollercoaster?" Raf suggested, his eyes twinkling.

She laughed. "Something like that."

Their gazes caught and held. For a long moment, Maggie hardly dared to breathe. Then Raf spoke again.

"I've had a great time out here, Maggie. Thank you for being the perfect host."

"You're welcome. And in case you've forgotten, you're entitled to do and see whatever you want. You own the place."

"Yes, but you're the one who's made it special for me and I appreciate the effort you've gone to this week to show me around and get me involved and to make me feel included."

She flushed. "That's all right. You're easy enough to be around and you're a quick study. Besides, I had an ulterior motive."

He compressed his lips. "Right. You want me to keep the station."

"Yes. But that doesn't mean you have to live here. Your late uncle rarely spent any time out here, and he never stayed overnight. It could be business as usual. The men and I and

Daphne have everything under control. You saw that for yourself."

"Yes. You're amazingly capable. All of you. I have nothing but admiration for your willingness to do whatever it takes to get things done."

"Except, maybe getting that air conditioning fixed," she mumbled. "We still haven't seen hide nor hair of that mechanic."

Raf frowned momentarily. "You're right. We've been so busy I forgot all about that. Leave it with me. I'll chase him up in the morning." He paused. "The thing is, I've enjoyed my time out here far more than I ever imagined, even without the air conditioning working, but I can't see myself ever living here permanently."

Comprehension suddenly dawned. Emotion tightened her chest. She blinked back a sudden rush of angry tears. "Oh, now I get it. This isn't a "thank you" for all the meals I've prepared for you since you've been here. This is a farewell dinner. You're leaving, aren't you?"

Raf flushed and averted his gaze. "No, this *is* a thank you dinner. You've been wonderful. I couldn't have asked for a better host."

"But you're still leaving," she said flatly.

He scrubbed at his hair. "I don't know what I'm doing! One minute I can imagine living here, eking a living out of the land, doing my day job remotely, like your brothers suggested. The next I think about my life in the city and how much it means to me, and I can't believe I'm even contemplating leaving it."

"Then go back to your precious city!" she cried. "You don't have to choose that life over this! As I said, you could be an absentee landlord. Come and go as you please. All I ask is that you retain ownership over this place so those of us who want to stay can. It would work out for everyone."

"But that doesn't solve my problem that I'm falling for you, Maggie Fairfax!" he exclaimed. "How does *that* fit into your tidy little equation?"

She gaped, speechless. "You're... You're falling for me?"

"Yes! No! Hell, I don't know what I feel! All I know is that I've never felt so strongly about a woman. It scares the hell out of me."

As she stared at him, hope blossomed in her chest. "I know how you feel. It scares the hell out of me too."

Raf slowly shook his head. "Then what do we do about it?"

Maggie drew in a deep breath and eased it out on a tremulous smile. Some of her anxiety eased.

"Why do we have to decide about it right now?" she asked. "Let's enjoy this delicious meal and we'll see what tomorrow brings. Deal?" She picked up her wineglass and clinked it with his.

"Deal," he said and smiled.

The early morning sunlight beamed in through the faded curtains Maggie had forgotten to draw the previous night. She groaned aloud and rolled over, turning her back on the offensive opening, but it was too late. She was already awake. Punching the pillow into a more comfortable position, she rolled onto her back.

She couldn't believe it was morning already. It felt like she'd barely closed her eyes. And that was probably true. She'd gone to bed late after spending a pleasant evening with Raf. She was still reeling from his admission that he had feelings for her. Though neither of them quite knew what today would bring, the fact he felt something for her was wonderful. Not that she'd get her hopes up. There was every chance he'd still return to Brisbane. The last thing she wanted was a broken heart. Better to move forward with caution.

A commotion outside her window momentarily interrupted her thoughts. She threw back the covers and padded across the room. Spreading the curtains wider, she blinked in surprise.

A four-wheel-drive vehicle had pulled up outside the front fence. Two young boys spilled out of it, calling out for Raf. They looked enough like him for her to do a double take. A woman, perhaps slightly older than Raf, climbed out from behind the wheel. Even from this distance, Maggie could tell she was beautiful. The woman went around the back of the vehicle and pulled out three suitcases.

Shock held Maggie temporarily mobile. She gaped.

It must be Raf's wife and kids.

She'd never asked him if he was married. She'd taken it for granted he was single when he wasn't wearing a ring. Anger at herself for being so gullible rose inside her. She was also angry at him. Last night, he'd said he had feelings for her! How dare he!

Storming across the room, she wrenched open the door to her wardrobe and hurriedly got dressed. She ran a brush through her hair and pulled it back into its customary ponytail. By the time she made it to the kitchen, identical twin boys and the woman Maggie presumed to be their mother were in the kitchen all talking at once, crowded around Raf, who was laughing and trying to get a word in. He saw her the moment she filled the doorway.

"Ah, Maggie. There you are. This is Allison. Ally, this is my station manager."

The beautiful woman Maggie had spied outside her window looked her up and down and then offered a pleasant smile. "Hello, Maggie. It's nice to meet you."

Raf ruffled the hair of both boys. "And these scallywags are Miles and Lucas. Say hello to Maggie, boys.

"Hello, Maggie."

The boys spoke simultaneously in a dutiful tone before returning their attention to Raf, each child tugging at a hand to get his attention. They were so cute. Dark hair and blue eyes, like their father. Allison was fairer. Tall and slender and dressed in the latest designer gear, she looked out of place in the old-fashioned kitchen.

Maggie's blood continued to boil. Had she been duped by a womanizer? A man who was married with kids. The hide of him! He was the worst kind of man imaginable. To think she'd fancied herself in love with him! How could she have been so blind?

Seemingly unaware of the tension that kept her body taut, Raf turned to the newcomers and grinned.

"Who's up for pancakes?"

Chapter Seventeen

♥

Raf passed around the plate of pancakes before taking a seat at the table across from his sister. The boys were having a great time pouring a combination of honey and maple syrup all over their breakfast and squabbling about who had the bigger stack. They were as rambunctious and full-on as a basketful of puppies.

Maggie sat away from them at the far end of the table. She picked at her food. He could tell she was upset, but he wasn't sure why and he couldn't exactly ask her in front of their unexpected guests.

He glanced at his sister. She looked like she always did. Tired and stressed. At thirty-five, she dedicated herself to raising her family. Twin four-year-old boys would be a handful for anyone. Every time he spoke to Ally on the phone, she sounded just as she looked.

Ally's husband, Rick, was an international art dealer and spent a lot of time overseas. Raf had urged her on a number of occasions to employ a nanny. It wasn't like she and her husband couldn't afford one. But Ally insisted she wanted to raise her boys on her own and refused to bring in help.

Raf didn't know if that made her a hero or stubborn to the point of crazy, but he stopped over at her place in Brisbane's leafy northern suburbs and spent time with his nephews whenever he could, just to give her a break. Though the time spent with his nephews made him glad that he could close the door on them and escape back to his bachelor pad, there were other times when he looked around his empty, inner-city apartment with its glorious views of the river and South Bank and wonder whether it was time to give serious thought to finding a mate.

Then he'd remember the chaos of Ally's household and the restrictions a wife and children would put on his life. He wouldn't be able to do as he pleased or go places at the drop of a hat. He'd have to consult his wife and seek her agreement, and goodness knows what else. Despite his casual musings of one day having a family of his own, the thought of being tied down like Ally was usually enough to bring him out in hives.

Maggie watched the interactions between Raf, his two boys, and his wife and grew increasingly despondent. They all got on so well together. The light banter between him and his wife made it clear they were very comfortable with each other. They'd obviously been together for a long time.

Her white-hot anger toward him had eased to a simmer—for now. As soon as she got him alone, she'd let him have it. To hell with trying to convince him to keep the place. She didn't want him there another minute. Despite that, she still found herself getting drawn into the cheerful scene. It was hard to remain aloof.

It was apparent his kids adored him. The boys took turns peppering him with cute questions. At one point, one of them climbed up into his lap. He gave the child a kiss and a cuddle and continued to hold him close with one arm while he attempted to eat breakfast with the other.

Without warning, an overwhelming wave of yearning took her by surprise. She held back a gasp from the impact of it. The happy family scene rolling out before her was suddenly too much to take. It was like watching her brother, Raine, and his wife, Isabella, all googly-eyed over their newborn. She realized just how very much she wanted what they had: a husband who adored her; kids who loved their dad.

Unable to sit there a moment longer, she stood abruptly, her chair scraping loudly on the kitchen floor as she did so. Conversation ceased. Four pairs of eyes turned to stare at her with various degrees of curiosity.

"I-I'm sorry," she stammered, her face aflame. "I need to go." Keeping her gaze steadfastly averted from the others, she made a beeline for the exit and left the room.

Rafs stared after Maggie in confusion.

What the hell's that all about?

He felt Allison's eyes on him.

"Is she always so rude?" his sister asked. "I understand that we've arrived here without prior notice, but you do own the place. I didn't realize I had to book in with your manager first."

He flushed. "I'm sorry. No, of course you don't have to book in. You're welcome anytime. But this is her house. I've been staying here with her. Unfortunately, there's nowhere else." He paused. "What are you doing here, anyway?"

Ally shrugged. "The boys were driving me crazy. I really needed a break. I thought a few days in the outback on their favorite uncle's farm was just what was required. So, surprise! Here we are! Now I realize it was thoughtless of me. Your manager's definitely put out."

"She's normally much more civil. Very pleasant company, in fact. Believe it or not, I've been enjoying my time out here. I'm not sure what's gotten into her."

"Perhaps she's feeling ill? She did look a little flushed. Maybe I should go and find her and apologize? Make sure she's okay?"

"No, it's fine. I'll go. Please excuse me. I'll be back soon."

Maggie leaned against the railing and stared across the paddock to where the horses were grazing. The morning sun that had woken her way too early had disappeared and had been replaced by an overcast day. The gloom matched her mood perfectly.

She was still trying to get a hold on her tumultuous feelings. She should never have let herself get close to Raf. She only had herself to blame. Except he'd *encouraged* her flirtation. There's no way she'd imagined his interest. Last night, he'd confessed to having feelings for her! And just like that, her anger re-surfaced again.

She was so immersed in her thoughts the crunch of footsteps on the hard ground was her only warning that someone had come up behind her. Spinning around, she caught sight of Raf. She narrowed her eyes at him.

"What the hell are you doing, sneaking up on me like that?" she snapped.

He frowned and held up his hands in a sign of surrender. At the same time, he took a few steps back. "Whoa. I'm sorry. I didn't mean to startle you." He paused and then added, "I just came to see what was wrong."

Her anger found its head. "What's *wrong?* You've got a hide! You've been flirting with me from almost the first moment you arrived. Last night you admitted to having feelings for me, and all along you're married! I don't know what kind of relationship you have with your wife, but I draw the line at married men."

To her consternation, Raf laughed. His inappropriate reaction only fueled her anger. She glared at him. Her breath came fast. "This isn't amusing. Not one bit. You should have told me."

Slowly, his expression sobered. "I'm sorry. I didn't mean to laugh. It's just that you've got it all wrong. I'm not married. Allison isn't my wife. She's my sister."

Raf watched as shock brightened Maggie's wide eyes. Her mouth gaped. She opened and closed it more than once before she finally recovered the power of speech.

"Your *sister?*"

Then her cheeks turned crimson. She buried her face in her hands. "Oh, God. I'm such an idiot!"

He hurried to reassure her. "Don't be silly. It's my fault. I should have told you. I didn't think. They weren't expected and... Well, you've met the twins. Things quickly got out of hand, and I didn't really think about the introductions."

Maggie lifted her head and looked at him with chagrin. "That's okay. You don't have to explain. I shouldn't have jumped to such a wild assumption. I'm sorry."

He shot her a sideways look. "Is that why you were so upset over breakfast?"

She compressed her lips and nodded. "Last night, what you said... I have feelings for you too. The thought that you were married... I was angry at you for being so deceitful and I was angry at myself. I should never have let myself fall for you so quickly. I barely know you."

His heart pounded at the fear and vulnerability in her gaze. He took a step forward and then another, until they were close enough that all he had to do was reach out and touch her, draw her nearer, kiss her.

Before he could stop himself, he reached out and cupped her cheek in his hand. "But you know enough, don't you?"

She gave him a long, searching look. Then she slowly nodded. It was all the affirmation he needed. As his head descended, her eyes closed. She made a little sound of surprise only moments before he pressed his lips against hers.

Her lips were soft and full and supple. She tasted sweet, like the maple syrup they'd had at breakfast. He kept the kiss light, their lips barely touching as he returned to taste her over and over again.

And then she pulled away, and it was over.

Maggie's heart pounded so hard she was surprised it hadn't already burst right out of her chest. She couldn't believe she'd just let Raf Hetherington kiss her! It didn't matter that it was the most amazing kiss she'd ever had, better than she'd even imagined. That changed nothing.

His life was in the city. Her heart belonged to the outback. Their future was still very much undecided; impossible, even.

She risked a glance in Raf's direction. His color was high. His breath came fast. He looked as disorientated as she felt.

"What's the matter?" he asked, his voice still rough with desire.

She eyeballed him and told the truth. "I liked that you kissed me. I liked it a lot. It was...amazing."

His blue eyes flared with an indefinable emotion. Before he could respond, she spoke again. "But there's no point taking things any further. There's a good chance that even if you keep this place, you're going to leave and go back to your life in the city. We'll likely never see each other again."

She paused, hoping he'd say that wasn't true, that he'd changed his mind, that he loved it out there; that he wanted to stay.

Instead, he chose not to speak, leaving her with no choice but to accept that things were exactly as she had said. Her chest went tight. It was difficult to breathe past the lump in her throat. Overcome by a sudden rush of disappointment and the need to put as much distance between them as possible, she clung to her self-control with her fingernails, clamped her lips together, spun on her heel and stalked away.

Raf stared after Maggie as she hurried away so fast it was as if the devil was on her tail. He cursed under his breath. "Shit."

He should never have kissed her. So what if it was amazing? So what if he didn't want it to end? No matter that he'd developed feelings for her, it had been a stupid thing to do.

She was likely right. At the moment, he couldn't see any future for them beyond a quick fling, and she wasn't the only one who didn't want that. Hadn't he just spent hours the night before convincing himself of that? Nothing had changed between then and now. As soon as his outback visit was over, he'd return to what he'd left behind. A successful career, his luxurious bachelor pad. His life of having fun with his mates, going to the beach. Attending parties with members of Brisbane's high society. Rubbing shoulders with famous and not so famous people. It was a good life. It was his life. He'd never imagined living any other way.

But that was before Maggie. He found himself attracted to her in a way he had never experienced with another woman. He wasn't sure if there was more than the physical attraction between them, but that was dynamite enough. Then there was the easy way she had about her. No-nonsense. A straight talker. And she was so amazing to kiss.

But there was no way she'd leave the outback, and the city was where he belonged. It wouldn't be fair to ask her to leave it behind. It was in her blood. The best thing to do would be to ignore the attraction between them and get the hell out of there as soon as he could. Just like he'd told himself over and over.

He grimaced. *Yeah, right.* He wished it was that easy. Somehow, over a very short period, she'd become important to him; had taken up residence in his head. He couldn't stop thinking about her. He wanted to be with her. Not just in the biblical sense, although that held powerful appeal. He also wanted to be near her; enjoy her company. It was all so confusing. He was being pulled in two directions.

His time at the station was ending, but he didn't want to leave early. He didn't want to leave at all. That didn't mean he was ready to upend his life and everything he'd known, but he couldn't deny he very much wanted to spend as much time with Maggie as possible. He'd deal with whatever happened when his two weeks were up. Until then, he wanted to be near her. Make her smile. Hear her laugh. Maybe even kiss her again.

If that made him an asshole, then so be it.

Maggie headed for the stables. She didn't expect to run into anyone, but just in case, she kept her head down, looking neither left nor right.

At times like this, when she was upset or overwrought, she always took refuge in her animals. Her little bay mare, Sunny, had listened to more than her fair share of Maggie's problems. Today she needed to vent like nothing else. She needed to talk through her disappointment and come to terms with the fact that the most amazing kiss she'd ever experienced had been with someone she could never pursue a relationship with.

Dammit.

Sometimes life wasn't fair. How many times had she prayed for a helpmate, someone who loved her above all others and who wanted to share her life? Now she'd met the most intriguing, sexy, interesting man, and he was devoted to the city. God certainly had a wacky sense of humor.

The clouds that had threatened earlier had begun to roll in and the sky had darkened, perfectly matching her mood. She walked into the stables and blinked to adjust to the dimness. As she passed the empty stalls, she came to a halt outside the one that housed Sunny.

She held out her hand to the horse. "Hey there, Sunny. How's it going?"

The horse knickered quietly and pushed her soft nose against Maggie's palm. Maggie gave her a pat.

"Sorry, old girl. I came unprepared. I don't have any treats for you today. But I hope you have some time on your hands because, boy, do I need you to listen."

The horse responded by stretching her head out further over the gate and nuzzled against Maggie's hand.

"Oh, Sunny. I knew I could rely on you. You never let me down. Not like some others I won't name." She pressed a kiss against the horse's velvety-soft nose and sighed. "Where do I start? I'm sure you've guessed already; yes, it involves a man."

She laughed, but the sound came out strangled. She hated she was so twisted in knots over someone she barely knew. She'd never believed in love at first sight. She had no experience of romantic love and wasn't even sure that what she felt for Raf could be defined like that, but she couldn't deny he'd touched something inside her that no one had ever reached.

"Maybe it's just because I'm lonely for the company of a man," she murmured against Sunny's neck. "Or maybe I'm just lonely. Period."

It had been so long since she'd gone into Roma for a night on the town. She'd been busy and going to the effort to dress up and drive more than an hour on rough roads and dodging wildlife was on the bottom of her list most of the time. There was also the fact she wasn't much of a drinker and on the rare occasions she overindulged, the inconvenience of having to stay in a sub-standard motel because she was over the limit had never held much appeal.

But perhaps she had to make more of an effort to socialize with people her own age. Or socialize with anyone, for that matter. Especially if she wanted to find a permanent mate. Or even a boyfriend. Yes, a boyfriend would be nice.

"There you are."

The sound of Raf's voice close behind her made her jump. She turned around and glared at him.

"Do you mind? That's the second time you've crept up on me."

"I didn't creep up on you," he retorted. "It's not my fault you didn't hear me."

She opened her mouth to argue back, but then closed it again. What was the point? The fact that she was consumed with talking to her horse and hadn't noticed his approach wasn't his fault.

"What are you doing in here?" she asked brusquely.

"I wanted to see if you were okay."

"I'm fine."

"Good."

She narrowed her gaze at him. "You can go now."

"I'd rather spend time with you."

"Too bad. I'm busy."

"Doing what?"

Thinking on her feet, she came up with a response. "I'm mustering cattle today," she lied.

"Great. I love mustering."

She shot him a sideways look. All the while, she fought a smile. "You don't know the first thing about mustering."

"True. But I'm a quick learner. You know that. I'm sure you can teach me all I need to know."

"Like riding a horse?"

He gaped. This time, she turned and hid her smile. She'd actually been planning to take a quad bike for the job, but an imp inside her had made her tell him they were going on horseback.

By the time she looked back at him, he'd overcome his initial hesitation. "Of course I can ride. It's been a while, but it's like riding a bike, right? You never forget how."

He gave her an uncertain smile. She shook her head.

"What about your sister and nephews? Are you just going to leave them here?"

"Yes. They'll be fine. They'll find something to occupy them. I've had a word with Bluey. He's going to let them watch him while he continues to break in that young filly and then Daphne's going to show them around the garden and get them to help her pick some vegetables for dinner."

Torn between wanting to spend time with him and wanting to guard her heart, Maggie stared at him. She tried again to dissuade him.

"They've come all this way to spend time with you. Aren't they going to be upset if you disappear for the day?"

A tiny frown appeared on his forehead. "Are we going to be away all day?"

She shrugged and expanded on her lie. "I'm moving a large herd of cattle from one paddock to another. It'll take at least half the day."

"Half a day? They'll be fine. When do we leave?"

She glanced at him over her shoulder as she turned back to Sunny, coming to a sudden decision. "Right now. Saddle up, cowboy."

Not waiting for his response, Maggie opened the gate to Sunny's stall and reached for the bridle that hung from a hook on the wall just inside. Quickly and efficiently, she pulled it over the horse's head. Then she slipped the bit into Sunny's mouth and led her out.

Raf stood where she'd left him, looking lost. Taking pity on him, she threw him a lifeline.

"Two stalls down, you'll find Remy. She's a beautiful dun mare who'll be kind to you. Her bridle's right inside the stall. If you need help, give me a holler."

With that, she led Sunny further down the stables to the railing fence where they kept the saddles. She found the one she usually rode in and saddled Sunny up. Securing the reins to the railing, she went in search of Raf.

He surprised her by getting the bridle on Remy without too much effort. It was obvious he knew something about horse riding. Curious, she asked him about it.

"How does a city boy know how to ride a horse?"

He glanced at her and smiled. "My parents believed in well-rounded children. Along with the dance lessons, they paid for Ally and I to learn to ride. Part of that included grooming and getting them bridled and saddled. It's been fifteen years since I rode, but I'm hoping those lessons will come back to me in my hour of need."

She made a sound of amusement in the back of her throat. She liked he was willing to give it a go, notwithstanding that it was obviously outside his comfort zone.

"You'll be fine on Remy. She's as gentle as can be."

"Was she born on the station?"

"No. We bought her from one of our neighbors. They no longer had any use for her, and they were going to put her down."

Raf looked alarmed. "But she's a perfectly good horse."

"Yes, she's a beauty, but she also costs money to run, and if there's no longer a use for her..."

"So, you saved her from death," Raf said.

Maggie shrugged, feeling uncomfortable with the admiration that now filled his eyes. "I guess so."

"That's so heroic."

"It was nothing," she mumbled. "We needed another good horse. Unlike some stations, we still use them from time to time."

With that, she took the reins from Raf's hand and led Remy over to where Sunny patiently stood waiting for her rider. With practiced efficiency, Maggie saddled Remy up and then adjusted the stirrups to where she guessed Raf might require them.

"If they're too short, let me know. I can adjust them a little more."

"No worries. Thanks."

"Don't forget to wear a helmet. We're all about safety here, remember?"

He frowned. "Do I need one?"

"I'm not sure. Do you? You've just told me you're an inexperienced rider. I think you should."

"Will you be wearing one?"

She shook her head. "No. But I ride all the time. It's not the same."

"What's it feel like to ride without one?"

She smiled. "Amazing. There's nothing like the feel of the wind in your hair when you're at full gallop." She paused and then added, "Not that we'll be galloping. In fact, given it's been so long since you last rode, it's likely you won't get any faster than a walk."

"Ouch! I'm hoping to do better than that. If it's all right with you, I think I'll leave the helmet behind."

Maggie nodded. "Well, it's your decision. After all, you're the boss. If you're ready, we'll head off."

Chapter Eighteen

♥

Maggie had been right. The feel of the wind in Raf's hair was marvelous. He probably wouldn't have felt that way if the sun was beating down, but the day was overcast and that kept the temperature pleasant. It took them over three hours to come upon the herd they were moving. Along the way, Maggie had pointed out where the wild dogs had attacked the cows. Fortunately, the stockmen had tracked the dogs and shot them dead a few nights earlier. Those dogs at least wouldn't be killing any more of their livestock. Of course, wild dog attacks would always be a problem and they'd always have to do what they had in order to protect the cattle. He understood that now.

"We might stop and have a bite to eat before we move the herd," Maggie said, interrupting his thoughts. "Are you hungry?"

Until she'd mentioned it, he hadn't been aware that his stomach had been grumbling. The only problem was, he'd brought no lunch. He hadn't realized when she'd returned to the homestead and left him with the horses that she'd gone to pack some food. No doubt she'd also brought water.

She pulled up a short distance ahead of him and slid off her horse. She tied the reins to a nearby tree branch and then busied herself at the saddlebags. He dismounted and looped Remy's reins over the same branch and then made his confession.

"I'm afraid I didn't pack any lunch."

She shot him a stern look. "You never leave home without food and water. It's the first rule of survival in the bush. Haven't you learned anything this past week?"

He flushed. "My bad."

She pulled a sandwich out of the saddlebag and a bottle of water. His stomach growled. She turned as if to walk away and then stopped and looked back at him.

"Here." She tossed him the sandwich. "Lucky for you, I packed two." She winked.

"Thank you," he said, catching the sandwich easily. "That was kind of you."

"Hey, it's not like I gave you much notice and I couldn't let you starve."

With that, she pulled out another sandwich and a second bottle of water from the saddlebag and strode over to another tall gum tree. They sat beneath its huge branches. Maggie unwrapped her sandwich. Raf followed suit.

They ate in silence for a few minutes. Raf gazed out across the wide-open land, dotted here and there with trees. The vastness of it continued to blow his mind. Not a car, nor another person in sight. Not even a building.

"There's a storm on the way," Maggie announced.

Raf frowned. "How do you know?"

She pointed to the clouds in the distance. They were dark smudges on the horizon.

He shrugged. "Looks too far away to me."

She chuckled. "Oh, so the city boy's now an expert on outback weather." She stood. "Come on, let's go."

With that, she collected their rubbish and returned it and the water bottles to her saddlebag. A moment later, she mounted up and was gone.

Raf followed more slowly. He wasn't afraid of getting lost. The wide expanse of paddocks allowed the dust kicked up by Maggie's horse to be seen for miles.

Remy ambled along, seemingly content with the slower pace. Raf had gotten used to her gentle roll. The stock saddle was worn and comfortable. Much more comfortable than the dressage saddles he'd ridden during the riding lessons his parents had insisted upon. The monotonous movement of the horse could almost put him to sleep.

Up ahead, beneath a stand of eucalyptus trees, he spied what appeared to be headstones. Riding closer, he dismounted. Leading Remy by the reins, he walked closer to what was clearly a graveyard.

The granite headstones were old and weathered. The writing on them was barely visible. From the names of those who lay beneath them, it was obvious this was a family cemetery that dated back to the 1800s. The name "McGregor" featured prominently. The first people to settle the land. He looked closer at the inscriptions. In particular, the dates caught his eye. Some headstones belonged to babies who'd obviously died at birth or shortly afterwards.

He recalled the entries he'd read in Eliza's journals. It had been a tough life. It had bred tough people. Yet they'd lived out here, created lives, families, memories. And they'd died out here.

As his gaze scanned the dozen or more headstones, he marveled at the number of graves. They spanned so many generations. The most recent headstone had a date in the 1940's. Maggie had told him the McGregor family had owned the property right until his uncle's purchase. No doubt later family members had been buried in Roma.

How amazing to trace one's family history over so many years...

These pioneering men and women put down roots and made the best of their circumstances. Sometimes they thrived. Sometimes they didn't. But they stuck it out. They faced the many challenges head-on. They were the definition of resilience.

Ever since he'd begun reading about them in Eliza's journals, he hadn't been able to stop thinking about them. Their strength and determination to carve out a life in such a hostile, unfamiliar land. Their courage in the face of adversity—drought, floods, bushfires, deaths. The lack of facilities. The isolation. And yet, they'd built a dynasty of which they could be proud, carried on by many generations. Just like Maggie's family.

He had nothing but admiration for the people who'd been there before him. Walked the land he rode over. Spent time beneath the tree that now shaded their graves, grieving their relatives, praying over them, gathering their courage and resolve to keep forging ahead.

As he stared at the headstones, a sudden burst of comprehension overwhelmed him that he'd been given the opportunity to start a family dynasty of his own. He'd inherited this station, with all its history, all its challenges, all its potential. All he needed to do was channel some of that courage the early McGregors had had in spades and take a leap of faith.

Am I up for it? Could I draw a line in the sand on my old life and start a new life in the outback?

Images of Maggie immediately crowded his mind. He snorted his impatience. He'd been there many times before and dismissed the possibility every time. He was a city boy. That's where he was most at home. Besides, he and Maggie barely knew each other. A few tender feelings and one kiss didn't make for an everlasting love.

No, the whole notion was ridiculous. He'd let himself get carried away by the trials of one family and the sobering proof before him. Best get back in touch with reality and leave silly notions where they belonged—in the journals of a woman long since passed and the testament on gravestones to young lives lost in an unforgiving land.

Maggie turned at the sound of hooves striking the hard ground. Raf was in full gallop on Remy, heading straight toward her. Her first thought was that the horse had taken off on him. Any moment and he could topple to the ground. But then she noticed how well he sat on the horse. How tall and confident he was in the saddle, holding his reins loosely along Remy's sides. When he'd told her he'd taken riding lessons in Brisbane as a child, she'd had some doubts about his riding ability. Now she realized she'd done him a disservice. It was obvious he was a fine rider.

As he approached her, he slowed his horse to a walk. She could tell by his expression that he was in an introspective mood.

"What is it? What's going on?"

"Nothing. I found some graves."

"They belong to the McGregor family. The people I told you about."

"Yes. I've been reading Eliza's journals. For a history buff like me, it's fascinating stuff."

She wanted to speak with him further about the journals, but she was also aware that the more they found things in common, the harder it would be to keep her distance, and that's exactly what she needed to do. Thankful she had a genuine excuse not to continue the conversation, she pulled on her reins and swung her horse around.

"We need to get these cattle moved before that storm rolls in." She indicated with her chin the dark clouds that had continued to gather on the horizon. "No matter what you might think, if we don't get a hurry on, we're going to get wet."

Not waiting for Raf's response, she dug her heels into Sunny's sides and clicked her tongue. The horse leaped forward, well trained in what needed to be done. Maggie leaned down to open the gate and held it open for Raf and Remy to walk through.

The cattle were gathered around the water trough. It was mid-afternoon, and they were drowsy from the indolent day.

"Where are we shifting them to?" Raf asked, eyeing the beasts curiously.

"To the northern paddock. There's more feed there."

"Which way is that?" he asked.

Maggie refrained from rolling her eyes. "North," she deadpanned.

"Oh, I see. North. Of course."

It was obvious he still didn't have clue in what direction they were headed. Taking pity on him, Maggie pointed in front of them.

"We're going that way. Through two paddocks and into the third. The gates are all in the same position—in the western corner, just like this one. We'll steer them in that direction, okay? Follow my lead. You'll be fine."

He suddenly smiled, and her stomach clenched in a sharp surge of desire. Dammit, he looked so sexy on the back of a horse, a tight T-shirt, Levis, and a five o'clock shadow on his cheeks. Determined to ignore the flare of attraction, she turned her horse away and cantered over to the cattle.

Whooping and shouting, she and Sunny did their job and herded the cattle together into a mob.

"What do you want me to do?" Raf yelled over the noise of the bellowing beasts.

"Stay out on the flank," she shouted back and pointed in that direction. "Don't get too close. We don't want to spook them."

To his credit, Raf did his fair share of keeping the cattle heading in the right direction. At one point, a steer took off away from the herd and Raf galloped after the beast and managed to turn him back. Maggie was quietly impressed that he'd picked up the knack of it so quickly. Of course, she wasn't surprised. He'd been a quick study all week.

Nearly two hours later, they had all three hundred head in the paddock where they needed to be. Maggie trotted over to where Raf sat on his horse and pulled up beside him.

"Job well done. Thanks for your help. We might make a station hand out of you yet." She winked.

He grinned. "Not bad for a city boy, right?"

"I guess so."

He pouted. "And here I thought you were grateful for my help."

She chuckled reluctantly. "Yeah, okay. For a city boy, you did okay."

"Does that mean you'll take me mustering again?"

The eagerness on his face was bittersweet. After all, his question was moot. He'd be heading back to the city by the end of the week. The thought filled her with disappointment, but she was determined not to let him see that. She had a responsibility to protect her heart, after all, So, she merely shrugged. "Maybe. If you hang around long enough."

Some of his earlier enthusiasm leaked from his face, but he smiled at her again. "Great." She shot him a dubious look. "Did you really enjoy it all that much? The dust, the noise, the smell of the cattle... It's not for everyone."

He grinned. "Smells like money to me."

He must have seen the disappointment on her face because he quickly added, "I loved the sense of teamwork, the shared responsibility. Like I was really helping you out. The feeling of achievement when the last of the cattle trotted through the gate was fantastic. As good as any feeling I've had during my career in high finance. It surprised me," he admitted.

Maggie could tell from his tone that he was speaking the truth. She couldn't help but be pleased about that. This was her livelihood, her office. The place where she spent most of her time. She loved it out there, but it wasn't for everyone. It was nice that he'd shared in the joy she'd experienced, even for a short time.

They were still several miles from home when the storm that had been threatening all day struck with a vengeance. Lightning flashed. Thunder rolled. Without warning, the heavens opened up. In minutes, they were drenched.

"What are we going to do?" Raf shouted above the noise.

Maggie pushed the wet hair off her face and answered him. "Take cover. By the look of those clouds, this won't be over in a hurry."

"Is there any shelter nearby?"

Maggie nodded. "There's an old stockman's hut a little further up the line. It's primitive, but it'll keep the rain out. Either that or we can forge on and try to make it home."

"How far away are we from the homestead?"

"In this deluge, it'll probably take us an hour or so."

Raf frowned. Before he could respond, a rumble of thunder was followed closely by another crack of lightning. The sound was deafening. Raf's horse bucked and shied away from the noise. With a startled cry, he went flying over Remy's head.

Maggie watched the drama unfold as if in slow motion. One moment, Raf was astride his horse. The next he was in freefall. Remy cleared out, terrified by the storm. Raf landed heavily on the ground. He didn't move.

Maggie's heart leaped in her throat. Blood pounded in her ears. Sunny became jittery beneath her. It took all of Maggie's skill to keep her horse under control. With chest tight, she quickly dismounted, taking care to keep hold of the reins. They'd already lost one horse. The last thing they needed was to be stranded out there with no means of getting back.

She hurried over to where Raf lay, so still and pale.

Oh, God. Please let him be okay. This is all my fault. I should never have suggested we go out mustering. I knew there was a storm on the way.

She was relieved to see his chest rise and fall, but she had no way of knowing how badly injured he might be. He'd fallen hard. He could have internal injuries. Or broken bones. Or any combination of those. And he didn't have a helmet on either. She should have insisted he wear one. Something else that was her fault.

As her panic grew, she deliberately forced herself to take deep breaths and get herself under control. Panic would get them nowhere. Raf needed her help.

Chapter Nineteen

♥

With her heart still thumping and mindless of the mud, Maggie went down on her knees beside Raf. His skin was ashen. With the reins twisted around her forearm, she pressed two fingers against the side of his neck. His pulse was faint and irregular, but at least it was there. Leaning down, she put her ear to his mouth and felt air, confirming that he was still breathing.

And then he startled her by opening his eyes and staring up at her.

"W-what happened?" he stammered, looking dazed.

"You took a fall," she explained, her voice wobbly with relief.

"Wow." He reached up and touched a gash on his forehead. It was bleeding, but the heavy rain washed the flow away as quickly as it formed.

"Where does it hurt?" she asked, taking care not to move him.

"Everywhere." He groaned. "My shoulder. My head."

"You have a graze on your forehead. You must have struck a rock. I'm so sorry, Raf! This is all my fault! I was the one who decided to go mustering. If it wasn't for me, none of this would have happened!"

"Stop. Not your fault."

Though she was grateful he didn't blame her, that didn't get them out of their current predicament. He needed medical attention.

"I'm fine," he rasped.

"No, you're not. You're bleeding and it won't be long before you'll have a goose egg to be proud of on your head. Can you move your legs?"

He grimaced in pain, but did as she asked. She was relieved all over again when he moved first one leg and then the other.

"Does that hurt?" she asked.

"No."

"Good. Let me look at your shoulder. Right or left?"

"Left." He gritted his teeth and then sucked in air as a wave of pain washed over him.

Maggie carefully felt around his upper arm and shoulder socket. The arm was hanging at an odd angle. "It's dislocated. I'm going to have to put it back in."

What little color he had left drained from his cheeks. "Do you know how to do that?"

"I'm no expert, but I've done it once before."

"Will it hurt?"

"A little bit, but not as much as it will if we leave it dislocated. That hurts like a bitch."

"You have that right," he managed through clenched teeth. "How long will it take?"

"Not long." She stared through the rain at the muddy ground around her and then found what she was looking for. "Here," she said, handing him a short stick that was about an inch thick. "Put this between your teeth and bite down on it as hard as you can. It'll distract you from the pain."

He stared at her in disbelief. "You want me to bite down on a muddy stick?"

"It'll help, trust me. Or don't. It's up to you. But I need to put that shoulder back in. We can't go anywhere until I do. Let me rephrase that. You won't want to go anywhere until I do."

Raf stared at her for a few more moments and then capitulated on another groan. "Okay. Do what you have to do. But hurry up about it. This hurts like hell."

With that, he shoved the stick into his mouth with his right hand and clenched his teeth around it. Maggie moved into position and, feeling with her fingers, quickly and efficiently popped his shoulder back into its socket.

"Fuck!" Raf shouted around the stick and then went limp. He spat out the stick and looked up at her with relief. "Thank you."

"You're welcome," she said, pleased to see some of the color returning to his cheeks.

Thunder crashed again. The rain continued to fall.

"We'll ride as far as the hut and take shelter until the storm's over. How does that sound?"

"That sounds bloody great," Raf replied with a smile.

Maggie stood and drew Sunny closer, patting the horse on the side, murmuring to her, calming her.

"Where's Remy?" Raf asked, peering through the rain.

"Unfortunately, the storm spooked her. When you fell off, she bolted. With a bit of luck, she's headed back to the stables."

"How am I going to get home?"

"You can ride with me. Sunny won't mind."

She leaned down and helped Raf to his feet. Staggering slightly under his weight, she slid her arm around his waist.

"Put your arm around my shoulder," she instructed.

He did as he was told. Together, they made it over to Sunny's side.

"I'll climb up first. Then I can help you climb up behind me, okay?"

Raf nodded. Maggie mounted her horse and settled in the saddle. Then she reached down for Raf. They gripped each other's forearms, and he heaved himself up behind her. She clung firmly to the reins while he got himself comfortable. His arms came around her waist, his hands clasped in front of her, pressing slightly into her stomach.

Her muscles clenched involuntarily from the contact. With the rain still pouring down around them and the night fast closing in there was nothing romantic about it and yet she was acutely aware of the feel of him pressed up against her back. The warmth of his body soaked through her wet shirt, making her even more aware of their intimate position. As Sunny sloshed and jostled forward in the mud, their bodies moved in unison with the motion of the horse.

A few moments later, Maggie spied the old hut she'd spoken about. She couldn't remember the last time someone had used it, but it was station policy that anyone who use the hut's supplies had to ensure it was re-stocked. That way, anyone who needed it wouldn't be caught out.

Holding Sunny firmly in place, she instructed Raf to dismount. He let go of her waist and slid off the horse. She was thankful that he remained upright.

"Hurry and get inside where it's dry," she said.

He stared up at her. "What about you?"

"I'll be in shortly. I'm going to tie up Sunny first and make sure she's okay."

He stood his ground, frowning. It was obvious he was reluctant to leave her.

"It's okay, Raf. I'll join you in a minute. Please, you're hurt. I need you to get out of the rain."

He looked up at her and nodded briefly before turning away and doing as she'd asked. She quickly dismounted and led Sunny to a sturdy fence rail that stood a short distance away, which had been erected for that very purpose. Securing the reins around the top rail, she gave the horse a reassuring pat and another quiet word before striding back to the hut. She opened the door and shut it softly behind her.

She blinked against the sudden darkness. Not all the light had left the day, but it was pitch black inside.

"Raf?"

"Over here," he called.

She picked her way carefully across the small room to a shelf where matches and candles were stored. Finding them, she struck a match and lit the wick. A pale orange glow pierced the darkness.

The hut was compact, measuring no more than twenty by fifteen feet. It was sparsely furnished with two wooden chairs and a small wooden table at one end and a makeshift bed at the other. The flooring had once been dirt, but somewhere along the line, one of the previous owners had added floorboards. The walls were rough-hewn pine that had been left exposed to the elements. The roof was thankfully made of tin and so far, was doing a good job of keeping the weather out.

"There should be a kerosene lamp here somewhere," she murmured.

Using the candle to light her way, she rummaged among the items stored on the shelf until she found what she was looking for, standing behind a tall can of kerosene.

"Here it is."

In short order, she lit the lamp. Brighter light filled the room. "There. That's better."

She set the lamp back down on the shelf, away from the can of kerosene. Raf had found his way to one of the two wooden chairs and lowered himself slowly into it.

"How's the shoulder?" she asked.

"Much better, thanks." He touched the graze on his forehead. "Is it still bleeding?"

Maggie picked up the lamp and shifted closer. Holding it high above his head, she inspected his wound. Though the bleeding had eased, it hadn't stopped.

"It's not as bad as it was, but it's still bleeding. I need to dress it for you. We should have a first aid kit around here somewhere."

She went back to the shelf, taking the lamp with her. Once again, after moving a few things out of the way, she found a first aid kit and pulled out some gauze, antiseptic fluid, tape, and a dressing pad. She took the items back to Raf, along with the lamp, which she set down on the table beside him.

"I'll need to clean it first."

He gave her a slight grin. "I thought the rain had probably already done that."

"True, but this is antiseptic fluid. It'll kill any germs the rain might have missed."

She poured some of the fluid onto the gauze pad and dabbed it on his wound. His breath hissed between his teeth.

"Sorry," she said. "This might sting a bit."

"Now you tell me."

"You're tough. I'm sure you can handle it."

So focused on tending to his wound, she didn't realize she'd stepped so close to him until her breasts brushed against his face. She gasped at the contact. Her nipples immediately hardened. Her face flamed.

"Sorry," she mumbled, and hastily moved away.

She felt Raf's gaze on her as she tried to concentrate on the task at hand. Now wanting only to put some distance between them, she quickly applied the dressing, secured it with tape, and stepped away.

"It's done. You're all good," she muttered and busied herself gathering up her equipment and returning it to the first aid kit.

She crossed the room and set the kit back on the shelf where she'd found it and then cast around for something else to do.

Maybe taking shelter here wasn't the best thing to do. Now I'm here with him in close confines and almost darkness, with nowhere else to go. Of course, I have no choice. Continuing home in that storm would be madness. I'll just have to deal with it.

From across the room, Raf watched in bemusement as Maggie became a flurry of movement and action. One moment she'd been tending his wound. The next it was as if there was a devil on her tail. He wondered if her sudden change of mood had anything to do with their accidental, rather intimate contact.

He hadn't missed the indentation of her pebbled nipples against her wet shirt.

After returning the first aid kit, she set about chopping kindling with a small ax from a pile of firewood stacked near the door. Then she lit a fire in the stone hearth that lined a good portion of one wall. As the orange flames began to lick the wood and then catch the larger pieces, Raf sighed. Whatever the reason for her sudden need to be busy, he was grateful for the heat that gradually seeped into the room.

He was wet to the core and even though they were now out of the storm, he was cold. No doubt a part of that was also a delayed shock to what had happened. After all, he'd been thrown by a horse, hit his head, dislocated his shoulder—all in the space of a few moments and in the middle of a raging storm. No wonder he'd started to shiver.

Wrapping his arms around himself in order to conserve what body heat he still had, he concentrated on stopping his teeth from chattering. He groaned aloud from the effort. Maggie swung around and looked at him. A frown marred the smooth skin of her forehead.

"Are you all right?" she asked.

"J-just c-cold," he stammered.

"It's probably shock setting in," she murmured, giving voice to his earlier thoughts. "You're also still soaking wet. You need to get out of those clothes."

He tugged ineffectually at the hem of his shirt. Somehow, the simple task of undressing seemed beyond him. What little strength he had was fast dissipating. All he wanted to do was sleep. He closed his eyes and slumped against the chair.

"Raf!"

The sharpness of her tone echoed in his head. He opened his eyes and found her standing beside him. Concern was etched into her face.

"Talk to me. Don't go to sleep. At least, not until I know you aren't suffering from a concussion. Do you have a headache? Pain anywhere?"

He shook his head. "N-no. I'm j-just tired."

"I understand, but I need you to stay awake. Just for a little bit, okay?"

"I-I'm still c-cold."

"You still have your wet clothes on."

"C-can't get them off."

He heard her sigh quietly. A moment later, her hands were tugging at the bottom of his T-shirt. She dragged it up over his chest and pulled it over his head and then tugged it off his shoulders. She moved the vacant chair closer to the fire and draped his shirt over it.

"J-jeans?" he asked.

In the dimness, a look of resignation filled her face, but she dutifully returned to his side.

"You need to help me. Can you stand?" she asked.

He struggled to his feet and undid his belt. Then he reached for the clasp on his jeans. He managed to slide down the zipper and then tried hard to shimmy the jeans off his hips.

But they were wet, and that made things more difficult than normal, and he was tired, so tired. After his third attempt, Maggie made a sound of impatience in the back of her throat.

"Here, let me," she mumbled.

Maggie tugged the sodden clothing off his hips and down the length of his legs. In some distant part of Raf's mind, he knew he ought to be enjoying the intimate attention from someone he was wildly attracted to. Here she was, removing his pants, and he was too weak to take advantage of the situation. Of all his luck.

She stopped at removing his underwear. He didn't know whether or not he was pleased. He wasn't ashamed of his body. Besides, she'd already seen him naked, even if most of that time he'd had the cover of the water to conceal most of what had been exposed to the eye.

Here, with the night swirling around them and the only source of light coming from the fire and a small lantern, there was an intimacy in the air that couldn't be ignored. She left his side and returned a moment later with a blanket. She draped it around him. He sighed.

"That feels so good. But what about you? Your clothes are wet too," he murmured. "Aren't you cold?"

"A little," she admitted.

"Then why don't you get out of them and get dry?"

Even in the dimness, he saw her flush.

"I will. Later. First, I want to fix us something to eat. Are you hungry?"

Until she'd asked, he hadn't realized he was. It seemed like a long time ago since their simple lunch.

"Starving."

"Good. That means you're still functioning okay. We should have a few tins of something here. I'll take a look."

With that, she turned away, hung his jeans beside the shirt, and then returned to the shelf where it appeared all sorts of useful things had been stored. He heard her foraging around, and then she turned back to face him, holding up a tin in each hand.

"Baked beans or spaghetti? Which would you prefer?"

"I'll take the beans."

"Good, because I prefer spaghetti." She smiled.

He felt the beauty of it all the way through to his gut. He wished he was in better shape to respond to it. Before he could contemplate it any further, she approached him with a plate and a fork. She set them on the table beside him.

"Here are your beans. I haven't heated them, but I can if you want to wait a bit longer."

"No, cold is fine. Thank you."

She smiled again. "You've stopped shivering. That's good. The fire must be working."

He nodded. "And the blanket. It definitely feels better without those wet clothes."

"Good."

He pulled his chair up to the table and tugged the blanket more tightly around him while he waited for her to sit down.

In silence, they devoured their simple meal. When they were done, Maggie leaned back against her chair and sighed.

"That was better than I imagined."

"Everything tastes better when you're hungry."

"You're right." She paused and then added, "How are you feeling? Still drowsy?"

He shook his head. "Not so much. The food did the trick, I think."

"Good."

She shivered suddenly. He frowned. "You need to get out of those wet clothes."

She grimaced. "Yes."

"It's not like I haven't seen you almost-naked."

Another blush stained her cheeks, but this time she held her ground. She eyed him in silence for a few moments and then, as if coming to a decision, she nodded. "You're right. I'm being silly. I'll be much warmer out of these wet things."

With that, she stood and stripped off her clothes, right down to her plain cotton underwear. Despite everything, his body stirred.

She was long and lean and toned, with curves and muscles in all the right places. She wasn't lean and sinewy like so many of the women he saw at his gym. Instead, she had the look of someone who did physical work for a living. He liked the way she looked. He liked it a lot.

In silence, she hung her clothes up on the same chair as his and moved it back closer to the fire. There was nowhere else to sit. Belatedly, he looked. His gaze fell on the wire-framed bed.

"You can sit here if you like. I'll take the bed."

"No! I want you to stay awake a bit longer. Just to be on the safe side."

"I'm fine. I don't feel groggy. Just tired. It's been a big day."

"It sure has. For someone who hasn't ridden a horse for so many years, I can understand if you're beat. On top of that, you had a fall and injured yourself...I should have insisted you wear that helmet..." Her voice drifted off. As if coming to a decision, she grimaced. "All right. I've changed my mind. You can take the bed."

"Are you sure?"

"I'm sure."

"Then, thanks. I'm not going to argue. Lying down after the day I've had is just what I need."

With that, he stumbled to his feet and crossed the short distance to the bed. Perching on the edge, the mattress let out a disapproving squeak.

"Feels like heaven," Raf murmured as he swung his legs over the side and stretched out, tucking the blanket around him.

Maggie remained silent, barely glancing his way. Instead, she moved around the small room collecting their plates and utensils and taking them over to a small sink.

"Don't tell me this place has running water?" he mumbled, almost on the edge of sleep.

She smiled. "No. Nothing quite as civilized as that. But we keep water in storage containers here for just this kind of emergency. I'll rinse them out with that."

"You could always leave them outside. It's still raining," he mumbled sleepily.

With that, he turned on his side and promptly fell asleep to the pattering sound of rain on the tin roof.

Chapter Twenty

Maggie stared across at Raf's sleeping form and gnawed at her bottom lip. She was still concerned he might have a concussion, even though he'd been able to carry on a conversation and appeared clear-headed enough. She was still shaken from witnessing his fall off the horse. It could have been so much worse. It could have been fatal. Watching him lying so still on the ground had nearly given her a heart attack.

In that moment, she'd realized just how much he'd come to mean to her, no matter that he didn't feel the same way. She'd fallen in love with him and her heart didn't seem to care that he'd be leaving soon and she'd most likely never see him again.

Stupid. Stupid. Stupid.

But she couldn't deny it was true. She wanted him like she'd never wanted any man, but it wasn't just a physical thing. She enjoyed being around him, sharing conversation. She liked everything about him.

She wanted to make love to him.

The thought came from nowhere and should have shocked her. After all, she'd reached the ripe old age of twenty-eight without being tempted to lose her virginity. Now she was prepared to throw it away on a man she barely knew and might never see again. It was madness!

Raf made a sound in the back of his throat, and her heart clenched with fear. She hurried over to his side.

"Raf? Raf? Can you hear me?"

He slowly opened his eyes. "Don't leave me. Please. Stay with me. Here."

With that, he scooted over in the bed, making room for her beside him. She hesitated, torn with indecision. He rolled over onto his back to face her.

"Please," he said. "We can keep each other warm. Please."

His gentle pleas did her in. With a sigh of capitulation, she climbed in beside him. For a while, she held herself apart from him. Her underwear was still damp. She didn't want to make him any colder. But when he put out his arm and drew her closer, she finally gave in. Turning on her side to face him she put her head on his chest. His skin was so firm, so warm beneath her cheek. His chest hair was as soft as she'd imagined. She couldn't help but sigh.

"Better?" he asked.

"Yes," she agreed. "Better."

With that, they both fell asleep.

Raf didn't know what time it was when he woke again, but it felt like he'd been asleep for hours. The rain outside had subsided. The room was still pitch-black. The fire that Maggie had lit earlier had died down to nothing but a handful of coals that glowed orange in the darkness. The air inside the hut was cool.

She still lay nestled against him on her side, relaxed in sleep. His arm was around her, holding her close. Her head lay on his chest. She felt so good in his arms, even when she was asleep. Her long hair was loose. It had dried and now fell in soft and silky lengths against his bare skin. When he turned his head slightly and inhaled, he could smell her shampoo. Something sweet and citrusy. It smelled good.

He couldn't remember ever noticing the smell of a woman's shampoo before. Probably because he'd never spent time lying awake with a woman in his arms. His relationships to date were limited to chance encounters with strangers, only one of which had lasted any distance. A mutual attraction often led to the inevitable conclusion. The only question that needed to be answered was whether they'd end up at her place or his.

He'd dated Stephanie on and off for the past year, but he'd never spent more than one night in a row at her place. He liked being on his own, surrounded by his own things. Apart from that, he'd never felt the urge to spend more time with a woman. Once the physical side of things had been attended to, there wasn't much to hang around for.

If that made him shallow, then he'd own up to that. He couldn't help the way he felt. But that was before Maggie. Before he knew what it felt like to want to spend more than a few hours with a woman. The feeling was strange, unfamiliar, and it scared him a little.

Is this what falling in love feels like?

The saner part of his mind immediately refuted the question. He was being ridiculous. There was no way he was falling in love with Maggie. They barely knew each other. They had next to nothing in common. She belonged in the outback. His heart was in the city. There was no future for them.

I've been over all this already... Why am I wasting time contemplating the same ridiculous questions all over again? It's not like anything's changed...

Maggie stirred against him. Her hand stole out and her fingers flexed, grazing over his nipple. The tiniest of touches, yet it jumpstarted his heart. She made a small, sleepy sound in the back of her throat. A sigh of contentment. And yet, it appeared she was still asleep. He wondered what she was dreaming about and whether any of her dreams involved him.

He was immediately bombarded with fantasies of her naked limbs wrapped around him, her body pressed against him, warm and wanton as she begged him to make love to her.

His breath caught. Blood rushed to his cock. When her hand slid over his chest once again, he tensed.

In the silence, he became aware that the sound of her breathing had changed. He stared at her through the darkness and saw the faintest glimmer of her eyes.

She's awake!

Wordlessly, her hand moved with more purpose across his chest, tentative at first and then more boldly as her fingers threaded their way through his chest hair and unerringly found his nipple once again. This time, she flicked at the sensitive nub with her fingernail.

Desire slammed through him. His heart pounded. He was shocked that such a tiny gesture could fill him with a need so great he felt like he might explode.

"Maggie," he rasped. It was both a plea and a prayer.

Fully awake now, she rose up on her elbow and leaned over him. Her silky hair teased his bare skin.

"Make love to me, Raf."

Her husky words were barely above a whisper, but the darkness couldn't conceal the desire he heard in her tone.

While the saner part of his mind demanded he turn down her request, his body had other ideas. His cock was hard and throbbing, desperate for release. Still, it was one thing to have meaningless sex with a woman he had no intention of seeing again, but this was Maggie. She wasn't like the other women. She was special. She made him feel things he'd never felt before. She made him think about the future. She made him want more.

As he continued to hesitate, some of her confidence dimmed.

"Don't you want me?" she asked in a quivery voice.

Shocked that she could have misread him so badly, he climbed out of bed and felt around for the kerosene lamp he'd noticed earlier. He wanted to see Maggie when he explained to her just how much he did want her.

Thankfully, the lamp was on the table where she'd left it, along with a box of matches. In silence, he lit the wick. A bright yellow glow filled the room. Leaving the lamp where it was, he returned to the bed and climbed back in beside her. Maggie sat upright with her back against the wall. Her arms were folded across her chest. Her chin was lowered, her gaze fixed on the blanket.

Raf reached out and cupped her cheek. "How could you think I don't want you? I've wanted you from the moment I set eyes on you."

She shrugged. Her bottom lip quivered.

"Maggie. Look at me."

The quiet command had its effect. She lifted her gaze to his. He ached at the vulnerability in her eyes.

"You're so smart and funny and beautiful. How could I not be wild for you?"

"Then why haven't you kissed me already?" she asked in a small voice.

He took one of her hands in his and threaded their fingers together. "You took me by surprise. I hesitated, not because I didn't want to immediately take you in my arms and make love to you, but because I'm not sure this is what's best for both of us. Have you thought this through properly?"

"Since I saw you take that fall, it's all I've been able to think about." She shook her head. "You could have died!"

"But I didn't. I'm okay," he whispered, squeezing her hand.

She sighed heavily and pulled her hand out of his. "Yes, and I'm so grateful. But from the moment I saw you lying on the ground, so still and silent, when I didn't know if you were dead or alive, I realized how much I care for you. Of course, it's way too soon." She gave a little laugh that was tinged with desperation. "Truly, I'm crazy for even thinking it, but... I've fallen in love with you."

Maggie's heart thumped so hard she was worried it might beat out of her chest. In the golden glow of the kerosene lamp, she saw Raf's eyes go wide.

Oh, God, He looks like a deer caught in the headlights. I've blindsided him. He's as shocked as I am about my revelation. Why did I have to tell him I'm in love with him? What a stupid thing to do. Oh, hell.

As the silence drew out between them, her face flamed with embarrassment. Her declaration of love had left him speechless, and she had only herself to blame.

What did I expect him to do? Declare he felt the same way? Promise me forever? Oh, God. I'm a fool.

With a sound of mortification, she buried her face in her hands and turned away from him. She inched to the bottom of the mattress and swung her legs over the side, intent only on making her escape. Before she could rise, his arm snaked out and snagged her around the waist.

"Please, Maggie. Don't go."

The quiet sincerity in his voice gave her pause. Still not able to face him, she kept her back to him and replied.

"It's okay, Raf. I'm sorry for making a fool of myself. Let's just pretend this conversation never happened."

"But I don't want to pretend it never happened. In fact, I very much want the conversation to continue."

With gentle insistence, he tugged on her waist until she had no choice but to face him. Her shoulders slumped on another sigh.

"You don't have to say that," she said.

He made a sound of irritation in the back of his throat and shook his head. "Would you just keep quiet for a minute and get over here?"

With that, he gently pulled her down beside him and into his arms. She tensed momentarily as their bare skin came into contact, but with Raf's arm pressed against her side, she had no choice but to give in to his silent urging and relax against him. He rolled onto his back and kissed her softly against her hair.

"That's better," he murmured. "Now, where were we?"

Her face flamed with fresh embarrassment. "I was declaring my undying love for you," she muttered.

"Ah, yes. Love. What a fascinating concept."

Something in the tone of his voice made her curious. "Have you ever been in love?"

"No."

"Not even close?"

"Not even close."

She contemplated that for a moment. "How come? Don't you believe in love?"

He was silent for a minute, as if contemplating his answer. "Do I believe in love? I guess so. There are enough books and movies written on the subject that it must exist. My parents are still happily married and so is my sister. I guess they know about love. As for why I've never been in love, I guess I haven't met the right woman. I've certainly been in lust. Does that count?"

He waggled his eyebrows at her and grinned lasciviously. She laughed. Her heart skipped a beat at the gleam in his eyes.

"Th-there's nothing wrong with a bit of lust, but it's not the same as love," she stammered.

He pulled a face. "Too bad, because you might have noticed that I'm very much in lust with you right at this moment."

With that, he half-rolled toward her and pressed himself against her. Even through the thin cotton of his boxers, the hot, hard length of his erection branded itself against her thigh. Her breath caught in her throat. A rush of heat surged through her and centered in her core. A wave of need washed over her, so strong that she trembled from the effects of it.

"Raf!" she gasped.

Taking encouragement from her response, he shucked off his underwear and then took her hand and pressed it against his cock. "Can you feel what you do to me, Maggie?"

His voice was husky with desire. Knowing how much he wanted her fueled the need that was already raging. She fleetingly recalled he'd spoken nothing of love, but right at that moment, that didn't seem to matter. All that mattered was feeling him inside her, assuaging her burning need.

She squeezed his cock and took pleasure in his answering groan of desire.

"Oh, Maggie. That feels so good."

She squeezed him again, and this time moved her hand up and down his shaft, tightening and releasing her hold. He groaned again and settled more comfortably on his back, giving her full access to his body. Emboldened, she came up on her haunches and ran her free hand over his chest, weaving her fingers through his soft chest hair, scraping her fingernails over his nipples. She continued to stroke his cock.

"You're killing me," he gasped.

"I've barely started," she teased.

Privately, she was astounded at the confidence she had around him. She'd kissed and done some heavy petting with her jackaroo boyfriend, but she'd never been naked with any man, let alone stroked and fondled and teased one in such an erotic way. Okay, so she still wore her bra and panties, but they hardly constituted clothes. It seemed that with Raf, she was a different woman, strong, confident, daring. A woman she barely recognized. And she liked her. She liked her a lot.

On another burst of courage, she maneuvered herself into position so that her head hovered just above Raf's cock. With her hand still encircling his thick shaft, she bent low and opened her mouth and took him deep inside.

"Oh, Maggie," he groaned. "Fuck."

She started out slowly, moving her mouth up and down his cock, sucking and licking, tightening her fingers around his shaft. It was awkward at first. She had zero experience. But she'd read about it, and she was relying on instinct. The moans of appreciation coming from Raf gave her the confidence to continue.

Keeping her mouth firmly over the head of his cock, she reached down and cupped his balls. They were full and heavy. Knowing how much he wanted her fueled her own desire. She burned with need between her thighs and yearned for him to touch her.

As if reading her thoughts, he shifted beneath her. "My turn," he murmured.

Coming up on his knees, he drew her up against him until her breasts were crushed against his chest. He bent his head and fused his lips to hers. Instead of the light touch he'd exhibited beside the horse paddock, the pressure from his mouth was earth shattering as his lips opened fully over hers. She was engulfed in the heat of him, breathing him in, clinging to him lest she lose her balance and fall.

He cupped the back of her head and held it in place while he continued to plunder her mouth. Then his tongue stole out and swept inside, filling her with liquid heat. She dug her fingernails into his skin, her heart pounding, as she kissed him for all she was worth. It was even more incredible than the first time.

By the time they broke apart, they were breathless.

"Oh, my goodness!" she gasped.

"Fuck," Raf mumbled.

Maggie touched her lips in wonder. "That was amazing."

Raf merely smiled and dipped his head. "And we're only just getting started."

"Can I kiss you again?"

She blushed at her forwardness, but Raf chuckled and waved her embarrassment away.

"Be my guest."

On a sudden wave of shyness, she lowered her eyes and inched closer to him. Framing his face with her hands, she slowly brought her lips to his. She kissed him lightly, tiny kisses at the corners of his mouth, before finally settling her lips against his. Letting her take the lead this time, he remained still while she explored his mouth.

His lips were firm and supple and so much softer than she'd ever imagined a man's lips could be. The stubble from his beard was a little scratchy, but she didn't mind. Kissing him was like sipping from the sweetest nectar with a pinch of spice thrown in. The sensuousness of it blew her mind. Never had she dreamed that kissing a man could feel so good.

But this wasn't just any man. This was Raf. A man who challenged her intellectually and made her laugh. A man who made her heart pound with excitement and her body sing with need. It wasn't any wonder she'd fallen so hard and fast.

Once again, she was reminded that he hadn't returned her profession of love and just as determinably, she thrust the thought aside. It didn't matter how he felt. Sometimes love took time, if it happened at all. That was out of her control. What she knew was that if she didn't make love with Raf right now, she might never get the chance again.

If they parted ways, then so be it. She wouldn't live with regrets. She wanted him like she'd wanted no man and she'd already decided that she wanted to experience her first time with him.

For a moment, she considered telling him she was a virgin, but then she dismissed the idea. Her virginity was hers to give away. It was really none of his business. There was also a part of her that was slightly embarrassed that at twenty-eight she'd never had sex.

Raf's hands skimmed her waist and then he reached around and undid the clasp on her bra. He tossed it aside. When his hands went to her hips, she helped him divest herself of her panties. He looked his fill in the lamplight's glow. His eyes glittered.

"You're so beautiful."

His voice was hoarse with desire, sending shivers of need coursing through her. He drew her even closer against him until nothing separated them except skin. Her nipples scraped across his chest, the scattering of hair turning them to hard little nubs. His erection pressed insistently against her stomach, a physical reminder of his desire. The feel of him only made her yearn to have him deep inside her.

"I want to make love to you," she whispered.

Raf kissed her deeply in response. "I don't have any condoms."

She shook her head. "I don't care."

Surprise flickered in his gaze.

"I don't have any diseases," she said. "What about you?"

"Of course. I've never had unprotected sex."

She smiled. "So, this is a first for you, too."

"I guess so." He grinned. "I'm game if you are. Are you using contraception?"

She flushed. "No."

He shrugged. "No matter. I'll pull out before I come."

The embarrassing talk about such intimate details had taken the edge off Maggie's desire. She wasn't used to having such conversations. As if sensing this, Raf stretched out on the bed and drew her down beside him.

"No more talk," he muttered and drew her into his arms.

He kissed her long and deeply, instantly reigniting the need that simmered just below the surface. Her arms crept around his neck, and she clung to him as he once again plundered her mouth. Knowing that they were going to make love only fueled her desire. She kissed him back with a passion that matched his own. Her heart pounded with a combination of excitement and nerves.

Slowly, he eased away from her and positioned himself between her thighs. Her legs fell open in silent invitation, and as his cock pressed against her entrance, she focused on his face. He thrust hard, and she yelped as a stinging pain engulfed her. Raf stilled. Surprise flooded his face.

"What the hell?" he muttered.

"Please, Raf. Keep going."

He stared down at her, indecision warring with desire on his face.

"Fuck, Maggie."

"I don't want you to stop."

"Are you sure?" His voice sounded strangled.

She reached up and pulled him down on top of her, staring into his eyes. "Yes. I'm sure. Please. Make love to me."

With that, he groaned in capitulation and moved once again. His strokes were long and sure and deep. She clung to his shoulders, gasping for breath, as desire burned hotly again.

Over and over, he entered her, plunging deeply into her heat, building her desire until she reached the peak. And then she was there, crying out as she climaxed, clinging to his shoulders.

A moment later, with his breath coming fast, Raf pulled out of her and tugged frantically at his cock. As he orgasmed and came on her stomach, he slumped against her in relief. She reached up and tenderly pushed the fringe of hair out of his eyes.

"Thank you. That was amazing," she whispered.

Chapter Twenty-One

♥

Completely drained, Raf collapsed beside Maggie and then reached out and drew her close. She rested her head on his chest and sighed quietly. The tension had left their bodies, and he could tell she was feeling as relaxed and replete as he was, but there was something he needed to know.

"Why didn't you tell me?"

She didn't pretend to misunderstand him. "Would it have made a difference?"

He frowned. "Yes! Maybe. Hell, I don't know. But you should have told me."

She shrugged. "Maybe I should have. What does it matter now?"

Raf tightened his arm around her and pressed a kiss against her hair. He wouldn't engage in an argument with her right after they'd made love, but he couldn't deny that he felt upset about taking on the responsibility of being her first lover without being informed beforehand. Not that the outcome would have been different. She'd wanted this as much as him. But he would have taken her virginity into account. Gone slower, been more gentle.

If he hadn't been so overwhelmingly aroused and desperate to be inside her, he would have noticed her inexperience. It was only now, in the aftermath, that he could see what should have been clear to him before.

Fuck.

He felt like a heel. Like he'd somehow treated her less than she deserved. It was nonsense, but the feeling was real. For him, the sex had been amazing. The best he'd ever had. In fact, it had been more than sex. A genuine connection that went beyond the physical. For the first time in his life, he'd felt like he was making love.

But had that really changed anything? His life was in the city. He couldn't imagine living anywhere else. Certainly not in outback Queensland, isolated from everything and everyone he loved. Though the knowledge wasn't new, it troubled him more than it had before. He wasn't someone who lived with regrets, but when he thought about the expectations Maggie might harbor now that they'd made love, his gut filled with dread.

As the sun broke through the clouds and filled the modest hut with early morning light, Maggie woke and stretched languorously. Though she was alone in the bed, she felt relaxed and replete and happy. Raf had made no promises the night before, but she was certain she wasn't the only one who'd felt the amazing closeness between them, a shared experience so wonderful that it defied words. She'd had no previous experience of making love to compare with, but surely, it rarely felt as good as this.

The scrape of a shoe on the floor drew her attention across the room. Raf stood in the dimness, his face silhouetted by the morning light. He was dressed in the clothes he'd worn the day before, now dried from the fire. She smiled at the sight of him.

"Morning," she said cheerily.

"Morning," he mumbled. He spun away from her and busied himself with something by the door.

She frowned. That wasn't exactly the response she'd been expecting. Not after what had happened between them the night before. They'd been as close and intimate as two people could be, and she was certain he'd felt as connected to her as she'd felt to him. At his continued silence, her shoulders slumped in a quiet sigh.

No doubt his distance had something to do with the fact she hadn't told him she was a virgin. He'd been upset over that. For her, not telling him hadn't been a big deal. What did it matter if he was her first? Someone had to be. And she'd very much wanted it to be him. She'd told him that.

But maybe there was more to his discomfort? Maybe he regretted making love with her, period? Maybe he was wishing even now that it had never happened?

The possibility filled her with disquiet. She couldn't help but wonder if she'd done the right thing. She'd given him her virginity. A man she'd fallen in love with, but who'd spoken no such words in return.

Fool.

The word burned into her consciousness. Her cheeks flushed with shame. She was disappointed in herself and in Raf. She also should have known better than to have unprotected sex. She wasn't taking any contraception. There hadn't been a need for that until now. But it had been stupid to take such a risk, even with Raf's withdrawal. She wasn't a naïve teenager. Pregnancy could occur despite that. And yet, last night, she hadn't cared about any of that. All she'd wanted was to feel Raf inside her, making love to her. And now he couldn't even meet her eyes...

As if aware of her tumultuous thoughts, Raf mumbled something about needing to go outside and then opened the door and disappeared through it. Maggie took the opportunity to dress and then sat back down on the bed, heartsick and disappointed. She didn't know what she'd expected to wake up to, but this surely wasn't it.

Perhaps he's running scared of the emotions we both felt last night? Perhaps this is all so overwhelming for him that he just needs more time...?

She sighed again. Whatever was going on in Raf's head, there was no way she'd regret making love with him. They had been the most magical, amazing moments of her life. Whether or not there was a future for them, she'd cherish those memories forever.

When Raf returned, Maggie climbed off the bed and excused herself to go outside. She desperately needed to relieve her bladder. No doubt that's what Raf had done, too. When she'd finished, she went over to Sunny, who stood calmly where she'd left her, tied up to the fence rail.

"Hey, girl. How're you doing? That was some storm last night, wasn't it?"

The horse nudged at her hands in search of food. Right on cue, Maggie's stomach growled.

She laughed and stroked Sunny's nose. "I wish I had something to give you. I'm hungry too. I might be able to find some baked beans or spaghetti, but you're going to have to wait until we return to the stables."

With that, Maggie returned to the hut. As if reading her mind, Raf had already emptied a tin of baked beans into one bowl and spaghetti into another. He handed her the spaghetti as she entered.

"It's not much, but it's better than nothing," he said.

"Thank you. My favorite."

"I could stoke up the fire if you want it heated."

"No, it's fine. I don't mind eating it cold."

With that, she took a fork from the drawer and sat at the table. Raf joined her with the bowl of baked beans. They ate the food in silence. Maggie kept sneaking glances at him from beneath her lashes, wondering if he was going to raise what had happened between them the night before. She wanted to say something, but his distant attitude didn't invite conversation. In the end, she shelved her thoughts until he'd had more time to digest the situation and was more approachable.

After cleaning up their breakfast things, dousing the coals in the hearth and replenishing their water supply, Maggie secured the door of the hut behind them and headed over to untie Sunny.

"How's your shoulder?" she asked Raf.

"It's fine."

"We're going to have to double again. Are you okay with that?"

"It beats walking."

With that, she mounted the horse and helped him to climb up behind her. He placed his hands lightly around her waist.

In an instant, she found herself transported back to the night before. Her skin burned beneath his touch. She swallowed a sigh and did her best to ignore him.

It was going to be a long ride home.

They were still at least two hundred yards away from the homestead when Maggie spied Bluey making his way across the flat toward the stables. Catching sight of them, he raised his hand in acknowledgement and continued forward. He walked with a more pronounced limp than usual. No doubt the wet weather had played havoc with his arthritis. Just another reminder of his advancing age and the unlikelihood of him finding work on another station if the worst happened and the new owner sent them all packing.

It was too bad she still hadn't been able to persuade Raf to keep the place. Now that she'd slept with him, there was no way she could approach him about that again. He might misconstrue her motivation and she didn't want him to think for even an instant that her decision to give him her virginity had anything to do with her desire to see the station remain in his hands.

Realization slowly struck her. She'd jeopardized everything by sleeping with him. She'd lost the high ground. She should have thought things through before she'd let her libido take over. How could she have been so thoughtless, so selfish? So many people were depending on her. She'd promised Bluey he'd be fine. Now she had to face the very real possibility that she wouldn't be able to deliver on her promise.

She groaned aloud in distress. Raf's hands tightened around her waist.

"Is everything all right?" he asked.

They were the first words he'd spoken to her since they'd left the hut. In an effort to regain control, she drew in a breath and eased it out before responding.

"Yes. Of course. Why wouldn't they be?"

She felt him shrug behind her, but he made no further response. It was obvious his willingness to engage in conversation had come to an end. That didn't matter. She didn't want to talk to him, anyway.

As she walked Sunny back to the stables, Bluey met them by the fence. He smiled up at them.

"I'm glad to see you're both okay. When Remy came back without her rider, we weren't sure what to think. Then the storm hit and forced us inside. It fairly poured down for hours. There was no point going out looking for you. We figured you'd find somewhere safe to hunker down and wait it out." He slid a curious glance in Maggie's direction, and then his gaze shifted to Raf.

Despite her best efforts, she blushed. She could tell from Bluey's searching look that he sensed something had happened between her and Raf, or at the very least, he had his suspicions. Not wanting to answer the unspoken questions in his eyes, she busied herself by holding Sunny steady while Raf dismounted.

"As you can see, we're fine," she mumbled. "Raf took a tumble and dislocated his shoulder. I managed to pop it back in. He also grazed his forehead, but it's okay, right?" She directed her question to Raf who stood nearby, half-turned away from them, his expression distant.

He touched the pad that still covered the wound and nodded. "It's fine."

She climbed off Sunny and pulled the reins over the horse's head before returning her attention to the old stockman. "We spent the night in the hut near the northern fence line. Luckily, it was stocked with food. We didn't go hungry, but Sunny could sure do with some hay. And the hut will need to be restocked with food and wood." She distractedly patted the horse's nose. "Is Remy all right?"

"Yeah. I stabled her overnight to wait out the storm. I checked on her this morning when I fed her. She's fine."

"Great. I'll take Sunny in there now."

As she led the horse toward the stable doors, Raf mumbled something about checking on his sister and nephews and strode off toward the homestead. Bluey stared after him, looking puzzled, as if he could tell something was awry, but he wasn't quite sure what. Unwilling to enlighten him any further, Maggie walked off.

Raf's long legs ate up the ground between him and the home-stead as if he was trying to outrun the tumult of emotions coursing through him. It had been hell riding for miles behind Maggie back to the homestead and not being able to hold her close, like he'd wanted to. He'd held her as lightly as possible around the waist because it wasn't fair to her to do anything else. He didn't know how he felt about her, about her giving him her virginity. He didn't know what to do about their connection, if anything. What kept circling in his mind was the thought there was no future for them.

That was the reason he'd kept his distance until now. The reason he'd vowed to stay away from her. Only his libido had taken over and all of his sensible decisions had vaporized.

On the way home, he'd kept conversation to a minimum and his answers brief. It was clear she'd expected him to talk about what had happened between them, and from the hope on her face, it was obvious she expected him to speak in positive terms. He was a coward not to address the issue, but what could he say? That it was the most fantastic sex he'd ever had? That he'd never felt so connected to a woman? That he wanted to make love with her over and over again? He also wanted to know why, after all this time, she'd given her virginity to him.

In a day and age when most people considered virginity as little more than an inconvenience to be disposed of as quickly as possible with the first person who came along, he wasn't sure what had motivated her to keep hers for so long. She didn't strike him as overly religious, and yet, she'd never had sex. It intrigued him, but he also felt weighed down by the responsibility handed to him, courtesy of her decision.

Why me? Why now?

They were questions he didn't feel he could ask her, especially when he wasn't ready to address the bigger issue at hand: *What happens next?*

Nothing changed the fact he lived in the city, hundreds of miles away, and her life was out here, in the outback, on a cattle station. It was an insurmountable difference and right now; he saw no way around it. He hated that his decision to remain silent had caused tension between them, but there was nothing he could do about that either.

Well, there is.

He could declare his undying love and to hell with his life in Brisbane and stay right there on the station. But that wasn't practical, and he still wasn't sure that what he felt for Maggie was enough to last a lifetime. He'd never been in love. He had no idea how it was meant to feel. What he knew was that he only intended to marry once. And right now, he was so confused he didn't have a hope in hell of making a rational decision.

Jogging up the wide steps that led into the homestead, his sister met him just inside the door. Ally was pale and her face was drawn with concern.

"Raf! Thank God you're back!"

"Hey, don't look so worried. I'm fine. It was just a little fall. A dislocated shoulder that Maggie popped back in with hardly an effort at all. It was only because of the storm that we had to stay the night. We—"

"Dad's had a heart attack."

Raf gaped at her. "W-what?"

"Dad. He's had a heart attack. He's been taken to the hospital by ambulance. I've chartered a plane. It leaves in an hour."

"Fuck."

"I spoke to Mum while she was on the way to the hospital. She found him unconscious in bed when she woke this morning. She started CPR. The paramedics took over when they arrived. Thank God they managed to revive him."

Raf's mind raced. All sorts of dreadful scenarios filled his mind. "Is he okay?"

Tears filled Ally's eyes. She hiccupped on a sob. "I don't know! Oh, Raf! I don't know!"

Her voice cracked with emotion. She threw herself into his arms. He held her close. "Hey, it's okay. He's going to be fine. I'm sure he is."

"You don't know that," she said, her voice muffled against his shirt.

"You said they managed to revive him. That's a good sign. And now that he's at the hospital, they'll be able to give him the full treatment, whatever he needs. Surgery, if necessary."

His sister drew back and nodded. With jerky movements, she swiped at her tears. "You're right. Yes. He's at the hospital. He's getting treatment. The best doctors available. He's going to be okay."

Raf could tell she was trying to convince herself as much as him, but that was all right. He understood. He needed to keep reassuring himself, too.

"Where's the plane coming from?"

"I chartered a private plane out of Roma. They'll fly us directly to Brisbane."

"Can they land on the station's airstrip?"

"No. Apparently it's too wet."

"Shit," Raf muttered, running a hand through his hair.

"Yeah, it sucks. Why did it have to rain now?"

He compressed his lips with a sigh. "Well, there's nothing we can do about that. You said the pilot will be ready to leave in an hour. It'll take us that long to get back to Roma. We'd better get moving."

"I've already packed up everything for me and the boys and put it in my four-wheel-drive. Your vehicle's right out front, beside mine. As soon as you can get your stuff together, we can leave."

With that, Raf immediately left his sister and strode down the hallway to his room. Quickly and efficiently, he packed his bag and prepared to leave. Five minutes later, he was outside on the front veranda, where he found Maggie waiting for him. Her expression was somber.

"Allison just told me about your father. I'm sorry, Raf. I hope he's all right."

He nodded grimly. "Thanks. I hope so too." He paused. This was so not the way he envisaged things turning out. While he might not have been ready to talk to her about their night together or their future, that didn't mean he was ready to take his leave. It seemed that fate had other ideas.

"Maggie, I... I'm sorry. I didn't mean for things to turn out like this. I hate that I have to leave... Especially now. We haven't had a chance to talk about... Well, you know what I mean."

"It's okay, Raf. Family's everything and you need to be with yours right now. Go. We'll catch up some other time."

He gave her a brief smile filled with gratitude. "Thank you for understanding. That means a lot to me."

She merely smiled and shrugged. "Of course. Now, go. And travel safely. Take care on the roads. They can be treacherous after so much rain."

With that, he turned and left her standing on the veranda. After checking that his nephews were safely strapped into the back seat and that Ally was okay to drive, he climbed behind the wheel of his rental. With a final glance in Maggie's direction, he swung the wheel around and headed toward the front gate.

Chapter Twenty-Two

Maggie stared after the retreating vehicle and immediately felt bereft. It was ridiculous. They'd only known each other for eleven days. She needed to get a grip.

She wondered fleetingly if his father was really ill or whether Raf was just running away. No, that wasn't fair. His sister and her sons had gone too. They'd left in an awful hurry, and the obviously upset Allison had no reason to lie.

She genuinely hoped their father was going to be okay. It wasn't Raf's fault she'd fallen in love with him. Or that she'd practically begged him to make love to her. A rush of heat flooded her face. She dipped her head in embarrassment, glad that there were no witnesses to her distress.

All she wanted was to crawl into bed and hide out for a while. Lick her wounds. Soothe her battered heart and her ego. It was probably good that there were things to be done around the station, like drenching and tagging and checking fences, particularly after last night's storm.

She sighed and squared her shoulders, mentally preparing herself for the day ahead. Having plenty of work to do would help to keep her mind off Raf and her own actions.

Raf paced up and down the corridor next to the intensive care unit waiting room of the Royal Brisbane Hospital. His father was still in surgery. He required a triple bypass. At least, that's what they'd been told by the surgeon who'd consulted with them briefly before disappearing in the direction of the operating theaters.

His mother and sister sat huddled together on hard plastic chairs, taking comfort from each other. His normally immaculately groomed mother was still dressed in her pajamas. That, more than anything, had shocked Raf into realizing the seriousness of the situation. She'd come straight from home to the hospital, not even taking the time to change. Her short gray hair stood on end, like she'd just climbed out of bed. As far as he could piece together, that's exactly what had happened.

She'd woken to discover his father unconscious in the bed beside her. She wasn't sure how long he'd been that way, but she'd immediately phoned for an ambulance and then had begun CPR. It had taken the paramedics nine minutes to arrive. Nine long minutes during which his mother had performed lifesaving treatment, all the while not knowing if her husband was going to make it.

No wonder she looks shattered...

It was hard enough for Raf to get his head around the possibility his father might not survive. His parents had been married for over thirty years. He couldn't imagine how it would feel to face the possibility of losing someone he'd spent so much time with, losing the love of his life.

An image of Maggie flashed before him. His heart gave a sudden jolt. He couldn't believe how quickly she'd become important to him. They barely knew each other and yet, that didn't seem to matter. The thought of her seriously injured, at risk of dying, made him feel sick.

Have I fallen in love with her? Is that what this is about?

No, surely not. Love didn't happen that quickly. Maybe in the movies, or in sappy romance novels, but not in real life.

What if I'm wrong?

Maggie had told him she'd fallen in love with him. Did he think she was lying? That she couldn't possibly have fallen in love with him so soon. No. When she'd spoken those words, his response had been to panic. Not because he didn't believe her, but because he very much thought she spoke the truth and he wasn't prepared to hear it. Or deal with it. Or think about it at all. Because that would require a response from him that he wasn't ready to give.

So, what did that make him?

A coward.

It wasn't the first time he'd thought about himself that way. The knowledge sat uncomfortably with him. He'd always been brave in the face of hardship or dissent in his professional life, and even in his personal life when he'd been tasked with making tough decisions, including breaking up with Stephanie after dating her on and off for the better part of twelve months.

He'd been well aware that she'd been angling toward a more permanent commitment and that she'd been shocked and hurt when he'd broken things off. The fact he'd helped to contribute toward her expectation that they had a future together by dating her for so long had filled him with guilt.

But that guilt hadn't been enough for him to continue their relationship when he'd accepted that he didn't like her enough to want to spend the rest of his life with her. He'd seen that kind of lifelong commitment between his parents and the deep love and respect that had bound them together for over three decades, and he knew he had nothing like that with Stephanie and never would. He simply didn't care for her that much.

While she was fun to hang around with and good in bed, what they'd had together wouldn't have been enough to last a lifetime. Their goals had been different. Once he'd arrived at that conclusion, it had only been a matter of time before he'd ended things.

Stephanie had been upset, but they'd parted on amicable terms. He hoped that if they ever ran into each other again, they could be civil at least, maybe even friends.

Not that any of that mattered right now. He had far more important things to consider. His father's life was on the line. Even now, the surgeons were fighting to save his life. So far, no one had given them any guarantees that he'd pull through. All they could do was hope and pray.

He'd never been much for religion and a higher power was nothing more than an abstract idea that rarely touched his consciousness, but now he murmured earnestly to whoever might be listening and to whoever might save his dad.

Slowly, he turned and retraced his steps until he took a seat beside his mother. Reaching for her hand, he squeezed it in silent support and reassurance. At the same time, he gave his sister a comforting look. He hated the fear and worry etched on their faces. The taut lips, the pale cheeks. The tears.

They'd been perched on the edge of their seats for hours, unable to speak past the occasional murmur, unable to move, unable to do anything but await the outcome of the emergency surgery they all hoped and prayed would save Bill Hetherington's life.

"How long has it been now, Raf?" his mother rasped.

Raf swallowed a sigh. "About three hours, Mum."

"Why is it taking so long?"

His mother's voice cracked on a sob. His sister put her arm around their mother's shoulders and hugged her close.

"It's okay, Mum. It's going to be okay."

"You don't know that!" their mother wailed. "You weren't there! You didn't see him! It was awful! I thought he was dead!"

"But he wasn't. He isn't. They're operating on him right now. They wouldn't be doing that if they didn't think he had a chance of pulling through. That's right, isn't Raf?"

His sister looked up at him, seeking reassurance. Raf swallowed hard and told her what she wanted to hear. What they all wanted to hear.

"That's right, Ally. No news is good news. Dad's always been a fighter. Remember that time he was T-boned in the old BMW? Broken leg, broken ribs, a bleeding spleen. Not to mention the punctured lung. The doctors had told us to expect the worst and yet Dad proved them all wrong. He's going to prove them wrong again. You'll see."

Raf spoke with a confidence he was far from feeling, but from the look of quiet hope that slowly seeped into his mother's face, his words had done the trick. He swallowed a weary sigh and sent up another silent prayer that he was right.

Maggie dropped the last skein of hay into Remy's food bin and gave the mare a pat. It had been a long day filled with the kind of endless chores that presented themselves regularly on a working cattle station. She'd ridden the fence lines with Bluey and had discovered a tree had fallen over during the storm, damaging one fence that bordered the eastern paddock. She and the old stockman had returned to the shed for the tools and equipment necessary for making the repairs.

Bluey had used the chainsaw to chop the tree trunk and branches into manageable pieces. Together, they'd lifted them off the fence and had then set about repairing it. That had taken them half the day. The other half had been spent going after the cattle who'd escaped into another paddock while the fence was down.

Now the sun had sunk low in the west, casting brilliant hues of red and orange and purple across the horizon. There was no sign of the wild storm from the previous night. Soon it would be dark, and it would be time to head inside. She'd spent countless nights out on the station alone and yet the thought of spending a night without Raf in the house filled her with a stab of loneliness and disappointment.

She hadn't heard from him all day. Not that she'd expected to, but she longed to hear his voice. Or at least to be told that everything was okay with his father. There was a lot that had remained unsaid between them, but she could wait for the right time for that discussion. His father's health took precedence over an emergency of the heart. But her phone had remained obstinately silent. Not even a text or a voicemail.

Despondency weighed heavily on her chest. She closed her eyes against the pressure behind them. A moment later, she shook her head and squared her shoulders, determined to throw off the negativity that surrounded her. He was just a man. She'd never let herself get depressed over a man. He wasn't the only man out there. If he wasn't her Mr Right, then so be it. She might have made a lapse of judgement in sleeping with him, but she'd get over that too. She was a good catch. She wanted someone who appreciated that. If that wasn't Raf, then that was his loss.

Pep talk over with, she gave Remy a final pat and then strode out of the stables. The homestead was dark. But there was nothing unusual about that. She never switched on lights ahead of time. Saving electricity was just one thing that came innately to her, living in the outback.

She climbed the steps and crossed over the front veranda. The old boards squeaked beneath her feet. It felt like a lifetime had passed since she'd farewelled Raf and his sister. And just like that, her thoughts were full of him again.

She made an impatient sound in the back of her throat, determined to forget about him. Her life had been just fine before he'd interrupted it. Now that he was gone, it would be fine once again. Just as soon as she got over her silly crush. Yes, a crush. That's all this was. She'd been ridiculous, fancying herself in love. How could she be in love with someone she barely knew? It was absurd.

With that, she kicked off her boots and made her way down the hallway to the kitchen. Pulling open the fridge, she stared inside at the measly contents. She hadn't been home long enough that morning to give any thought to taking something out of the freezer for dinner. Raf's family emergency and his sudden departure had been all that was on her mind. Then he'd left, and she'd gone directly to the stables, needing a distraction from the sudden emptiness that enveloped her.

She pulled out a container of leftovers. Some of Raf's Beef Wellington. The fact that the very sight of the dish brought back a flood of memories was almost enough for her to leave it in the fridge. But preparing something fresh was beyond her. She was drained. The Beef Wellington would have to do.

Raf was the first to spy the surgeon dressed in scrubs approach them from along the corridor. It was the same surgeon who'd spoken to them briefly before the surgery had begun.

Raf sprang to his feet, his heart in his mouth. He tried to gauge the surgeon's demeanor from his expression, but the man's eyes gave no clue as to the success or otherwise of the hours' long surgery he'd just performed.

As Raf's mother and sister became aware of the doctor, they got to their feet and stepped forward, clinging to each other, their expressions reflecting equal parts hope and dread.

"Doctor, how is he?" Raf asked.

The doctor gazed at them and then offered them a weary smile. "He's a fighter, that's for sure."

Raf's shoulders slumped on a sigh of relief. He grinned toward his mother and sister. "See? I told you so."

"He's not out of the woods yet," the surgeon cautioned, "but so far, so good. He's been moved to the ICU and we expect he'll be there for at least a few days. It's a good thing he's otherwise fit and healthy. That'll help with his recovery, no doubt."

"Oh, thank goodness!" Raf's mother gasped, holding her hands up to her mouth. "Thank you, Doctor. Thank you so much."

The doctor inclined his head toward her. "I'm glad I could help. I understand you were the one who first started CPR?"

Raf's mother compressed her lips and nodded. "I've never been so scared in all my life. I had no idea if I was doing it right. All I knew was that Bill would die if I didn't do something."

"Well, it's lucky that you had some knowledge, and that you were brave enough to try. There's no doubt you saved his life."

"When can we see him?" Raf asked.

The doctor turned slightly to face him. "He's sleeping now and the best thing he can do for his recovery is to rest. I'll ask the nurses to come and find you when he wakes. They have your contact numbers. While you're waiting, there's a great little café downstairs. They serve a mean cappuccino. It looks like you could all do with some caffeine."

Raf's mother held out her hand toward the surgeon. "Thank you, Doctor. You can't know how grateful we are for everything you've done."

The doctor shook her proffered hand and nodded. "Like I said, I was happy to help."

After accepting both Raf's and Allison's gratitude and shaking their hands, the surgeon took his leave. As if all the wind had suddenly been taken from her sails, Raf's mother sagged against his sister in relief.

"Thank goodness he made it through the surgery," she whispered.

Raf nodded, feeling just as relieved. "He's going to be all right, Mum. He's going to be all right."

On his way downstairs to the café, following behind his mother and sister, Raf's thoughts centered on how tenuous his hold on life could be. One moment he could be on top of the world and the next he could be dead. It made him realize how short life was and that it couldn't be taken for granted. A health scare like his father had just endured sure helped put things into perspective. No one was promised tomorrow. He only had today. Best make the most of whatever time he had.

Chapter Twenty-Three

♥

Maggie woke the next morning to the sound of a vehicle pulling up outside the homestead. Her heart leaped into her throat.

Raf!

Jumping out of bed, she threw on some clothes and hurried outside. She was brought up short by the sight of one of her brothers crossing the wide expanse of the front yard.

"Lachlan! What are you doing here?"

He bounded up the steps, ruffled her hair, and then pecked her on the cheek. "Is that any way to greet your favorite brother?"

She grimaced. "Since when did you become my favorite brother?"

He grinned, exposing a dimple in his cheek. "Since now. Wait until you see what I have for you in the back of my truck. Got anything to eat? I'm starving. I left home before breakfast. I haven't even had time for a cup of coffee."

With that, he pushed his way past her and strode on into the house. Bemused, Maggie followed him. She filled the kettle and set it to boil before pulling out two cups and spooning instant coffee into them. She added sugar to both of them. Even though it had been three years since she'd lived at the family homestead, she still remembered how Lachlan took his coffee.

"So," she said, leaning back against the counter and folding her arms over her chest. "What amazing thing do you have for me hiding in the back of your truck?"

Instead of answering, Lachlan opened the fridge and stared inside for a few moments before shutting the door. Then he latched onto a Tupperware container on the bench. He opened it and found the banana bread that was left over from the first day Raf had arrived at the station. It seemed like a lifetime ago.

Lachlan grinned in triumph. "Home-baked banana bread. My favorite. You must have known I was coming."

Without bothering to get a knife, he broke off a chunk and stuffed it into his mouth. Maggie rolled her eyes and shook her head. Some people never changed.

At twenty-five, Lachlan was three years younger than she was. There were another two brothers younger than him, along with three younger sisters. Maggie was one of the oldest in the Fairfax family lineup.

He held up another chunk of cake. "It's a bit stale. Not as good as Mum's."

Maggie opened her mouth in outrage, then caught the teasing glint in Lachie's green eyes just in time. Swallowing her words of protest, she grabbed the tea towel from its hook near the stove and flicked him with it.

"Ouch!" he complained.

"Brat," she responded. "Just so you know, I baked that banana bread almost two weeks ago. I'm surprised it's not moldy."

He choked. "Why didn't you tell me? What if I get sick?"

"You'll be fine," she said.

The sound of the kettle boiling distracted her. She spent the next few minutes making coffee. She handed Lachie a cup.

"Thanks," he murmured and took a grateful sip. "Ahh. That's good."

"I'm glad to see I can do something right."

He grinned again. "Now, now, now. Don't be like that, big sis. I come bearing gifts, don't forget."

"Yeah, yeah, yeah. So you keep saying. So, what it is? Come on. Spit it out."

"I was in Roma yesterday."

"So?"

"I ran into Jeremy."

"Jeremy who?"

"Jeremy Baker."

"Who's Jeremy Baker?"

"He's an apprentice. He moved here from Townsville. Apparently, he's sick of living on the coast. Go figure. I think it'd be cool being able to hang out at the beach whenever you wanted. Anyway, he just started working for—"

"For goodness' sake, Lachie! Get to the point!" Maggie interrupted, her patience at an end.

"I am!" her brother protested, his eyes wide with innocence. "Like I was saying, Jeremy just started working for Luke's Air Conditioning."

Maggie frowned. "Luke? As in Aaron Luke? The one and only air conditioning mechanic in Roma?"

"One and the same."

"I called him nearly three weeks ago. He still hasn't returned my call."

Lachie smiled smugly. "I know. I heard all about it from Jeremy. Aaron's been super-busy doing a big installation job out of town. Although, according to Jeremy, Aaron had you penciled in for the end of the week."

"The end of the week? He told Raf he'd be here last week."

The moment at the words were out of her mouth, she wished them back. She desperately hoped Lachie hadn't heard her, but one look at the avid curiosity that now flooded his face and she realized that hope was gone.

"Raf? You mean the new owner I met the other week?"

"Yes."

Lachie's eyes narrowed on hers. "What's the go with the two of you? Is there something going on between the two of you?"

Her face flamed. "No! Why would you say that?"

Lachie's frown deepened. "I don't know. I couldn't quite put my finger on it at lunch, but something just felt...off."

Maggie averted her gaze and buried her nose in her coffee cup. "You're imagining things."

Lachie shrugged and looked around him. "So, where is he?"

"He... He's gone. He got a call to say his father was seriously ill. He left yesterday morning."

As if sensing there was more to the story, Lachie's gaze turned probing. "When's he coming back?"

Heat crept up her neck. She turned away before Lachie could notice her discomfort. "I... I don't know. He was meant to be here for two weeks. He's still deciding about whether to keep it or sell."

"But what about you and the other guys? Bluey and Daphne? The jackaroos? Where will they go?"

She drew in a breath and compressed her lips. "I guess we'll work that out when the time comes. Who knows? Raf might even decide to keep the place yet."

"Then you have to do everything you can to convince him," Lachie replied. "Bluey and Daphne are too old to start somewhere anew. I mean, we could probably employ them on Marlowe Downs in the short term, but we don't really need any extra hands right now. Then there are the others. As much as I'd like to, we can't find a job for them all."

Maggie turned back around to face him and nodded. She was all too aware that her family was still doing what they could to rebuild their herd after suffering through a terrible drought. That had been followed by a flood that had left just as much devastation in its wake. It was a tough life, eking out an existence from the land when there were so many variables out of everyone's control.

"Let's hope it doesn't come to that. I had ten days with Raf before he had to leave. I tried to convince him to keep the place, but I'm not sure how successful I was."

Lachie's frown deepened. "Why? What did you do? Surely someone of your charm and persuasion could have had some impact."

Anger stirred inside her. "Why do you think it's something I did? I told you. I did my best. That's it. I have no power over the man. I can't force him to keep the station if he wants to sell. Hell, I barely know him."

Her face was on fire. Her breath came fast. Lachie's eyes narrowed with suspicion.

"What's going on, Maggie?"

Her flush deepened. She turned away from him once again, refusing to look at him. "Nothing. I don't know what you're talking about."

"Is he single?"

"What does that have to do with anything?"

"Is he single, Maggie?"

She stared at the floor. "Yes, as far as I know."

"Ahh. Now it all makes sense."

"What makes sense?" Maggie asked, irritated.

"Why you're not sure if he's coming back. You like him, don't you? You like him a lot. In fact, you might have even done something stupid like making a pass at him. "

Her cheeks turned crimson. Her brother pounced.

"So you have made a pass at him." He *tut tutted*. "Oh, Maggie. That probably wasn't the wisest thing to do."

Her anger found its head. "Don't you dare go giving me advice about my love life! As if you've had a world of experience in that area. Remind me of just how many girlfriends you've had in the past, Lachlan Fairfax?"

To her irritation, rather than getting embarrassed, a smug expression filled his face. "A gentleman never kisses and tells, but let's just say I've had more than you know."

She snorted. "Yeah, right. Like you ever get off Marlowe Downs long enough to meet anyone."

Lachlan merely grinned. "You'd be surprised, sis. You'd be surprised." He winked.

She waved her hand in dismissal. "Whatever. I don't care how many women you've slept with. That has nothing to do with me. Or my situation. The truth is, if Raf Hetherington sells, all of us here could very well be without a place to live, as well as unemployed. It's a daunting possibility for all of us. I really thought I could convince him to keep the station."

"How do you know you haven't?" Lachie asked in a quiet voice.

Maggie's shoulders slumped on a defeated sigh. All of a sudden, she felt the need to unload, to share the burden with someone who cared.

"Because I went and ruined everything and now he's gone. It's just as you said, only worse." She paused and looked at him. "I didn't make a pass at him. I slept with him."

To his credit, Lachie barely reacted to her confession. It was as if he sensed how distressed she was over the whole sorry situation and decided to hold his tongue.

"You don't know that's impacted his decision to leave. Didn't you say his father was ill?"

"Yes. Apparently, he had a heart attack."

"Well, hell. That's reason enough to leave in a hurry. It sounds like Raf's abrupt departure had nothing to do with you."

She gave a tight smile. "Perhaps. Anyway, I guess we'll have to wait and see. But thanks for trying to cheer me up. I appreciate it."

"No worries. That's what brothers are for, right?"

"Right."

"When do you expect to hear from him?"

"I'm not sure. I hoped he'd at least call or text to let me know how his father was doing, but I haven't heard a word."

"If he's any kind of decent guy, he'll call you, and I won't believe you would have slept with someone you didn't think was decent."

"Thanks. He's decent enough. I just don't know if he wants to keep the station. He's a city guy. His life's in Brisbane. There's nothing out here for him."

"Except you," Lachie said pointedly.

Maggie closed her eyes briefly on a sigh. "Yes. But I don't know if that's enough. He left before we had a chance to properly talk. I don't know what's going on in his head. I wish I did."

Lachie chuckled. "Hey, if you ever gain the ability to read minds, please give me a heads up."

She smiled and picked up her coffee and took a sip. "You still haven't told me what's in your truck."

Lachie grinned. "Why don't you come and check it out for yourself?"

With that, they set their coffee cups down on the counter. Maggie followed her brother outside. He went around the side of his four-wheel-drive and lifted a tarpaulin that covered three large cardboard boxes.

"What are they?" she asked.

"They are brand-new air conditioning units. Three of them. Split systems. That means both hot and cold."

She rolled her eyes. "Thank you, Lachlan. I know what a split system is."

"Then you know what they're for."

She frowned. "Hang on. I'm confused. I left a message for Aaron to say my air conditioning had stopped working. I didn't order any new units. I don't have any authority to spend money like that. I've always had to clear capital purchases through Arthur. With him gone, I guess that means I'll have to speak to Raf. I'm sorry, Lachie, but you've wasted your trip. I can't accept these."

"Oh, but you can. Apparently, your new boss was the one who asked Aaron to replace the old units with these."

Maggie gaped. "Raf ordered these?"

"That's what Jeremy said. That's why he asked me to bring them out here. Aaron will be out soon to install them."

Maggie blinked rapidly, trying to get her head around what Raf had done. It was such an incredibly generous gesture. The current air conditioning units were old and rundown and had been repaired more times than she cared to remember. Replacing them was a dream that she'd never expected to become a reality because of the sheer cost involved.

Like she'd told Raf, his uncle was always happy to spend money on livestock and anything on the station that generated income, but he'd been far less willing to pay for things around the house. That included new air conditioning units.

She couldn't help but wonder if Raf's generosity indicated that he was thinking about keeping the place. Why else spend money on such things? It wouldn't make any difference to him if the homestead was air conditioned or not if he were no longer the owner.

The whole situation was curious and definitely bore more thinking about...

Chapter Twenty-Four

Raf was relieved to see his father sitting up in bed the next time he visited him at the hospital. He'd been moved out of the ICU and into a cardiac ward two days earlier and was doing well. He certainly looked much improved. His color was good, and he was engaged in a lively conversation with his grandsons when Raf walked into the room. His sister was perched on a chair in one corner, reading a magazine.

"Dad. How's it going? You're looking better."

"Thanks, Raf. What do you have there? I hope it's Chinese takeaway. The food here is awful."

Raf laughed. "You must be feeling better if you're complaining about the food." He set the paper bag he'd been carrying down on his father's beside table. "I'm afraid to disappoint you. There's only a container of fresh fruit salad inside."

His father screwed up his face. "Fruit salad? What are you trying to do? Kill me?"

Raf's nephews giggled.

"Of course not, Grandpa!" Lucas exclaimed. "Why would Uncle Raf want to kill you?"

"Grandpa's only kidding," Ally admonished, coming forward and pecking Raf on the cheek. "How are you, brother? It's good to see you again."

"Yeah, I'm fine. Where's Mum?"

"She left a little while ago. She went home before the traffic got too heavy."

"Tell me about it. Peak hour's a bitch. It took me over an hour to get here and my office is literally three miles away."

"Uncle Raf said a naughty word. Uncle Raf said a naughty word!" Miles chanted.

Raf patted the small boy on the head. "You're right, and I shouldn't have said that. I don't want to hear any naughty words out of your mouth, okay?"

"Okay," Miles dutifully responded.

"Come and tell me about your time in the outback," Raf's father said, patting the bed beside him. "With everything that's been going on, we haven't had a chance to talk about it. I still can't believe Arthur left you a cattle station. He knew better than anyone what a city boy you are. What was he thinking?"

Raf stepped closer and chuckled. "I don't know. But to answer your first question, it was great. So different to what I'm used to. So many wide-open spaces."

His father laughed. "You can say that again. Does anyone actually live out there, other than the cows?"

Raf smiled. "Of course they do. Who do you think takes care of all those cows? And don't you worry, there are plenty of cows. And steers. And bulls. And calves. More cattle than I've ever seen."

"Sounds like it was an adventure. So, when are you putting the place on the market and investing the proceeds in something more practical, like a new block of townhouses?"

Raf shrugged and averted his gaze. "Yeah, I'm not sure. I haven't really had enough time to think about it. I was only there for ten days, but the time I spent there was amazing. The natural beauty of the place is breathtaking. I never thought I could live anywhere but the city, but after spending time out there..." His voice drifted off.

His father's eyes widened in shock. "Don't tell me you're actually contemplating living out there? Have you lost your mind?"

Before he could come up with a suitable response, Allison cleared her throat and smiled.

"Ask him what her name is, Dad."

Their father frowned, and then comprehension slowly dawned. "You've got to be kidding. I should have known there was a woman involved. What's her name, Raf?" he asked dryly.

Heat exploded across Raf's face as all eyes turned toward him. He shifted uncomfortably, not sure how to respond. But then he realized how much he wanted to talk about Maggie. It had been nearly a week since he'd seen her, spoken to her. A hastily worded text message advising her that his father was on the mend was the only contact he'd had with her since he'd left. Her response had been just as brief.

"Her name is Maggie Fairfax," he said. "She's the station manager. She's been out there for three years and has done an amazing job. Her family owns the neighboring station. She's the most capable woman I've ever met."

"She's also drop-dead gorgeous, single and of marriageable age," Allison added smugly, giving Raf a wink.

Their father gaped. "Don't tell me you've fallen in love with her?"

Raf flushed. "Of course not."

"Liar," his sister said. "It's written all over your face."

"No, you're wrong," he said, his tone tinged with desperation.

Allison shrugged nonchalantly. "I've seen the two of you together, remember?"

"How could I be in love with her? I barely know her."

"I think you know her well enough," Allison replied.

Raf refused to answer. When the phone in his top pocket rang, he snatched at it in relief. He checked the screen. It was from one of his friends. Grateful for an excuse to bring an end to their conversation, he stepped outside of his father's room to take the call.

"Hi, Simon. How's it going?"

"Good, mate. What are you up to?"

"Just visiting Dad at the hospital."

"I heard he'd had a heart attack. Is he okay?"

"Yeah, he's fine. Thank God."

"That's good to hear. Listen, the reason I'm calling is that Dylan and Ivy are having a housewarming party tonight. Everyone's going to be there. I just thought you might be interested in letting your hair down for the night."

Raf contemplated it for all of about three seconds. Dylan and Ivy were friends of theirs from way back. They were always fun to be around. It had been so long since he'd had a night out on the town. With the visit to the outback and then his father ending up in hospital, there just hadn't been time. A night out was exactly what he needed to clear his head of the woman who'd dominated far too many of his thoughts and dreams.

He grinned. "I'll see you there."

Maggie sat on one of the cane wicker chairs that stood on the back veranda and sipped from a glass of wine as she enjoyed the dying rays of the sunset. Nature had put on another magnificent display. Unfortunately, even the glorious sunset couldn't lift her spirits from the slump she'd been in ever since Raf's departure.

She hated that she missed him so much. She hated that he consumed her thoughts. Watching the sunset reminded her of sitting out there with him on the back veranda, drinking wine and watching the day draw to an end.

Earlier, she'd driven past the stockman's hut on her way to inspect some cattle and had been reminded of him all over again. In fact, everything on the station reminded her of him. He'd spoiled the place for her. Maybe it was best if he sold the station and she was forced to move on. Go somewhere memories of him couldn't haunt her. Too bad he'd also invaded her dreams.

She groaned aloud and took refuge in her wine. She was on her third glass of one of Arthur's bottles and then remembered they now belonged to Raf. Everything belonged to Raf. The house she slept in. The chair she sat on. The wine she sipped. The precariousness of her future was stamped on everything.

It was made even worse because she hadn't heard from him since the single, one-line text advising her that his father was on the road to recovery. She had no idea whether he'd thought about her or the station since he'd left. Not knowing was difficult. She hated the waiting. It wasn't only for herself that she was concerned. Raf owed it to Bluey, Daphne, and the other employees to let them know what he planned and to give them as much notice as possible.

Anger stirred inside her. No doubt he'd barely given a thought to the lives and livelihoods of the people who currently depended upon him. He'd be so engrossed in his city life with his city friends that it probably wouldn't cross his mind that there were people anxiously awaiting his decision.

While it had only been a few days, the more time that went on, the more she was convinced his plan was to sell up. He'd made it clear over and over that his life was in Brisbane. She just wished he'd rip off the Band-Aid and get on with it so they could all put it and him behind them and get on with their lives.

The party was in full swing when Raf arrived a little after nine. Women wearing designer dresses and impossibly high heels stood shoulder to shoulder with men who were resplendent in black tie. They filled the spacious penthouse and spilled out onto the balcony that served up a magnificent view of the Story Bridge. Raf recognized an actor from a popular TV show. There were also a few sporting identities, along with some of the wealthiest people in town.

The pop music coming from the state-of-the art speakers that were affixed discretely in the walls was loud enough to force the crowd to shout over the top of it. Raf could barely hear anything over the sound of so much chatter. Already, a headache had formed.

He looked around the room for Simon, but didn't see him. Snatching a glass of champagne off a tray held by a formally dressed waiter, he muttered his thanks and then elbowed his way outside. He found his friend in one corner of the balcony, holding court among three glamorous women who could have come straight off a fashion runway. They looked like they were hanging off Simon's every word.

Simon spied him a moment later and greeted him effusively. "Ah. Raf! There you are! Good to see you, mate."

The two men shook hands. Simon patted Raf enthusiastically on the shoulder.

"Meet my beautiful companions," Simon continued. He indicated the woman on his left. "This is Sybil." He quickly followed through with introductions of the other two women. "This is Molly. And this is Fiona. Say hello to my friend, Raf, ladies."

They turned in unison and offered him almost identical smiles. Straight, white teeth. Bright red lipstick. Botoxed lips and cheeks.

Since when did women begin to look so fake?

He murmured appropriate greetings, already wishing he hadn't come. To think he used to enjoy parties like this, filled with beautiful people who'd never worked a day's manual labor in their lives. And he'd been just like them. Flitting from one ritzy party to the next. Sharing small talk with strangers. Hooking up with a beautiful woman for the night.

One woman—Sybil, or was it Fiona—moved closer to him, deliberately brushing her breast against his arm. The avid interest in her eyes was clear to see. Not so long ago, he'd have been eager to take her up on her unspoken invitation.

Suddenly, he felt claustrophobic, no matter that the air outside was fresh and cool. Murmuring his apologies to Simon and the ladies, he escaped back inside. Intent on leaving as quickly as he'd arrived, he didn't even notice Stephanie until he almost collided with her near the front door.

"Stephanie! Hi. It's good to see you," he said, taking a few steps backwards.

Recognizing him, her eyes went wide with surprise and then filled with obvious delight.

"Raf! How wonderful to see you!" She stepped in close and kissed him full on the mouth.

He broke the kiss off before it could get started and put some distance between them.

Stephanie pouted. "Where have you been? It's been ages since I last saw you. I thought you'd dropped off the face of the earth!"

Raf offered a tight smile. "I've been around. Busy. You know how it is."

She gave an exaggerated sigh. "Don't I ever! You're always working." She paused and then once again sidled up close to him. She ran a long, manicured finger down his chest. "But that doesn't mean I don't miss you. I do. I miss you a lot, Raf."

Her hand flattened on his chest and slid lower, across his stomach. When she made a move to go lower still, he closed his hand over hers and gently removed it.

"You look good, Stephanie. Single life obviously agrees with you."

And it was true. She was as stunning as always. As tall as him and with a body most women would die for, her full breasts strained against her low-cut dress, threatening to spill out at any moment. The floaty red dress skimmed her slim hips and fell almost to the floor. She was gorgeous, utterly desirable and yet... She left him cold.

The problem was, she wasn't Maggie. She wasn't the beautiful, capable, strong, smart woman he'd left behind in the glorious red outback. Allison was right. He'd been lying to himself. He was head over heels in love with Maggie Fairfax, and there was no longer any point in denying it.

He could have any number of beautiful women. They were his for the taking, but he only wanted her. It was as if a light had been switched on in his brain. He knew with complete certainty that he was willing to turn his life upside down for her. To leave his job. To move to the outback. Perhaps he could go into business on his own? He could do that from anywhere. He'd have to get better Internet at Hetherington Station, but so what? That was easy to arrange.

As his excitement built, he couldn't help but grin. Mistaking his lightened mood, Stephanie once again moved in on him.

She draped her arm around his neck and pulled him in close. "How about you and I go somewhere private?" she whispered in his ear.

Gently extricating himself, he looked at her and shook her head. "I'm sorry, Stephanie. It's been lovely to see you again, but you and I are done. Find someone who can love you the way you want. You deserve that. I want you to be happy, but unfortunately, you're going to have to find that with someone else. I'm sorry. Good night."

With that, he set his glass of champagne down on a hall table and left.

Back out on the street, he drew in a deep and cleansing breath. He felt almost light-headed with anticipation and exhilaration.

I'm in love with Maggie Fairfax!

He couldn't wait to tell her, but he didn't want to do that over the phone. No, he needed to tell her in person, to see her face. To hold her. Something this momentous, this life-changing, deserved nothing less.

He took a cab home and striding back into his apartment, he felt like he was walking on air. He wanted to leave immediately, but of course, it was far too late to charter a flight. The best he could do was to arrange for one to leave the following morning and fly directly into Roma.

On his way to the airport, he'd also call his lawyer and tell him he was going to keep the station. He looked forward with anticipation to working side by side with Maggie, helping wherever he could. Not that she needed his help, or that he'd be very good at being a cattleman. But, whatever. At least they'd be together.

The thought of putting down roots and raising his family on the station filled him with a sense of rightness. They could continue the dynasty first started by the McGregor family so many years ago. Okay, so he and Maggie were far from pioneers, but leaving his comfortable city life for the outback felt very much like stepping into a new frontier. He couldn't wait for it to begin.

The next morning, Raf woke before his alarm, even though he'd barely slept because he was excited to see Maggie again. He left for the airport more than an hour earlier than he had to. He didn't want to risk missing his flight.

On the way, he called his lawyer and told him he was keeping the station.

"If you don't mind, would you come into the office?" his lawyer asked.

Raf frowned. "What, now?"

"Yes, if you don't mind."

Raf glanced at his watch. He was well early. Besides, he wasn't sure how long it would be before he was back in Brisbane. With a quiet sigh, he agreed.

His lawyer greeted him with a smile and a friendly handshake. "It's good to see you again, Raf. Thanks for stopping by."

"No problem, Jeff. But just so you know, I'm on my way to catch a flight. If you don't mind, I'd like to make this quick."

"I can do that," the lawyer agreed.

He led the way into his office and then took a seat behind his desk. He indicated for Raf to take a seat opposite him. Then he handed Raf a sealed envelope.

"What's this?" Raf asked, turning the envelope over in his hands. He noticed his name scrawled across the front in his uncle's familiar, bold hand.

"It's a letter from your uncle. He wrote it the last time he made amendments to his will. He asked me to keep it safe until you agreed to keep Hetherington Station."

Raf frowned. "But he had no way of knowing my decision. What would have happened if I'd told you to sell?"

The lawyer calmly folded his hands together and sat them on the desk in front of him. "Then the letter would have been destroyed, pursuant to your uncle's instructions."

Chapter Twenty-Five

Curious, Raf turned the letter over again and at last slid his finger along the top to open it. He pulled out a single sheet of handwritten paper. Once again, he recognized his uncle's hand.

Dear Raf,

If you're reading this, then I am dead. Don't be sad. I'm okay with it. We all have to die sometime, right?

Anyway, I'll get to the point. How are things going between you and Maggie? She's such a beautiful girl. The fact that you're reading this also means you've decided to keep the station. I hope Maggie has had something to do with that.

For years, I've watched you flit from this woman to that. All beautiful, all accomplished. But none of them were your match, your soul mate. Believe me, I know what it is to meet your soul mate. Foolishly, I let her go, and she married someone else. That's a decision I lived to regret. I don't want you to make the same mistake, or to settle for anything less.

Call it meddling by an old man, but I hope you and Maggie have fallen in love. It would make me so happy to know that the two of you have found each other in the midst of the outback and, despite all obstacles, including your obsession with the city.

Another one of my regrets is that I didn't spend more time out there and that I didn't insist on bringing you with me. Perhaps you could have met and fallen in love with Maggie while I was still alive. That's something I'd have given anything to see.

Still, it wasn't to be, but I can't be too upset. You've agreed to keep Hetherington Station, and that's enough. I wish you all the happiness in the world and I pray you live a long and happy life. That you and Maggie build a life and a family and grow old in a place I grew to love.

Take care now,

Your loving Uncle Arthur

The letter was dated six months before his uncle had died. Raf read the letter twice, still blown away by the discovery that all along Uncle Arthur had wanted him to meet and fall in love with Maggie. That's why he'd left him the station. Now it all made sense.

His uncle had known they'd be perfect for each other, and he'd been right. Knowing he and Maggie had his uncle's blessing filled Raf with indescribable peace and an even more urgent desire to get to her and tell her how he felt.

The bright sunlight that shone through Maggie's bedroom window belied the misery she felt inside. Another day alone on the station. Another day without Raf. Her dismal mood was getting monotonous, and she could tell it was effecting her staff. Even Bluey had told her to pull herself together and to either go after the city slicker or set aside her pining and wipe him from her mind.

If only it was that easy...

On a surge of determination, she threw off the covers and climbed out of bed. It was the beginning of a new day. The first day where she was going to refuse to let Raf's departure affect her attitude. He was gone and so far, there was no sign that he was coming back. The best thing she could do was to accept that sometimes life didn't turn out the way she wanted. It was time to get on with it.

Raf's gut swarmed with nerves as he neared the turnoff to Hetherington Station. He'd wanted to surprise Maggie with his visit, so he hadn't called ahead. Now he questioned the wisdom of that. She could be anywhere. She might have gone mustering for the day, or even left the station. After all, he'd given her no indication that her future was secure. A stab of panic went through him at the thought.

He hadn't come all this way not to find her there. Then again, if she was gone he'd simply find out where she was and track her down, even if she'd moved a thousand miles away. He was in love with her, and he wouldn't rest until he'd told her.

He hoped she'd accept his declaration of love. After all, not that long ago, she'd told him she was in love with him. Surely her feelings couldn't change that fast.

Then again, he hadn't spoken to her for a week. What if she thought he'd abandoned her? That he wasn't coming back? He wouldn't blame her for thinking that. For a while, he hadn't been sure himself. But all that had changed now, and he couldn't wait to tell her.

As he flicked on his indicator and turned off the high-way into Hetherington Station, nerves continued to swirl. The four-wheel-drive he'd hired from Roma Airport bounced over fresh ruts in the dirt road. At least it was dry. He hadn't been keen for a repeat of the slipping and sliding he'd done in the mud the last time he'd driven on that road.

As he looked in the rearview mirror at the dust blowing behind his truck, he couldn't help but smile. Who would have thought that a boy from the city could feel so at home with red dust? Of course, it was all about the woman he was driving to meet. A few more miles and he'd be there. He couldn't wait.

Maggie was on her way to the stables when she saw the dust of a vehicle approaching in the distance. She paused. At the sight of the white Land Cruiser, her heart skipped a beat.

Raf.

Then she told herself not to be stupid. There were hundreds of Toyota Land Cruisers just like that one owned by people on neighboring farms. They were the only vehicle that could stand the tough outback conditions. The sight of one shouldn't be cause for anything more than mild curiosity. It could even be one of her brothers.

Raf had no reason to come back. He'd seen all he'd wanted to see. No doubt he was busy back in Brisbane meeting with real estate agents. He'd made no bones about wanting to sell. She was sure he'd returned to his life in Brisbane. It was time for her to accept that.

As the vehicle drew closer, she could see the shape of a man behind the wheel. He had short dark hair and wore sunglasses that concealed his eyes. But when the truck came to a halt and Raf opened the door and climbed out, her heart stopped.

A second later, her pulse took off at a gallop and hope flared in her stomach. Not knowing what he was there for, she tried desperately to rein it in.

"W-what are you doing here?" she croaked.

Overjoyed at discovering her there, Raf had to restrain himself from the urge to rush over and take her in his arms. He saw the hope and hesitation warring in her eyes. He took heart from it. Hope meant she was glad to see him. That had to be a good thing. He couldn't expect her to come running at him with open arms. After all, she had no idea why he was there.

"Hello, Maggie."

His voice came out all rusty, as if he wasn't sure what to say and now that the moment was upon him, he felt strangely tongue tied.

"What are you doing here?" she asked again, this time in a stronger tone.

"I wanted to see you again."

"Okay. You've seen me. Now you can leave."

"No! I mean, I don't want to leave. Please don't tell me to go. The thing is, I've fallen in love with you."

Instead of the enthusiastic response he'd expected, she gave him a barely there smile.

"Congratulations. I'm sure that's been hard for you."

Her voice was as dry as the yellowed grass he'd passed on his way in. This was going to be harder than he'd thought.

"It's true, Maggie. I love you."

She merely shrugged. "Your life is in the city, remember? You told me so, repeatedly. And I'm not leaving the outback.

So, I guess that means we're back to where we started. I love you and you love me, but it's never going to work."

He grinned, relieved. "I'm so glad to hear you still love me. I wasn't sure, seeing as it's been more than a week since you told me, and I haven't exactly been blocking up your phone."

Her expression turned fierce. "It still doesn't matter, Raf. Nothing's changed. I'd never ask you to leave the city, just like you know there'd be no point in you asking me to leave here."

He took a step toward her, holding out his hand. It nearly did him in when she retreated a few steps.

"You don't understand, Maggie. Hell, I'm making a mess of this. You see, you don't have to go anywhere. *I'm* the one moving in. Permanently. That's if you'll have me."

Her eyes went wide with shock, as if she couldn't believe what she'd heard. And then she confirmed it.

"Say that again."

He took a few more steps toward her, and this time, she didn't move. He came to a halt in front of her and stared into her beautiful eyes.

"I love you, Maggie Fairfax. And I want to spend the rest of my life with you. Right here, on Hetherington Station."

She chewed at her bottom lip. Indecision was evident on her face. "Why?" she demanded.

He frowned. "Why what?"

"Why do you want to move out here?"

"Because I love you and I'll do whatever it takes to be with you. Even if that means moving to the end of the earth."

A small smile tugged at her lips. "We're hardly at the end of the earth."

Taking heart from humor, he reached for her hands. "Maggie Fairfax, will you stay and be my wife? Raise a family, create memories and history we can pass onto the next generation, like Angus and Eliza McGregor and all those others who have gone before us?"

He was nearly breathless when he finished speaking. His heart pounded so loudly he could barely hear her response.

"I'd love to."

With that, she smiled with joy and threw herself against him. He caught her and held her tightly. She felt so good in his arms. She felt like home.

And then they were kissing each other like they couldn't get enough. When they finally came up for air, Raf chuckled and suggested they go inside. Maggie laughingly agreed. Hand in hand, they walked across the front yard and up the wide concrete steps, stopping to exchange kisses now and then.

Maggie led him into her bedroom, where it was pleasantly cool. He glanced up at the brand-new air conditioning unit.

"I see they arrived."

She laughed. "Yes! You should have said something! It was a delightful surprise."

"I'm glad you appreciated it."

"Absolutely. I'm just glad you now also get to enjoy it."

He nuzzled her neck. "There's plenty more for me to enjoy."

She tilted her head back, giving him greater access. "Oh, Raf."

Raf's body was on fire. His cock was so hard it felt like he might explode. He'd never been so happy, or so turned-on. That Maggie was still in love with him and was willing to be his wife was the best thing that had ever happened to him, and he had his uncle to thank for it.

As he took her in his arms and kissed her for all he was worth, all thoughts of his uncle disappeared. The only person he could think of was the beautiful woman kissing him back. His tongue probed her lips, seeking entrance. She opened her mouth and let him in. Their tongues danced and tangled as they took from each other all that the other could give.

He reached for the buttons on her shirt, desperate to feel her bare skin. At the same time, she tugged at the hem of his T-shirt and released it from his jeans. She pulled the offending garment over his head and flung it to one side. He did the same with her shirt and then started on her bra.

In no time at all, they were naked and pressed together on her bed. Her breasts were crushed against his chest as he kissed her once again.

This time, he took things slower, deliberately taking the time to kiss her eyelids, her cheeks, her chin, her nose, before finally settling his lips on hers once again. Their kisses became deeper, gentler, as they learned the taste and texture of each other. This time, there was no urgency, despite the aching in his body.

He was determined that this time he'd take things slowly, to make sure she enjoyed every moment of the event. He wanted to show her everything he knew about making love.

Rolling her onto her back, he teased her with his fingers, flicking at the hard little nubs of her nipples before bending his head and taking first one, then the other, into his mouth. Her little gasps of desire and delight only fueled his own need, but he made a conscious effort to ignore his body's urgings and continued his exploration of her body.

Moving lower, he kissed his way across her abdomen and flicked his tongue into the small indentation of her belly button. She squirmed beneath him.

"Does that tickle?" he asked.

"A little," came her shy response.

Undeterred, he continued lower until his mouth was on the very heart of her femininity. Licking and sucking and kissing her most sensitive flesh, he reveled in the sounds of her growing passion.

"Oh, Raf!" she gasped, digging her fingers into his hair.

He continued the rhythmic stroking until she stirred restlessly beneath him, her movements became increasingly frenzied.

"Yes, Maggie. Come for me. Let yourself go."

He increased the pressure of his tongue and was rewarded with a cry of passion. Her grip on his head tightened. Her hips bucked wildly. And then she cried out again, a mixture of pain and relief. He watched tenderly and with satisfaction as her body spasmed and then finally came to rest.

She opened her eyes and stared at him.

"Good?" he rasped.

"Amazing."

"There's plenty more where that came from."

She chuckled in a self-satisfied way. "I'm very glad to hear that."

And then she wriggled out from beneath him and pressed him down on the bed. Sitting astride him, she gazed down at him with a wide grin.

"My turn."

Chapter Twenty-Six

♥

Maggie was relaxed and replete, but sitting astride Raf, her desire for him reignited. She wanted to show him how much she loved him, just like he'd shown her. Mimicking his actions, she bent her head and suckled his nipples. His sharp intake of breath told her how much he liked it. Encouraged, she threaded her fingers through the soft pelt of his chest hair and kissed her way across his well-defined pectorals, down over his taut abs before moving lower still.

Determined to give him as much pleasure as he'd given her, she encircled his cock with her hand and then lowered her mouth. First licking the rim and then swirling her tongue over his sensitive head. Then up and down his shaft, before taking him fully in her mouth. She didn't really know what she was doing, but she hoped he liked whatever she did. From the groans of contentment coming from him, she gathered she was on the right track.

Sucking him hard into her mouth, she tightened her hand around his shaft. Sucking and tightening, she kept up a rhythm that appeared to be driving him wild. His hips shifted and bucked. He flung his head from side to side. When she tasted fluid on the end of his cock, she knew he must be close.

Before she could suck him through to orgasm, he sat up and pulled gently away.

She frowned. "Don't you like what I'm doing?"

He gave her a pained smile. "To the contrary, I like it too much. If you keep that up, I'm going to come."

"That's okay. You let me come."

"Yes, but I want to come inside you. Is that okay?"

She nodded and said, "I'm not taking any contraception."

He chuckled. "That's okay. I want to build a life with you, a family. There's no time like the present to start making babies. What do you think?"

Her heart filled to overflowing. "I think that sounds wonderful."

With that, he drew her into his arms and once again kissed her deeply. The hard pressure of his erection against her stomach reminded her that they weren't quite finished.

As if reading her mind, he gently pushed her back down on the bed. Then he crouched and positioned himself between her thighs. As he stared into her eyes, his cock probed her entrance. With a single fluid thrust, he was inside her.

She gasped at the feel of him, huge and hard inside her. Stretching her, filling her, igniting a fresh wave of desire. He moved slowly at first and gradually picked up his pace, rhythmically stroking her with his cock.

As need built inside her once again, she clung to his shoulders, loving the feel of him, loving him.

And then she was there, at the peak, and he was right there beside her. Their cries of triumph were mingled with tender kisses and gasps of relief. They fell asleep in each other's arms.

Sometime later, Maggie woke to find Raf lying on his side and staring at her, his eyes dark with unspoken questions. Disquiet stirred inside her.

"What is it?" she asked.

"Why were you still a virgin?"

She blushed but bravely held his gaze. "I guess I'd found no one I wanted to sleep with."

"But surely there must have been other men in your life? Boyfriends?"

"Not that many. You'd be surprised. I just never felt strongly enough about them to have sex with them. I wanted to wait until I found someone special."

His gaze warmed with emotion. "That makes me feel incredible."

She shrugged. "It's true." She reached for his hand and threaded her fingers through his. "Now it's my turn to ask a question. What changed your mind about living out here with me?"

Raf sighed quietly and rolled onto his back. He stacked his hands behind his head. "I got back to Brisbane, and I couldn't stop thinking about you. It didn't matter that my father was seriously ill, even at risk of death. You dominated my thoughts. When my sister accused me of being in love with you, at first, I denied it, but then I realized it was true. I was. I am. And I was so happy about it. I couldn't wait to see you again."

She brushed away the hair from his eyes. "Are you sure you're going to be able to live out here, so far away from everything?"

"I'll live wherever you live. My life, my heart, is where you are."

She melted at the sincerity in his eyes. "That's so sweet. I love you so much."

"I love you too." He paused and then added, "Who would have thought my dear old uncle could be so right?"

Maggie frowned. "Your uncle? What are you talking about?"

He told her about the letter. "By then, I'd already decided, but it's nice to know he was on our side."

Maggie shook her head in disbelief. "Wow. I can't believe it. All that time, he was plotting for us to get together. He never said a thing."

"I guess that makes it even more special, right? We chose each other long before we knew my uncle had already decided we were destined to be together. Now I can't imagine wanting to be with anyone else. Or anywhere else. You're stuck with me forever, under the outback sky."

"Sounds good to me." She smiled.

The End

Get a free book when you sign up for Chris Taylor's newsletter at: https://christaylorauthor.com.au/

If you enjoyed Maggie and Raf's story, don't forget to leave a review at your favorite digital retailer. Every review is greatly appreciated and will help other readers find my books.

A Cattleman's Secret Baby is the next book in the Fairfax series. It is due for release in November 2024.

Other books by Chris Taylor

The Munro Family Series
(in order)

The Profiler
The Investigator
The Predator
The Betrayal
The Deception
The Negotiator
The Christmas Vigil (A novella)
The Ransom
The Defendant
The Shooting

A CATTLEMAN'S DAUGHTER

The Maker

The Sydney Harbour Hospital Series (in order)

The Perfect Husband
The Body Thief
The Baby Snatchers
The Final Bullet
The Debt Collector
The Lab Test
The Stolen Identity
The Cliff-top Killer
The Likeable Fraudster

The Sydney Legal Series
(in order)

An Accidental Murderer
At the Hand of her Father
A Woman Scorned
Lies and Deception
Ordinary Evil
The Ties that Bind
The Perfect Crime
A Toxic Inheritance
Malicious Love

CHRIS TAYLOR

The Craigdon Family Series
(in order)

Callum
Joel
Isabella
Nicholas
Sophia
Flynn
Noah
Logan
Elizabeth

The Barrington Family Series
(in order)

Broken Lives
Broken Promises
Broken Bonds
Broken Spirits
Broken Minds
Broken Vows
Broken Hearts
Broken Dreams
Broken Homes

The Fairfax Family Series (in order)

A Cattleman in Disguise
A Cattleman's Quest
A Cattleman's Daughter
A Cattleman's Secret Baby
To Catch a Cattleman
The Doctor and the Cattleman
To Rescue a Cattleman
A Cattleman's Heart
For the Love of a Cattleman

Bachelors and Brides Series (in order)

Matilda
Austin
Farrah
Benjamin
Verity
Denver
Ebony
Tyrone
Willow

Books by Chris Taylor
Writing as
Bella
Christian

This Is Where It Ends Series
(in order)

Jessie's Story
Ryan's Story
Holly's Story
Sarah's Story
Veronica's Story

Love audiobooks? Check out Chris Taylor Books on audio
iTunes   Amazon   Audible

Join Chris Taylor's Facebook reader group/fan page and be
among the
first to receive news of book releases, read and review books
prior to release
and other amazing offers.

Join Now!

Acknowledgments

As usual, no book comes into being without a lot of help and support by my friends and family. A world of thanks must go to my wonderful editor, Nicole Guihot. Thank you for your excellent editorial comments, proof reading skills and suggestions. I hope you like the final result.

To the fantastic writer organizations such as Romance Writers of Australia, Romance Writers of America and Romance Writers of New Zealand for all the help, support and encouragement they offer new and aspiring writers, including me.

To my readers, thank you for your support and love for my stories. Your encouragement and enjoyment make this journey all worthwhile.

And lastly, to my friends and family, especially my husband and children. Thank you for putting up with late dinners and even later conversations as I've emerged day after day from the sometimes scary but always enthralling world I've created on my computer.

About the Author

Chris Taylor grew up on a farm in north-west New South Wales, Australia. She always had a thirst for stories and recalls writing her first book at the ripe old age of eight. Always a lover of romance and happily-ever-afters, a career in criminal law sparked her interest in intrigue and suspense. For Chris to be able to combine romance with suspense in her books is a dream come true.

Chris is married to Linden and is the mother of five children. If not behind her computer, you can find her doing the school run, taxiing children to swimming lessons, football, ballet and cricket. In her spare time, Chris loves to read her favorite authors who include Richard North Patterson, Sandra Brown, Kathleen E Woodiwiss and Jude Devereaux.

You can find out more about Chris and get a free book when you sign up for her newsletter at her website:
http://www.christaylorauthor.com.au

Join Chris on Facebook at:
    https://www.facebook.com/christaylo-rauthor/

* 9 7 8 1 9 2 5 4 4 1 2 2 2 *